Un-Followed

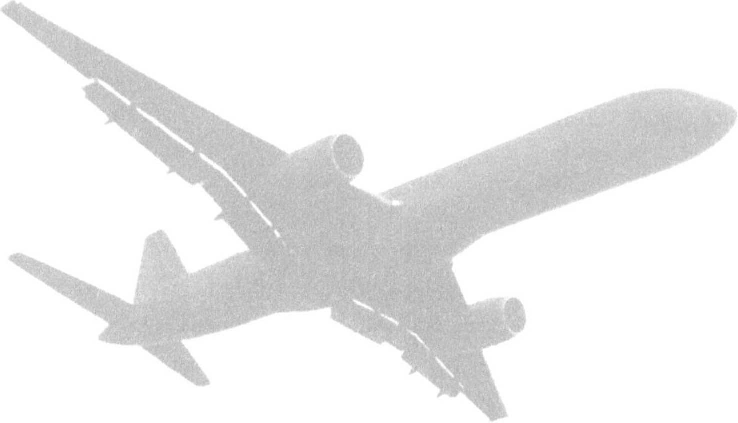

A NOVEL

The Flight Risk Spy Series: Book Four

SHELLY SNOW PORDEA

LITTLE BLACK BOOK

PUBLISHING

Contents

Prologue

Undisclosed Location, Canada

DEEP WITHIN THE OPERATIONS center, time seemed to move differently from the world above. Machines spoke in code and static, whispering their secrets into the manufactured dawn of the control room. Stephen Hopkins stood at the center of it all as rows of monitors washed pale blue light across the analysts' faces. Their expressions stayed unblinking, detached, almost reverent as they watched the screens. Beyond the glass, the rest of the world slept beneath a blanket of snow.

A single feed filled the center screen, playing images of a woman moving in real-time. She stood in the middle of a Manhattan street, coat half-buttoned and hair whipped by the wind, her breath rising in pale bursts against the freezing air. She was struggling to manage several pieces of luggage, the sound of wheels scraping across salted pavement.

"She's on the move," a young technician confirmed. "This feed is from the security cameras at the Bryant Park Hotel."

Director Hopkins didn't answer right away. He watched as Amanda's image blurred and damp flakes hit the lens, melting and streaking across the glassy surface, the streetlights haloing her in muted gold. The weight of years rested lightly on his shoulders, hair silvering at the temples, but his posture carried the steadiness of someone who had commanded silence all his life. It was ironic that he was about to step out of the shadows during his twilight years.

"And Montgomery?" he asked.

"She left his place minutes ago—alone," the tech reported.

Facial recognition was this guy's specialty. His precision software linked surveillance networks across every major city Amanda had visited, trained to isolate her features with near-perfect accuracy. In months of observation, it had only registered two false positives.

They watched Amanda's silhouette move toward the building and through the gilded doors, bumbling on as she pushed and pulled her bags before a young man came to her aid.

"Alright. Alert me when she emerges," the man in charge said, "I'm going to turn in for the night."

"Yes, sir," the technician replied, readying himself for an overnight shift, but the boss hesitated before leaving.

"Is Agent Harrington on site?"

"Yes, sir. She arrived last night," an agent monitoring another screen said.

"Good. Arrange a meeting. 8 a.m. I think it's high time we deploy our main objective. Amanda's ready."

His nod came slowly, less like assurance than an attempt to push doubt aside, conflict drawn across his face like a roadmap. Perhaps it was sheer mercy that he planned on retiring; this final intelligence mission would have undone him if leaving the service hadn't already been decided *for* him rather than *by* him.

"Will do, sir," the agent said.

"Try to get some shut-eye when you can," Hopkins said. "You'll learn soon enough that the better you take care of yourself now, the more you'll appreciate sensible habits when you're older, young man," he grinned.

"Copy that," the agent smiled.

As Hopkins moved down the corridor to his quarters, one thought trailed him: youth never understands the cost. He surely hadn't. His bed had been made years ago, and now he lay in it the only way he knew how.

CHAPTER ONE

New York City: The Morning After

THE SCENT OF COFFEE drew Amanda from sleep, followed by the muted rhythm of Cooper moving around the suite. A blanket had been draped across her shoulders during the night; she was still on the sofa, still in the clothes she'd arrived in. Across the room, an art deco clock—with lines instead of numbers—glowed faintly: 8:16 a.m. For a moment, disorientation clung to her like a second skin. The silence pressed in, hollow and strange, edging toward dread.

The last thing Amanda remembered was standing in Tristan's doorway, exhaustion collapsing her from the inside out. Everything after that was fragments—the soft click of the door, the weight of the room, her own voice unraveling as she tried to apologize for something she didn't have words for.

But as morning poured through the window in a thin wash of light, the thought of the man she ran to—not the one who'd cast her out when the truth surfaced—somehow steadied the world. Cooper sat at the small table, looking at his laptop screen. His sleeves were rolled to his elbows, hair slightly disheveled as if the night had asked more of him than sleep could give back.

The blanket still held a trace of his warmth, the faint scent of coffee, and a darker note that seemed to thread through the air rather than the fabric. His back was to her, shoulders broad beneath a white shirt, the morning light catching in the curve of his neck. For a moment, she just watched him move, his rhythms unsettlingly intimate.

He glanced up when she stirred, hesitation spreading across his face before a small exhale escaped him—a subtle mix of relief and feelings unspoken, like a burden he hadn't realized he'd been carrying had finally shifted. "Morning," he said.

Amanda sat up slowly, fingers pressing at the bridge of her nose. "I'm so sorry," she murmured. "I shouldn't have—"

"Don't." Cooper's tone was gentle but firm, threading through her like a pulse. The authority in his voice was borrowed, unnatural to him, but after years of playing the part and keeping measured, Cooper's control made her want to lean closer even when she knew she couldn't.

"You were wrecked," he said. "I wasn't about to turn you away. Besides, you know how I feel about *shouldn'ts*."

She gave a small, brittle laugh. "I can't even imagine what you must think."

"I think you've had a hell of a few months," he said, crossing to her. "And that you need coffee." He handed her a cup, the cardboard warm against her palms. Their fingers met—barely a brush—but it was enough to send a spark through the quiet. He felt it too; she saw the hint of restraint in the way he stepped back, as if distance could cool the air that had already warmed between them.

"It's strong enough to resurrect the dead," he warned as Amanda lifted the cup.

She smiled faintly, taking a careful sip. The taste was bitter, the heat soothing against her lips.

"Thank you," she smiled. "For... everything. I didn't mean to impose."

"You didn't." He took the armchair opposite her, leaning forward, his forearms solidly on his knees. "I'm not exactly overwhelmed with company these days, anyway."

Amanda nodded, eyes drifting toward the window. She tried to remember how long it had been since Tokyo, how long he'd been broken up with his fiancée. Wasn't it just weeks ago? Was it months? *He was supposed to marry her.* The thought hit Amanda before another one toppled it: *she* was supposed to marry Tristan. Was any of it ever real? She couldn't know. Not at that moment.

The city stretched beyond the glass, pale and precarious under the cold.

"It's strange," she said, "Waking up and feeling safe." Her fingers tightened on the warm cup as if anchoring herself to the moment. The sensation of heat against her palms, the muted hum of the radiator, even the weight of the blanket still across her shoulders made the word "safe" feel tangible again—fragile, but real. "I think I'd forgotten what that felt like. Is that crazy?"

He studied her for a moment. "You *are* safe here. You know that, right?"

Amanda looked down at the coffee in her hands, watching the surface tremble slightly. "I want to believe that."

"Then start there," he said simply.

They sat in silence for a while, the hotel's vibration steady—the kind of near stillness that comes after everything has broken and no one knows how to rebuild.

"Cooper, I can't just drag you into this," she said, the disbelief of her situation softening into concern for him.

"No, I'm serious." His tone sharpened. "No apologies. You came to the right place," he repeated his sentiment from the night before.

He rose slowly, his eyes never leaving hers. The scent of him—soap, coffee, and that faint, unmistakable musk that was uniquely his—reached her before he did. When he sat, the cushions dipped, gravity pulling her closer to him. For one suspended breath, they shared the same pocket of air, and his hand found hers, firm but shaking, as if gripping her was the only thing that tethered them both to reality.

"This wasn't an accident. You were set up," Cooper whispered.

Amanda's mind raced, fragments of facts clattering against one another until panic threatened to spill over. She swallowed hard, forcing herself to breathe through the pulse hammering at her throat.

"I know," she blurted.

He didn't move, only searched her face. "You *know?*" The question sounded less like surprise than disbelief.

"Of course I know, Cooper." Amanda shifted, heart pounding.

"How *much* do you know?" he asked, his voice slow and measured.

"How much do *you* know?" she returned, keeping her tone soft but unyielding.

Cooper hesitated, then leaned closer. "I know it's no coincidence that you and Tristan ever crossed paths. He's been obsessed with you for years."

Amanda blinked. "How could you possibly know that?"

"Have you ever heard of a group called *Anonymity?*" he asked.

A glimmer of surprise crossed her face, her brow lifting slightly. "The vigilante hacker group? Sure. Who hasn't?"

Cooper exhaled through his nose, bitterness cutting through his voice. He closed his laptop, not because he was finished with it but because the conversation deserved his full attention.

"Most people know the name," he said gently. "But not what they really are."

Amanda waited, sensing the shift in him.

"They're not just hackers," he continued. "They're...people who walked away from systems that stopped being worthy of them. Coders, whistleblowers, analysts who saw too much to pretend anymore. They step in when institutions look the other way—when someone needs to pull a thread before everything unravels in the wrong direction."

He stopped there, eyes lowering for a beat before returning to her.

"They don't go after power for the thrill of it," he added quietly. "They go after the people who abuse it."

Amanda's breath caught—not because of the words, but because of the way he said them, as if speaking from a place that had shaped him long ago. But she couldn't think of their history in that moment, pushing aside the idea that his involvement could have ever been anything more than knowledge about them from without.

"And?" she asked, her voice careful.

"When Anonymity moves," he said, "it's because someone with no agenda but the truth puts their name—sometimes their whole life—on the line to make it happen."

His voice gentled, almost imperceptibly, as he leaned in. "I have been part of the group for a while, but Tristan's been deep in it for over ten years—one of the best, and he knows it. When talk started about him angling for a facilitator role, it blew back—*hard*. We weren't sure of the name behind the handle, but a few months ago, there was a leak. Someone exposed that it was true—he was the guy trying to seize the role by coercion. Turns out, the members had started connecting the dots, figuring out who he really is."

She stared at him. "And?" she asked again.

Cooper exhaled slowly, his gaze dropping to his hands as if steadying them before he spoke.

"And for years, before he ever met you, he used to talk about the girl of his dreams—someone he saw one night in Chicago. He said he knew this girl just had to be his perfect match. Then, I don't know, about a year ago, he said he found you. He'd carried out all this research to ensure that his 'head and his heart were in alignment.'"

A hollow scoff left him, his thumb brushing once along the ridge of his knuckle—a small, unconscious gesture. "He even bragged about not 'mixing his genes with anyone stupid.'"

Amanda's breath hitched, horror dawning in fragments. Her fingers tightened slightly against the edge of the table, as if grounding herself.

"Then one night," Cooper went on, his voice lower now, "he posted that it was time for a blind date with his dream girl. After that, he stopped mentioning anything about his love life. Just coding chatter here and there. But when the news showed you with him..."

He hesitated—long enough that she felt the air shift between them.

"I realized you were the girl, Amanda. Billionaire Tristan Montgomery was trying to take over the group, pushing this invasive technology he'd been developing, and of all people in the world, he was dating you—the girl he'd been obsessed with for years."

Amanda stared at him, her pulse roaring in her ears. Cooper's hand rested near hers on the table—close enough to feel the warmth, not quite touching, but unmistakably there. A reminder that even shaken, even fractured, they were still leaning in the direction of each other.

"That's when I decided to finally give in and take a job with my dad," Cooper said softly, "I had to come to Tokyo. To see how much you knew—or warn you about what kind of man you were really with."

The words landed like a dissonant note between them. Amanda's mind reeled as the edges of the room seemed to warp and stretch.

"Warn me?" she repeated, not in denial but in the dawning awareness that his earlier cautions had barely grazed the truth. "About the kind of man he really was," she murmured, the realization settling slowly.

Cooper nodded once, slow and deliberate, as if even motion might shatter what little composure remained between them.

Amanda looked away, focusing on the condensation gathering on the window, watching it tremble with the faint vibration of the heating system. The room vibrated softly, alive with the machinery of comfort, but her skin prickled as though she were standing in the open air.

"You think I didn't know," she whispered. "I mean, obviously, I didn't know all *that*, but... I knew some of it... and that I was only being shown what they wanted me to see."

Cooper's eyes flickered—half empathy, half suspicion. "Then tell me what you saw."

Amanda exhaled, her breath shaking out in small fractures she couldn't quite steady. The words hovered at the edge of her mind before she found the courage to give them shape.

"I've seen so much, but..." She paused, feeling the weight of the last few months settle into the space between them. "I don't know. I keep trying to make sense of him. Of us." Her fingers tightened around her legs, anchoring herself. "I guess—God—maybe I always knew something was...off. The way everything around him felt arranged. Not fake exactly, but always obviously precise and curated."

She swallowed, the truth pushing forward in hesitant pieces.

"His charm, his spontaneity—the way he acted like the whole world could bend if he just wanted it badly enough." She shook her head, almost apologizing to herself. "I told myself it meant passion. Vision. Romance. I wanted to believe that. I *did* believe it."

Her voice thinned. "But now, after last night, I... I see it differently." She drew in a breath, forcing herself to meet Cooper's eyes. "What felt like brilliance looks more like calculation to me now."

Cooper leaned forward, elbows braced against his knees. "And he made you part of that calculation."

Amanda met his gaze. "Not exactly. But, I *was* put in his path."

Something in Cooper shifted. His hand—warm a moment ago where it rested near hers—stilled, then withdrew with a slow, almost reluctant hesitation, as though the truth she was circling had its own gravitational pull.

"What do you mean?" he asked, his voice low and careful, bracing for whatever came next.

"Katherine came to me," Amanda said, the confession leaving her in pieces. "She showed up in Rome, said she knew who I was. She had a photo of us, and convinced me I was in danger.

In exchange for protection, I had to do one thing—keep an eye on Tristan Montgomery.”

The color drained from Cooper's face. “My father sent her?”

Amanda's throat tightened. “Yes. She said he was the one funding her operation. Not by name—not at first—but who else has ever made me sign an NDA in my entire life? It wasn't hard to connect the dots.”

She let out a thin, shaky breath. “I didn't know what to believe about the past or how much it would bleed into my life now, but when Katherine showed up like she did with your dad behind her...” Amanda stopped, a short, nervous laugh slipping out before she could stop it. “It was like I was seventeen again. Everything in me went straight back into survival mode.”

She ran her fingers through her hair before interlacing them behind her neck, gazing upward.

“I know it didn't look that way,” she went on. “I pushed back. I tried to lose her that night in Rome. I told her I didn't want any part of whatever she was doing. But underneath all of that...I was still that kid who'd learned what happens when powerful people decide they want something from you.”

She dropped her hands, lowering her eyes again to meet Cooper's gaze.

“So—I didn't go along like a lamb. But I also wasn't as untouchable as I wanted everyone to believe. If I said no, they really could have blown up my entire life. And part of me reacted before I even understood what I was reacting to."

Cooper's pulse visibly ticked in his throat. "So you *work* for him?"

"I don't know, Cooper," Amanda said breathlessly. "Do I?"

His eyes searched hers as she felt the heat of his skin press against her, even through the inches remaining between them. Still, the air changed—not exactly electric, but heavy and dense with the possibility of mutual demise.

"He told me Katherine was a consultant. He said she vetted people for security clearance, that she was helping us assess leaks. And now, she's head of Helion's ethics committee. I never thought..." His voice trailed off, the sentence dissolving into the hotel room.

"Your dad used us both," Amanda said, the words tasting like rust. "You through loyalty, me through leverage."

"That sounds like him," Cooper said, a huff escaping his lips with an inadvertent sigh.

Amanda sat back, her body folding into the sofa next to him, finally allowing herself to feel his touch.

"So what happens now?" She tried to silence the pulse of memory, the thought of his hands groping for her skin, the taste of his lips on hers. She straightened her back with a jolt. "We've both been used," she said. "We've both lied. And I'm sure there's so much more to tell."

"But, you still don't see it," he said, his voice low and urgent. "You were never just a pawn, Amanda. You were the fail-safe. If Tristan failed, you were the backup plan."

Her head snapped toward him. "Backup for what?"

"For control," Cooper said. "For the Grid. My father's been positioning himself for months. If the Helion board rejects the ethical review, he's ready to push the technology through political channels. You were given a prototype, right?"

She nodded toward him, answering without a word.

"Yeah, if he couldn't get you both, he knew he could at least control *you.*"

Amanda's heart pounded. Of course, she knew Hansen was after the prototype; that's what had brought Melody into this mess, but she couldn't tell Cooper about investigating Russell Drake's death and her side gig as a vigilante Spyce Girl. At least, not yet.

"But Tristan found the one I did have—that's why he kicked me out last night. He found the prototype stuffed in my bag, and there's no reason in the world his fiancée would have it, you know?" Bitter regret curled at the edges of her words. "I should've known this would all blow up in my face."

Cooper's voice cracked slightly. "You were leverage wrapped in affection," he said before his voice softened. "That's how he operates. My father doesn't need to control you directly—he just needs to control the person you love. Because he knows love makes people second-guess themselves. He knows it makes you hesitate. He knows it makes you willing to do things you'd never do for anyone else."

Cooper shook his head, grief and anger braided through the motion.

"If he could keep you tethered to Tristan, he'd have access to Tristan. And if he had access to Tristan..." Cooper's jaw tightened. "He'd have everything he needed to secure his power. That's James Hansen's specialty—turning intimacy into weaponry."

Amanda leaned forward, staring at the floor, light slipping across the grain of the wood like an afterthought. She nodded slowly, a faint tremor in her jaw.

"I wanted to believe Katherine was different. Every piece of this feels like someone else's story that I got written into by mistake."

"That's what manipulation feels like," Cooper murmured. "It convinces you that you had a choice."

Amanda let the truth sit between them. It was heavier than grief, more intimate than confession. She felt stripped to the bone.

"So," she said at last, "what are we supposed to do now?"

Cooper looked at her for a long moment before answering. "We start with the truth. No matter how ugly. No matter who it hurts. It's the only thing that will save us. I can't deal with the lies anymore."

Amanda's laugh was soft, but bitter. "You make it sound simple."

"It isn't," he said. "But the truth is the only thing left that hasn't been weaponized."

She studied the exhaustion lining his face, the veiled wreckage in his eyes of the many painful truths she'd revealed to him. Whatever steadiness he'd shown was a thin veneer over desperation. He wasn't calm; he was clinging to the edge.

"You know this could destroy us," she said.

"It already has," he replied. "But if we're careful, maybe it doesn't have to end us."

Amanda looked at him—really looked into the face of a person she'd loved half of her life—and saw not the boy she once thought would save her, but the man who understood what it meant to survive.

"So, we stick together," she said. "And if we do this, we'll have to be smarter than the people who made the rules. Katherine. Your father. Tristan. Julius."

"Yep, and we'll write our own rules," Cooper said, his voice resolute.

"Okay, it's a pact, then?" she asked. "We tell the truth. No matter what."

Cooper's jaw tightened, and for the first time in what felt like forever, his voice carried a kind of peace that sounded real. "Yes," he said. "No matter what."

He extended his hand, and Amanda took it in a firm shake meant to be brief. But Cooper didn't let go. He guided her toward him, easing back into the couch until his shoulders met the cushions, settling into a loose recline. Amanda followed the pull, her face finding its place against his chest as if it had remembered being there a hundred times before.

Neither of them moved for a long while. The sound of the city returned: a car horn, a far-off siren, the heartbeat of a world that had no idea what had just changed.

And yet, as Amanda looked up at Cooper, meeting his eyes, she felt it—something like recognition, maybe even faith, germinating in the ruins.

Chapter Two

Undisclosed Location, Canada: Two Days Later

THE HELICOPTER CARVED THROUGH the dawn sky like a blade through silk, its rhythmic thrum coursing through Amanda's ribs. She sat rigid in the rear seat, headset pressed tightly to her head, the static a restless whisper in her ears.

The pilot, a stoic man who never looked directly at her, spoke only in clipped commands. She didn't mind, and she didn't need reminding that she wasn't the one flying. Losing command of the air—the one place that had always belonged to her—left her chest taut, and her pulse sharp.

Fixed-wing crafts obey reason and physics; they are loyal to logic. A helicopter is another creature entirely—alive, unpredictable, trusting chaos over its pilot. Each jolt vibrated up her spine, and every sway through the currents reminded her that control was an illusion. Yet the pilot's hands were sure, his movements practiced. They skimmed the edge of the wilderness, treetops rushing past like a blur of dark watercolor. Below, Canada stretched wide and indifferent—evergreen and ice, lakes fractured into shards of light under the rising sun. It was breathtaking and isolating in equal measure.

Amanda pressed her forehead to the window; the glass steadied her, biting her skin with cold. She wondered if Cooper had slept since they parted. She hadn't, not more than a few scattered hours. His words still threaded through her mind like a mantra: *truth between us, games with everyone else.* It was the only anchor she had left in a world that trafficked in deceit.

The radio crackled. "Five minutes," the pilot said, but his voice was swallowed by the mechanical roar.

Amanda inhaled slowly. Her breath fogged the glass, a brief apparition that vanished as quickly as it came. She closed her eyes, the noise around her thinning into memory: the sound of wind in Rome, Tokyo's neon buzz, Tristan's voice fading into silence. She wiped an exhausted tear from her eye. The machine tilted, slicing through a low sheet of mist. Pines speared upward through the fog like sentinels, guarding whatever waited below.

The helicopter dropped into a clearing where snow billowed upward in diaphanous plumes. The skids hit ground with a hollow thud, and before the blades had fully slowed, the cold rushed in—piercing and animate, a predator with teeth. Amanda pulled her hood tight, boots breaking through a crusted surface of brittle snow. The wind clawed at her, a feral welcome to nowhere.

By the time she reached the edge of the landing pad, the helicopter was already lifting off again, swallowed by clouds and noise. What remained was silence—an absence so total it seemed to deafen. Ahead stood a small compound with three low, gray buildings, symmetrical and severe, shouldering the base of a mountain. There was no insignia or flag, just the authority of a place that didn't need to declare itself.

A figure waited at the main entrance, flanked by two others in long, dark coats. Even from a distance, Amanda knew the stance—poised, unhurried, and impossible to mistake: Katherine Harrington. The escorts beside her were motionless, their attention fixed outward, their identities unimportant.

Katherine had summoned her here for a *final mission*—at least, that's what the message said. And, coming from Katherine and Hansen's orbit, anything described as final sounded like music to Amanda's ears. So here she was, reporting for duty.

She expected dread as she approached, but her body felt something closer to readiness—acceptance of whatever waited beyond. Amanda wasn't sure which version of Katherine she'd face today: the manipulator, the mentor, or something in between. The older woman's silver hair caught the pale light, her expression softened into an almost-maternal calm that Amanda had come to distrust.

"Amanda," Katherine greeted, voice crisp but composed. "You made good time."

"I wasn't the one flying," Amanda said with a faint smirk. "You'd have been too hard to find."

"That's the point." Katherine's reply came with the ghost of amusement. She turned, gesturing toward the door. "Come along. You'll want to warm yourself before we begin."

Snow hissed underfoot as they crossed the short stretch to the entrance. One guard moved ahead, pulling the heavy door open, its hinges exhaling a low metallic sigh. As Amanda and Katherine stepped inside, the two silhouettes resumed their post outside—dark figures against concrete and snow, sealing the world behind them.

The slight fragrance of antiseptic and old paper greeted them as they entered—a sterile familiarity that pulled Amanda backward in time. The room was precise rather than warm, its order deliberate: glass walls, steel fixtures, massive wooden beams, and the muted whir of machines working in patient, disciplined rhythm. It could have been a near-perfect replica of the London compound where she'd first been trained—clinical, restrained, built to make obedience feel like safety.

"This is... quaint," Amanda said nervously, the dryness in her voice gentler than her nerves.

"Rather," Katherine replied, the corners of her mouth refusing to lift. "Sit," she said.

Amanda took her seat, the sound of wood against tile harsher than it should've been. At the utilitarian counter along the wall—an afterthought of comfort in an otherwise austere space—Katherine lifted a kettle and poured two cups, watching the liquid darken and steam, her eyes never leaving the swirl of liquid. She nudged one toward Amanda, a thin line of steam curling between them, almost like a breath withheld.

"You've been compromised," Katherine stated matter-of-factly.

"Oh, that's how we're starting this?" Amanda's nervous laughter took over, coming out thin, the sound skittering across hard surfaces.

"Communicating in brief texts isn't ideal," Katherine went on, her tone even. "Let's lay it out. Tristan has the prototype, and you are no longer in communication, *yes?*"

"Not exactly," Amanda admitted, her voice low but steady.

Katherine's eyebrow lifted slightly, the movement so precise it felt rehearsed. "And yet, I'm looking for exactness."

Amanda exhaled through her nose, leaning forward until her elbows pressed against the table's cold edge. "Okay, he's texted. But look, I have been compliant, scared, confused, and probably really stupid throughout this whole thing. If you want *exactness,* then I do too," she spat the word right back at Katherine. "You said if I came here, I'd receive my final mission, right?"

Katherine didn't respond at first. She merely lowered her head a fraction, chin dipping while her eyes lifted to meet Amanda's—a deliberate gesture that carried both patience and command, and an unspoken assurance that she had said exactly what she meant.

"Great," Amanda continued, sitting back and crossing one leg over the other. "Then you tell me, I tell you. Cool?"

Katherine's lips parted slowly before stretching into a smile that showed just enough teeth to feel dangerous. It wasn't amusement, it was appraisal, the kind of expression a cat gives while deciding whether to pounce.

Amanda shifted in her seat, her pulse picking up as she tried to match the older woman's composure.

"Cool," Katherine finally said, the single syllable ludicrous on her lips, soft but with an edge like glass.

Amanda let out an involuntary snicker, more reflex than humor. "Yeah, cool," she said, her laugh tapering into a jittery exhale. Her fingers toyed with the edge of her teacup, turning it slowly and methodically, as though control of that small rotation might steady everything else. "So, you first."

"Very well. What *exactly* would you like to know?" Katherine said the word "exactly" as if it were now an inside joke that only the two of them could understand.

"How are you gonna get me out of this, and what do you expect me to do next? Now that—" Amanda's voice trailed off, leaving the words, *now that Tristan knows I've been lying to him,* unsaid. The danger she assumed she'd put herself in was disorienting and nearly unfathomable.

Katherine leaned an elbow on the table. "Well, Tristan is a man in love, so I am not all that surprised that you've spoken with him. But I believe answering your questions of what's next depends on my knowing what has transpired and what has been said. Have you called off the engagement?"

"Isn't it obvious?" Amanda huffed.

"Seemingly, yes," Katherine admitted. "And does he know you spent the night with Cooper Hansen after you left his loft?"

Blood rushed to Amanda's ears, heat rising in her chest. "I... don't know." That they could track *her* was no revelation; she'd lived with that shadow for months. But hearing Katherine drop Cooper's name so effortlessly still sent a cold weight through her. "But... nothing... happened," she stumbled through the words, sounding completely unbelievable. "I swear."

"This isn't about judging you, Amanda. It's about safety."

"For whom?" Amanda scoffed.

"Everyone," Katherine said, her reply immediate and hushed. "The Ocular Grid isn't a product anymore, Amanda. It's a movement, and Tristan is at its center."

Amanda's mind drifted back to the thought of his charm, his precision—it had all seemed so truly idealistic at the beginning. Now his ardency seemed like the playbook of a zealot.

"What do you need from me?" she asked.

Katherine studied her. "Perspective. And patience. Pieces are moving you don't yet see."

Amanda's jaw tightened. "I'm here to follow orders, remember?"

Katherine smiled faintly. "You're here to understand what you're fighting for... and for a way out."

She slowly turned one of the folders toward Amanda, the motion deceptively simple. The tab brushed Amanda's fingers, feeling as light as a breath, but as heavy as a fault line. Inside lay documents stamped with classified headers and a name she had spent most of her life trying not to acknowledge. Until Katherine and Julius suggested she had been orbiting the espionage world far longer than she realized, destined to be in it merely because of her bloodline, she hadn't let the name hold meaning.

Stephen Hopkins.

Amanda's throat tightened around the name. "What is this?" she managed. "Why do you have a dossier on my father?"

Katherine's voice gentled, adopting a softness that felt almost like an apology. "He has been stationed here for a few weeks," she said, unhurried, as though delivering news that was expected rather than seismic.

A strange unsteadiness swept through her, as though the room had tilted by a degree she couldn't correct, the air stretching thin around her.

"Here?" she finally whispered. "I—I thought he was *dead*. You spoke about him like he was a legacy—someone you referenced, not someone you briefed."

"That is what you were meant to believe," Katherine replied, her poise undisturbed. "He chose it that way. Rather firmly, I might add."

Amanda pushed back from the table, the chair scraping sharply across the tile. "Why would he do that? Why would you let me think—" Her voice tangled, rising despite her effort to contain it. "None of this makes sense."

"It will, in time," Katherine said, though even she seemed aware of how little comfort the words offered. "He worked on an early intelligence initiative—the groundwork that later evolved into what Tristan disastrously co-opted as the Grid. Your father did not design *that*, of course, but he contributed to the architecture long before it resembled anything Tristan built."

Amanda lifted a shaking hand, cutting her off. "Stop. Please." Her breath wavered, her pulse a drum in her ears. "You're telling me my father is part of the same world that stalked me across continents? That you and Julius pulled me into with a dossier and an ultimatum? You're telling me he's alive, in this facility, and you waited until now to mention any of it?"

"When he realized Tristan had taken an interest in you, he kept a close watch," Katherine said, her tone low and remarkably steady. "And when Hansen entered the picture—"

"Don't," Amanda whispered, almost choking on the word. She moved to the narrow window, the snow beyond drifting in soft, indifferent spirals, and pressed her palms to the cold glass as though it might steady the unraveling inside her. "You can't expect me to absorb all of this at once. You've had months. Why now?"

"Because you must understand," Katherine replied, her voice measured but no longer gentle, "that you were never incidental. You were always a variable—one with consequences far beyond your own field of vision. And your father... he has been waiting for this moment rather longer than you have."

Amanda's breath caught in her chest, refusing to move. "No," she whispered, though the denial felt weightless. *"This* moment? You can't mean—"

She couldn't have said more if she wanted to, the door behind them opening with a click. Amanda turned, her heart knocking hard against her ribs as the moment elongated, stretching thin and fragile enough to break into a thousand tiny pieces. A man stepped through—older, smaller, worn by years she had not witnessed. His hair, silver threaded with ash-dark strands, framed a face marked less by time's cruelty than by its accumulation. But it was his eyes—steady, searching, and devastatingly familiar—that held her still. The same eyes she had scanned in photographs as a girl, hunting for pieces of herself she never found anywhere else.

She had always imagined she would recognize him by the static stillness of a memory, but it was the movement that undid her—the slight inclination of his head, the controlled sweep of his gaze as he took in the room, as though he had been preparing for this moment far longer than she had.

Her breath gathered sharply, trembling against the weight of the moment that would not release her.

"What is this?" she whispered.

He didn't answer—just lowered his gaze, the muscles in his jaw shifting once before going still again, as though he'd rehearsed this silence a hundred times. Then suddenly, he closed the distance between them and drew her into his arms. For a heartbeat, the sterile air shifted into warmth.

The scent of wool, the tremor of age in his hands, the solidity of a body she thought long gone. She let herself exist there—suspended between bliss and indignation—before she could think what it meant.

When he pulled back, his eyes glistened. "You've grown into your mother's courage," he said.

Amanda swallowed hard. "All these years. You could have come. You could have known me… or at least told me you were alive."

"No, I couldn't." His voice was low, heavy with the kind of regret that doesn't beg forgiveness. "I was never safe. Keeping my distance kept you alive. I thought anonymity was mercy."

Her hands trembled, the chill from the window finally catching up with her skin. "You call this mercy?"

"I call it survival." His gaze moved past her for a moment, toward Katherine, then back. "I never meant for you to be pulled in. But men with more power than I will ever have don't always take no for an answer."

Katherine stepped forward, her tone soft but steady, like a current shifting the boat back onto course. "There's a war coming, Amanda. Not one fought with bullets or borders, but with information and influence. Some insist control is the only way to preserve peace. They would fashion a world governed by data—a technocracy that demands obedience under the illusion of kindness."

Stephen's jaw tightened, his eyes not leaving his daughter. "Quite," he breathed in, the single word weighted with agreement. "Some of us still believe people must be trusted to think for themselves."

Amanda looked between them—the woman she had never fully trusted, and the father she had never stopped longing for. "And which side are you asking me to be on?"

Her father's answer was quiet, almost kind. "We're not asking. You've already chosen."

She shook her head, the gesture small and disbelieving. "I didn't choose any of this."

"You did," Katherine said. "Under duress and coercion, initially, yes, we understand that. But, your loyalties have been apparent from the start—you're on the side of free thinking."

Amanda's mouth opened, but, at first, no sound came. The compound breathed around her—the muted drone of machinery embedded in stone, the steady vibration of generators anchored somewhere in the mountain's spine. Light filtered in through the narrow windows cut into the building, revealing only a sliver of the snow-laden world beyond.

"You talk about sides as if they're fixed," she could barely get out more than a whisper. "But everything I thought was true came from people who lied to me. And yet... not all of it was untrue. I don't know what or who to trust anymore."

Her father's expression softened. "You don't have to, not yet. That's why we need you."

"*Need* me?" she repeated, nearly laughing. "For what? You've got intelligence, soldiers, and algorithms that predict every move. I'm the one who keeps tripping over the truth."

Katherine studied her, arms folding loosely across her chest. "You're the bridge between what was built and what must be undone. You've witnessed enough to question the shape of the truth—exactly what is needed now."

Amanda's eyes burned. "That's not power, Katherine. That's torment."

"Maybe," Katherine said. "But it can also bring clarity."

Silence fell again, heavy as snowfall around them. Amanda watched the frost edge the corners of the window and thought of Cooper—his voice, his steadiness, the promise of truth between them. It seemed less like a couple of days and more like a lifetime ago, and yet he felt closer than anyone in the room.

She turned back to her father. "What exactly do you expect me to do?"

Stephen's gaze drifted toward Katherine, a silent exchange passing between them before he spoke. "Tristan's been reaching out, hasn't he?"

Amanda's fingers stilled in her lap, *of course, they already knew that.* "A few times. Texts. Nothing dramatic." Her voice softened. "He wants an explanation."

Katherine angled her head toward Amanda, assessing. "And do you plan to give him one?"

"I told him I would," Amanda admitted. "Just not over the phone. I wanted to buy time."

Katherine's mouth curved faintly, a half-smile that didn't pretend to be kind. "Then that's your opening."

Amanda blinked. "My *opening?*"

"To go back," Stephen said. "To talk, listen, and to see what he's hiding."

Amanda's breath caught, quiet but piercing. "You think he's selling control above ground while inciting chaos below?"

"Mmhm," Stephen confirmed, "We just don't know how deep."

Amanda looked down at the folder again. The paper seemed to thrum faintly under her fingertips, as if some part of it were alive. "And you want me to find out?"

"We need proof," Stephen said gently. "Not rumors. Not code fragments. Something verifiable, something that ties him to both Helion and Hansen that predates the fiasco in Tokyo."

Amanda shook her head slowly, a resentful laugh slipping out. "You're asking me to walk right back into the mess I just escaped."

"Not walk," Katherine said, her tone smooth as glass. "Step carefully."

Amanda's pulse stirred, the words sinking in like cold water. She thought of Tristan's last message—polite, almost tender in its restraint. *We both got caught in something bigger than us. We can still talk when you're ready.* There was no apology in it, not really, but the precision of his phrasing—measured, careful, and so painfully Tristan—was enough to unsettle her all the same.

"What if I go," she began speaking the words, not quite ready to think about the possibilities, "and he's innocent? What if all of this is wrong?"

Katherine's eyes softened, though her posture didn't. "Then you'll know the truth. And knowing is never wrong."

Amanda turned slightly toward her father. "And if he's *not* innocent?"

"Then you'll have seen it yourself," Stephen said. "That matters more than anything we could tell you."

The wind pressed faintly against the windows, a hollow, intermittent sound like a breath held too long. Amanda stood, the chair legs scraping lightly against the tile. She didn't feel dramatic or brave; she was just certain that standing was the next logical thing to do. Maybe to shake off the bombshell of information she felt buried under. "Okay, when?" she spouted.

"There's a helicopter arriving in forty minutes," Katherine said. "We've arranged your return to New York. You were never meant to remain here. Tell Tristan you're coming to explain, to make peace. He will *want* to believe you. He is a man in love who desires love. Use that to your advantage."

Amanda lifted her eyes toward the window. Snow had started to fall harder, flakes tumbling sideways in the wind, erasing the horizon in slow motion. The world outside looked blurred and borderless, as if it, too, was between versions of itself.

"I'll go," she said finally, her voice even. "But I won't go as your operative. You called this my final mission, right? You promised. If I do this, it's for freedom, not allegiance. "

Stephen inclined his head, a hint of pride passing through his expression. "Alright."

Katherine didn't smile, but her tone gentled. "Then it's settled."

Amanda pulled her coat on, turning slightly toward the door but not moving yet. For a moment, she caught her reflection in the glass—a faint double exposure of the woman she was and the one she might still become.

CHAPTER THREE

Tristan's Loft: Four Days After the Breakup

"YOU DIDN'T HAVE TO bring flowers," Tristan said.

The words came softly, without sarcasm, but they landed with the weight of unspoken accusations.

"They go well with an apology," Amanda said, standing in the doorway, her fingers tightening around the paper-wrapped bouquet.

The cold still clung to her coat, a small collection of winter flowers trembling in her hands—white, deep red, muted green, and silver eucalyptus threaded between the colors like a breath turned visible in winter air.

"I didn't know what else to bring," she answered, her voice shaky, but still steadier than she felt.

Tristan stepped back, leaving the door open. "As long as you brought yourself and an explanation, that's enough," he smiled tersely.

Amanda hesitated, watching the light from the window stretch across the floor. *The last time she stood here, her bags had been waiting by the door.* The memory flickered like static.

She padded into his apartment, the door closing with a muted click behind her. The loft felt cavernous, all glass and silence, the kind of space that amplified distance. Tristan took her coat, hanging it on the rack before they fell into step beside one another, footsteps whispering across the wood, echoing once before fading into a silence laden with everything unsaid. The scent of coffee weaved through the air, steam rising from a cup on the counter, and a laptop glowing faintly beside it sat half-lit, as if Amanda had caught him in the middle of a workday.

"So, this is the part where you tell me everything I don't understand." Tristan leaned against the kitchen island, hands braced on the edge as though the surface itself were keeping him grounded.

Amanda set the flowers down, their stems dripping faintly onto the surface. "There's a lot you don't understand," she said. "And I don't blame you for any of it."

"Who's to blame?" His voice carried a note she couldn't name—maybe anger, maybe curiosity, maybe fatigue.

She took a breath, choosing her words like chess moves—each one deliberate, none without consequence. "I lied to you. That's true. But not about us. Not about what I felt." Though her feelings had been waning, that part was truer than anything she knew she'd say. The love she felt for him—sometimes *still* feels for him—was real.

But Tristan let out a laugh, short and bitter. "You were holding a prototype of my invention without my knowledge, Amanda. I think that counts as a pretty big infraction."

"I wasn't working against you, though," she said. "I was trying to keep you safe. Even when I didn't know what I was really protecting you from."

He looked at her, really looked—eyes sharp, expression unreadable. "You make it sound like you were doing something noble."

"It wasn't noble," she said. "It was desperate."

The brief silence that followed felt almost gentle, the kind that precedes either forgiveness or collapse.

"Who are you working for?" Tristan asked.

Collapse it is.

"I'm not working for anyone," she said. "I was blackmailed by someone. I knew I was in danger, and I didn't know what else to do."

Tristan's brow tightened. "Blackmailed? By whom? What could someone possibly have on you?"

"I..." She hesitated, her throat tightening. "You know the Governor."

"Yes," Tristan said slowly, the word landing like a test.

"He's not who you assume him to be," Amanda managed, her voice small but steady. "He isn't just another political figure trying to partner with you, or with Helion, or whatever he's telling you. He's been in this longer than you think."

Something flickered across Tristan's face—a slight disbelief, yes, but braided with subtle fear: the possibility that he had misjudged a man he'd considered predictable. His gaze searched hers as if he were looking for the version of her he wanted to believe in.

"You're saying Hansen blackmailed you?"

She nodded once, the motion barely perceptible. "Yes."

Tristan didn't move or speak—the pause a demand.

Amanda's pulse raced, and every word she spoke now had to balance enough truth to sound clean and enough silence to stay safe.

"You know how I said I knew the family?" she began. "It wasn't just from our school functions overlapping. It was because Cooper and I dated for a while. His family didn't approve, but we got caught."

Tristan's expression flickered—there was no surprise, only confirmation. The truth didn't wound him; it settled, slow and inevitable, like something he'd already known in his bones. He shifted his weight, one hand braced on the counter, the other curling loosely at his side. "Go on."

Amanda nodded faintly, lowering her eyes to the floor and back at him again. "But the Governor, Cooper's father—and his grandfather too—they both had their own secrets. I stumbled onto one of them, something that could have ruined them if it ever came out. They made me sign an NDA and threatened to bury me if I spoke about it. And they could have. They nearly *did*. It was because of them that I never pursued my academic dreams."

Tristan leaned closer, his voice low, eyes fixed on her. "What kind of secret?"

"The kind of secret that doesn't stay buried forever," she said. "But that's not the point. They wanted control over me—over everything in that town. And now, it seems Hansen has his eyes set on something much larger. Control of the Grid. Control of you."

Tristan's jaw tightened, the faintest movement betraying a shift under his calm exterior.

"I thought I was rid of them," Amanda went on. "But when I was in Rome, someone from their circle approached me and said they could keep me safe if I helped them. And I—" she paused, arms crossing over her chest, fingers pressing into her sleeves—"I thought I was protecting both of us."

"Rome?" Tristan's voice caught on the word as if it cut him. This surprise wasn't rehearsed—it was real, perhaps the most vulnerable he'd been since she walked in.

Amanda bit her lip, the air between them contracting. *Had she said Rome? That wasn't part of the plan.*

Tristan straightened, searching her face. "So, you're telling me that you knew who I was the night we met?" he asked.

She had known nothing but the assignment—no history, just a target she was meant to reach. And even then, it was clunky and elusive, and done all wrong.

The corner of her mouth tightened, her pulse pounding. "Hold on a second," she said, her tone edged with defense. "You have no room to talk. Do I need to remind you that I'm the *'dream girl'* you obsessed over for years? So *romantic,* "she added, the word laced with accusation. "Are you really telling me a man like you didn't do his own digging into the details of my life before showing up there that night?"

Tristan's eyes darkened. "Okay," he said. "So what if I did? Can you blame me? I knew who you were, and I didn't lie about it."

Amanda drew a slow breath, trying to steady herself. "Then don't stand there and act like I'm the only one who kept secrets."

Tristan's laugh was short and humorless. "Secrets? Amanda, I run a global tech empire. Secrets are currency. What matters is *why* you kept yours." He pushed off the counter and took a slow step toward her. "So let's hear it. How did you get the prototype?"

Her spine stiffened. "You wouldn't believe me."

"Try me," he said, the softness in his voice disarming.

Amanda's hand instinctively went to her throat, fingertips brushing the base of her collarbone. "It wasn't stolen," she said. "Not by me. It was given to me."

"By whom?"

Her silence was enough to make his expression turn into a glower. He exhaled, running a hand through his hair, the motion controlled and tense.

Tristan shook his head, a grim smile ghosting across his face. "You think I don't see the game being played here? You think I don't understand how Hansen operates? Of course I do. He's not naïve, he's strategic—and I respect that. Men like him don't bluff; they build leverage. And if he came after you, he thought facing off with me was worth the risk."

He clasped his hands together as if to solidify the claims he was making. "That's why I have Julius. He's been where I am. He knows how to read men like Hansen—how to make their threats look like opportunities. But you—" his voice dropped, low and resigned—"you handed them exactly what they wanted."

Amanda searched her mind for the right words before speaking again. She took a step towards him. "I was just trying to protect you," she said. "You think I didn't see what was happening around you? Piranhas waiting for prey?"

"Then why didn't you come to me?" he asked.

Her throat felt like a wire drawn too thin, one vibration away from snapping. The question landed like a blow, but Tristan's gaze didn't leave her eyes.

"You could've trusted me... You *should* have trusted me," he said, his voice steady but stripped of any warmth. "I don't play the fool, Amanda. Not in business, and not in love."

Amanda's breath became shallow, her composure splintering. "I didn't come to you because I didn't know how," she said. "You think everything can be solved with control, with precision, but this—this wasn't something I could manage."

Tristan's eyes flickered. "You mean you didn't *want* to manage it?"

She shook her head. "No. I mean, it was bigger than us. I was told what would happen if I said a word. If I even hinted at what I knew."

"By whom?" he pressed, the question sharp enough to pierce her flesh.

Amanda's fingers gripped the back of a nearby chair, grounding herself. "You wouldn't understand."

"Try me," he said again, the words severe and weighted.

Her shoulders dropped, a small surrender as she exhaled slowly. "You think power looks like owning a company, standing on a stage, or being quoted in magazines. But the kind of power these guys are talking about—" her voice faltered, "—it doesn't show up in headlines. It moves in silence. It listens. It records. It decides what *survives.* And that's what your tech gives them the possibility to do."

She tried to say the words without implying that she was starting to lump Tristan in with these men she was only referring to as "them." And she wasn't sure she was pulling it off.

Tristan's expression hardened, but not with disbelief. "And you think Hansen wants to leverage it all for total control? Gain the White House, then have surveillance on the rest of the world?"

"You don't?" she said with a hint of shock in her voice.

Tristan shrugged, either to think it through or to deflect, trying to hide that he already knew it.

"Well, in Hansen's case, I *know*," Amanda said. "He doesn't just want control of the Ocular Grid—he wants control of the people who know it best. You. Julius. Anyone who could make or break him."

Tristan leaned back against the countertop, crossing his arms. "So, you thought keeping me in the dark would protect me?"

"I thought it might buy us time," she said softly. "And maybe keep me safe long enough to find out who was pulling the strings."

He watched her for a long moment, jaw tight, unreadable. "And did you?"

Amanda hesitated, the truth dangling precariously on her tongue. "I don't know," she admitted, "I don't think so."

The silence that followed felt like the moment before a fuse reached its destination—stifled sparks, airless until the deafening sound of explosion. When no eruption came, Tristan's voice filled the void instead. It was low and careful, dangerously close to honesty.

"You know what's maddening about all this?" he said. "You could lie to my face, vanish for weeks, walk back in here and tell me half a story, and I'd still believe you before I'd believe anyone else."

Amanda looked into his eyes, startled by the confession wrapped in accusation. He stepped closer to her, the remembrance of his skin on hers enough to make her breath hitch.

"I've spent years surrounded by people who want something from me—contracts, leverage, a name they can attach to their cause. But you..." He shook his head once, the movement almost disbelieving. "You make me want things I can't quantify. That's how I know you're the right one."

Her breath caught. "Tristan."

"No, listen." His tone softened, steely resolve bending to something that sounded like fatigue. "Maybe that's why this hurts. Because even now—after everything—I still see you as the only person who never asked me for anything I didn't already want to give."

Amanda's eyes burned, the weight of it pressing through her chest. "You probably don't even know what you're saying."

The corner of his mouth lifted—not a smile, just a wisp of resignation and desire. "I know exactly what I'm saying. I just don't know what to do with it anymore."

Amanda's pulse tripped. He was close enough for her to feel the warmth of his breath, the scent of coffee, and the faint trace of cedar clinging to his collar. Her body betrayed her before her mind could intervene—every nerve drawn toward the gravity of him, the pull that had never really faded.

"Tristan," she repeated his name softly, a whisper more than a warning this time.

He reached up, not touching her yet, only tracing the line of her jaw before tucking a piece of hair behind her ear. The gesture was restrained and reverent, maddeningly patient.

"Tell me you didn't betray me," he said. "Or tell me you don't love me."

Her breath shuddered out, barely audible. "I can't." Even she wasn't sure which part of his sentence she was referring to.

The city light caught on the glass behind him, washing the room in a pale gold that felt almost unreal. Then, slowly, his hand found the edge of her sleeve, fingertips brushing the fabric.

For a fleeting moment, she let herself believe in the reality of her actions—that she'd done what she came here to do, that this was the first step. *I did it. I'm in.* The thought steadied her like a mission checklist, something solid to hold onto.

But underneath, her heart moved, quiet and dangerous. The ache that came with seeing him like this, close enough to touch, was the same ache that warned her not to give in. Her training told her to compartmentalize, to build walls inside herself—one compartment for loyalty, one for truth, one for feeling. But somewhere between them, stockades had started to crack.

She told herself this was strategy, the clean edge of control she'd promised she could maintain. But as Tristan's touch lingered—barely there, barely allowed—her resolve began to fray.

It would be easier if he were cruel, if his ambition looked like absolute greed instead of conviction. But that was what made him so perilous—he *believed* in his own virtue. She wanted to believe in it, too—in the possibility that power could be used without corruption, that the boy who'd grown into a billionaire might still remember how to love something he couldn't own.

And yet, even as she stood there, the echo of another voice threaded through her mind as steady as the ground, familiar and inveterate. *Truth between us. Games with everyone else.*

Cooper's words rang with piercing ting.

Amanda turned away before Tristan could see the conflict burning in her eyes. Whatever this was—whatever it always had been—she couldn't let it pull her under completely.

You can't save him and love him at the same time, she reminded herself. She just didn't know yet which one she was still trying to do. One of them would lose.

CHAPTER FOUR

Tristan's Loft: The Next Morning

MORNING SUNLIGHT SPILLED ACROSS the loft in long, deliberate strokes, touching everything—revealing rather than softening, exposing the sharp edges of a night left unfinished.

Amanda lay on the couch, the wool blanket drawn to her chin, the faint trace of Tristan's cologne clinging to the air around her. Her sleep had been shallow and dreamless, the kind that hovers at the edge of awareness, refusing to let her forget where she was—or what almost happened.

Tristan had wanted her close; that much was certain, and it's not like her body didn't crave it too, but lies had blasted a cavernous wedge between them. With every brush of their hands, or accidental nudge as they talked long into the night, the gap had shrunk, though—his voice low and calm, his movements deliberate. The space between them narrowed until it had become electric and fragile again, reminding her of what they'd had. And for one suspended moment, she'd nearly let it all break. But the thought of what she was here to do—why she had come at all—pulled her back from the edge. A breath. A word. A shift in tone. Just enough to draw the curtain closed before anything irreversible could slip through.

He hadn't pressed her after she said, "Tristan, we shouldn't... not yet."

Instead, he offered the couch, maintaining his signature ease. He was warm and tender in his restraint, and it sent Amanda's head spinning. The revelations about Tristan were still rearranging themselves in her mind, reshaping her sense of what had been real.

They had said goodnight, leaving behind a silence too unreasonable to explore before daylight. With her eyes as heavy as her heart, she had drifted to sleep.

Now, in the thin dawn of morning, the room felt altered, making her more aware than ever that she had accepted a mission. The air was colder, more exacting, as though even it had chosen sides. A hiss from the steaming shower carried through the apartment, and Amanda turned onto her side, her eyes tracing a glare slanting across the floorboards when the buzz of her phone startled her. She swung her legs over the couch, sitting upright to scan the room before picking up the device. There was one short message.

Status check. Confirm embedded. No names. No calls. Maintain access. –K

She typed a reply, hands steady even as her chest felt anything but.

Inside. Will report.

The water stopped, and she deleted the thread, dropped the phone face down, and stretched her arms with a deep yawn as Tristan emerged. His hair was damp; he wore a white shirt unbuttoned at the collar, sleeves pushed up like a man ready to do business. He caught her watching him, and the air whispered an undeniable pulse between them.

"I didn't wake you, did I?" he asked, as casually as ever.

"No, I just... couldn't sleep anymore," she said.

Tristan's eyes lingered a beat too long before he forced himself to look away, busying his hands with the espresso machine. The motion was practiced, almost soothing—precisely the sort of thing a man would do to hide the fact that wanting her and resenting himself for it had begun to feel indistinguishable.

"Too bad," he said with a half-smile, nodding toward the bedroom. "You'd have been more comfortable in there."

Amanda managed a small smile of her own, though it felt tight at the edges.

"Maybe," she said lightly. "But I doubt I would've slept any better."

His look narrowed as if he recognized the truth she wasn't admitting and chose to either graciously or strategically let it be.

"I just couldn't turn my mind off," she added.

Tristan grinned, not pressing her further. "Breakfast?"

"Sure," she answered.

He turned toward the counter, put on an apron as if having a casual breakfast was the most natural thing for the two of them to do, and began working. Soon the scent of morning filled the air—toasted bread and coffee mingled with orange peel from fresh-pressed juice, and butter melting on warm ceramic.

Amanda watched him work in silence, the faint purr of appliances layering the air with sounds where words might have gone, thankful she didn't have to fill the space. Even with his culinary skills, Tristan moved with the kind of focus that made the smallest gesture seem choreographed, a faint smile on his lips giving the impression of expertise in each movement. It was no wonder the world saw him as a golden boy. She'd once seen an article describing him as "the genius of everything." And though he looked exactly like the man the world adored, she felt herself slipping more out of sync with that reality every moment.

As Tristan cracked the eggs into a skillet, he looked her way and said, "I suppose this feels strange for you."

"What does?" she asked, startled at the bluntness of his statement.

"Being here again," he replied. "After everything."

"Yeah, a little. I was surprised you called, I'm not going to lie," she admitted.

He looked over his shoulder, the edge of his mouth lifting with a mischievous grin. "I told you last night, I'm not interested in apologies. But I *am* interested in the truth."

The word didn't so much land as linger, circling her thoughts until she could no longer tell whether it comforted or accused her. "Truth?" she repeated the word as if it were a question.

He nodded, continuing to stir. "You already know what my system is capable of. Surveillance, predictive data, behavioral coding—none of it's a secret. You know what the Grid does, so why pretend there's privacy between us?"

Amanda's throat tightened. "What are you trying to say?"

Tristan didn't look up from the pan as he answered, his voice carrying a gentle lilt of affection.

"I'm saying I can find out anything. About you. About the people around you." He plated the food with deliberate, unhurried strokes. "Maybe I was naïve to think I wouldn't have to. Or just too buried in launching this project to keep my guard where it should've been."

The mildness of his tone made the words land harder than if he were truly scolding her. Amanda forced her shoulders to stay loose.

"But the truth," he went on, sliding the plates toward the table, "is the only way this works. You know—being open with each other." The ease in his voice made it sound like surveillance was a favor he was doing her. "Sit. Eat." He motioned to the table.

Amanda moved slowly, every gesture measured. Obedience felt like the only safe response. He poured orange juice, the bright color startling against the gray morning, and set a plate before her. The porcelain scraped softly against the hardwood, the only sound in the room while Amanda's thoughts raced in her head.

"You know," Tristan said as he sat opposite her and reached for the coffee, "I spent part of that first night running a few diagnostics."

The fork stilled in Amanda's hand, suspended above her plate. "On what?"

He didn't look at her right away. "The prototype," he said finally, as if delivering a conclusion he had reached long ago. "The one you carried halfway across the world and insist you didn't understand what it was."

Amanda's chest constricted, but she made her voice stay calm. "I told you what I know."

Tristan gave a soft, indulgent laugh. "Perhaps you told me what you hoped I'd believe. There is a difference."

He sat opposite her, elbows braced on the table, the coffee warming his hands. "You should know," he said, "that the device was designed to identify itself the moment it enters my network. A kind of digital self-awareness. Smart enough to know its home—and when it's far from it."

Something cold slid through her stomach. "I don't understand."

"I'll explain." Tristan's voice dropped, the intimacy of it worse than anger."When you stayed behind in New York, and I moved on with the tour, I checked the system from the road. Helion's involvement meant tightening security, so I was watching things more closely than usual."

He drew a slow breath in. "At first, it looked like nothing. A small blip in the activity log. I assumed it was just background noise from the devices already connected here since we'd been traveling so much. I didn't think much of it."

He looked down, his thumb brushing the rim of the mug before he lifted his eyes back to hers. "But when I got home..." he tightened his jaw. "I went back through the logs. And I saw that the signal originated from inside this apartment. Not a guest device. Not anything I recognized. Something... out of place."

Amanda's pulse thudded. "And that's when you knew?"

"That's when I saw something was here that shouldn't be," he said. "I didn't know you had a prototype on you until I started checking the apartment."

Amanda's pulse climbed sharply into her throat."So, you weren't—" she swallowed "—just going through my things?"

"Why?" the left side of his mouth curled into a half-smile. "Because that would have crossed a line, Amanda?"

"Tristan, I told you—someone forced me."

"Yes, yes, blackmail," he said, nodding. "You've said that part. But what you haven't said is *who* gave it to you. That's the piece that still doesn't add up."

"I can't—" she stared, but he didn't let her finish.

"Don't say you can't," he interrupted, his tone still hushed, yet landing with a heavy blow. "You *won't*. And that's fine, but you must understand what that tells me."

A thin breath caught in Amanda's chest before she steadied it. She lifted her chin just slightly—enough to make it look like poise rather than bracing. "What does it tell you?" she managed, each word measured to keep her hands from trembling.

"That you're protecting someone." Tristan tilted his head, the faintest flicker of amusement crossing his face. "And that makes me think you can play both sides."

"I'm not—"

He interrupted her again gently, his voice all warmth and reason. "Amanda, look at me."

She acquiesced, letting her gaze meet his even though every instinct told her not to.

"This isn't an interrogation," he smiled. "It's a conversation. I just want to know what game we're playing, and whether we're playing it together or not."

He then rose, crossing behind her, the faint scent of citrus and coffee following him, warm and crisp.

It hit her the way certain memories do—first with comfort, then with consequence. She had loved that smell on him once, the clean brightness of it, the way it lingered on his collar every time they spent the night together. It used to mean morning, possibility, and a man whose brilliance felt like gravity.

But now it carried something else beneath it, like the after-taste of a lie or the heat of a machine running too long. She still craved the familiarity of it—craved what it reminded her of—but beneath that craving ran a thin, undeniable thread of fear: that she couldn't know which parts of him were real and which parts were curated for effect.

"You think I'm angry because you had the prototype," he hovered, his voice steady. "I'm not, babe. But here's what you don't realize—it was easier to trace from here on my home network. And I know it was the one in Julius' possession. There was a strict protocol when those were assigned."

Amanda turned her face to meet his eyes. "It *was* Julius?" she whispered.

If it really was Julius Babb's prototype, then Katherine was telling the truth, and the model sitting at the bottom of the sea was, in fact, a decoy. At least she could chalk one mystery up as solved. But it's not like Amanda could even decipher what game she was playing and whose side she was on. Not fully.

"I was angry at first, obviously," Tristan continued talking as if she was listening intently, "but I'm actually quite impressed, Amanda." He kept using her name, and she was starting to bristle at the sound of it. His hand brushed her shoulder, lightly enough to be viewed as affection.

She could feel his breath close and steady as he leaned in. "So what happens now?" she finally uttered.

Tristan smiled, setting his cup beside her plate. The metal of his watch glinted in the light, distracting her gaze from meeting his eyes as he came into view.

"Now we stop pretending we don't understand each other. You tell me who gave it to you, and I make sure neither of us pays for their mistake."

"I don't want to fight with you," she said softly.

"I know," he replied. He pulled an empty chair from the table and scooted it next to her, taking a seat and brushing his fingers lightly along the back of her hand. "And I don't want to lose you."

When he bent into her, his lips grazing her cheek, the warmth startled her. For a fraction of a second, her body remembered what it had loved about him. But this wasn't love; it was possession masquerading as tenderness. She breathed in deeply as Tristan drew back and looked at her, his eyes unreadable.

"Who was it?" His voice was melodic, but the demand was unmistakable.

"Katherine Harrington," she said.

"The Helion Ethics Committee Chair?" Tristan laughed as Amanda nodded, confirming that was, in fact, what she had just said.

She wasn't sure why it came out. *Truth is better than lies,* she thought. Even she couldn't see how to explain her way out of this one. Perhaps she was at the point where hiding didn't matter. What more could they take from her now? Her thoughts splintered.

"Brilliant move, Julius," Tristan said, smiling as though that settled everything, then he turned casually to refill her glass.

Amanda didn't say another word. She saw her bag still resting near the counter, her phone face down on the coffee table—every device, every screen, every way to be traced. *Get out,* her instincts whispered. *Now, before he decides to test the story you just gave him.*

Tristan straightened, brushing his hands together. "Well. That's that." No further questions—just a bright, efficient pivot. "I've got to run. Meetings stacked to the ceiling."

The whiplash of it sent a cold ripple through her. He had folded the interrogation neatly into nothing, as if the threat of a moment ago had been a shared hallucination. Her eyes darted around the apartment—not for escape, but for certainty of her own footing.

"I've got a meeting downtown. The Grid summit call with Zurich," he said lightly, glancing at his watch. "You're welcome to stay, babe. I'm not kicking you out. We're building trust here." He smiled, waving his finger between them like it was a promise instead of a warning.

She managed a quiet, "Thanks," keeping her eyes on the half-empty plate until she heard the faint click of his shoes on the marble and the whisper of the elevator doors closing behind him.

The stillness pressed against her ears as she scanned the loft—eyes tracing corners, ceiling beams, a faint red blink that might've been a sensor or could have just been her imagination. Every polished surface looked suddenly suspicious.

She grabbed her purse, leaving her phone, watch, and computer exactly where they were—dead weight if anything, potential eyes she couldn't risk carrying. The door clicked shut behind her as she stepped into the hall, down the elevator, and out of the building.

By the time Amanda reached Forty-Second, her breathing was measured enough to pass for sanity rather than reveal her internal frenzy. A short cab ride later, she slipped into a narrow café tucked beneath the street level—a place of low ceilings, steamed windows, and the smell of espresso cut with burnt sugar. It was the kind of place Tristan would never frequent, so at least there, she could assume anonymity.

Cooper was already waiting at the far end near a wall of frosted glass, coffee mug cupped in both hands. He didn't smile when she entered, just stood slightly, enough to acknowledge her, before nodding toward her purse.

She slid into the seat across from him, lowering her voice. "He didn't follow me."

"He doesn't have to," Cooper said, eyes flicking toward the window, then back to her bag. "You could be lit up like a beacon right now."

"I left everything, no phone—" she started, but a thought hit mid-sentence. She dug into the bag, her fingers running the seams until she found a small hole. With one tug, the stitches tore, and she turned the lining inside out, dumping everything onto the table. "Nothing," she sighed.

"Good." Cooper leaned in, voice barely more than a thread. He didn't ask why she looked paler than she had last night; he already knew.

A waitress drifted by, setting a fresh cup in front of her before disappearing again into the café's blur of voices and clinking dishes. Amanda stared at it, startled. The tea was exactly how she drank it—light, no sugar. She hadn't said a word when she'd walked in; she barely remembered walking in at all.

"You ordered this?" she asked, curling her hands around the warm ceramic, letting it soak into her cold fingers.

"I figured you wouldn't take the time to stop at the counter," Cooper murmured, eyes flicking briefly toward the door as if expecting Tristan to spill through it.

She smiled, lifting the cup, breathing in the steam like it was the first real breath she'd taken since leaving Tristan's apartment.

"So," she began, "Tristan found the prototype in my suitcase because it pinged some kind of network or log when we got to his apartment. He was too busy to notice right away, but after he got back, he was checking the logs or something. And when I was out wedding dress shopping, of all things—with his mom and sister—" she paused, not for dramatic effect but to absorb the truth as it left her mouth. "Yeah. He went on a hunt."

"And I told him," she added, fingers tightening around her cup. "About Katherine. That she was the one who gave me the prototype in the first place. I panicked, Cooper. I didn't know how to lie to him without making everything worse."

Cooper's jaw tensed, not at her, but at the thought of her being pushed into a confession she never should've had to make.

"Okay," he murmured. "Then we plan for that variable too."

He reached into his jacket and slid a small unmarked drive across the table.

"This is a shell clone," he said, turning the device over in his hands. "Basically an empty version of Tristan's system. Once we get his main computer to mirror onto it, this one becomes a full copy: files, messages, signatures, everything he thinks he's hidden."

Amanda blinked. "You can really do that?"

"It's easier than breaking into his actual machine," he replied. "We're not hacking him—we're tricking his system into talking to itself."

Amanda blinked at it. "You make it sound simple."

"It's not." His eyes softened briefly, the tension in his features shifting but not lifting. "He's too good. Every keystroke on his system is tracked, and any anomaly trips a security relay. And right now?" He shook his head. "He's watching everything. He may not show it, but he is."

Amanda narrowed her eyes. "Cooper... when did you become good at all this?"

He glanced up, surprised not by the question itself, but by how long it had taken her to ask it. "What do you mean?"

"This." She gestured to the drive, the planning, the quiet precision of his movements. "This isn't just 'I read a manual once' good. And you were never—" She caught herself, shook her head. "You weren't an IT kind of guy before."

A faint, rueful smile curved at his mouth. "No. I wasn't. But it's been a long time since you've known the guy I used to be."

"So?" she pressed. "When?"

Cooper set his cup down with care, aligning it with the edge of the saucer. When he finally spoke, his voice had dropped into a lower, more private register—one she'd only heard from him a handful of times.

"West Point opened a few doors," he said. "And after that... doors inside doors."

"That's not an answer."

"It's the beginning of one." He leaned in slightly, elbows on the table, shielding the conversation with his body. "When I was deployed, I got pulled into a small unit—off the record, hybrid operations. They needed people who could blend. Look ordinary. Think fast. Learn things on the fly."

"Special ops?"

"Not the kind you picture," he said. "Less kicking down doors, more slipping through the cracks. Signals intelligence, digital infiltration... reading patterns no one was supposed to see."

Amanda blinked, trying to merge the boy she used to know with the man across from her now. His expression softened, something like regret threading through it.

Cooper's gaze lifted to hers, steady and unflinching. "I learned what I learned to keep people alive, Amanda. And right now... that includes you."

Her stomach tightened, but for the first time since leaving the loft, her fear didn't feel shapeless. It had direction—edges, an ally across from her who wasn't pretending everything was fine.

Cooper glanced down at her hands, at the faint tremor she tried to hide, and reached over to touch them, to steady her.

"You'll have to get into his office when he's gone, plug this into the auxiliary port on his workstation. Leave it for two minutes. That's all I need."

Amanda frowned. "He's never more than a few feet from his computer," she said.

"Then wait until he's in the bathroom."

Amanda dropped her head.

"I know it's risky," Cooper said, curling his fingers into hers and bringing her hand closer.

"I know. It's okay. I'll do it. You'll be remote?"

"Yep," he answered quickly. "I'll get a signal as soon as it goes online."

The way he said it made her chest tighten. "And if he sees it?"

Cooper's voice stayed calm, but his expression carried the weight of the risk they were taking. "Then we're both done."

For a moment, she saw him as he'd once been—the boy who'd been taken from her, trained to obey, to march in straight lines until emotion became a liability. That discipline, despite being unnatural, lived in his posture, in the exactness of his words. He was all mission now, barely any softness left—and that, she realized, was exactly what they needed.

"But if we pull it off, we'll have the proof—his communications with Julius, his access logs, his network routes. Enough to dismantle the entire illusion of his innocence. But whatever we do, cloning his computer has to look like routine background data on his end."

Amanda sat back, letting his words settle. The noise of the café faded, replaced by the low rush of blood in her ears. She exhaled, the air escaping her lips trembling slightly. "What if I can't do it?"

"Then you don't," he said. "You walk away. But if you can…" His other hand rose, enveloping her free hand, drawing her an inch toward him with a restraint that felt perilously close to slipping. The movement was minimal—barely a shift in space—yet their faces hovered close enough that she could see the faint pulse at his throat, steady but not calm.

"Then we end this. For good," he said.

His touch lingered longer than it had any right to. Just the grip of their hands—and yet the temperature of the room seemed to tilt around the point where their skin met.

"Cooper," she whispered, the word slipping out before she could cage it.

He exhaled, slow and controlled, as he eased his hands back, each inch a deliberate withdrawal. "We can't afford to…" he swallowed his thoughts. "Not here," he said.

"I know." But her words felt thin, as if they'd been drained of all meaning on the way out.

Cooper exhaled slowly, the moment folding back in on itself. His fingertip brushed the slim drive between them, nudging it toward her with a speechless finality. Amanda reached for it. For a beat, she simply held it, feeling its cold weight settle against her palm, before she slipped it into her bag.

He rose swiftly, as if this part of the mission was successful, his movements deliberate as he shrugged into his coat.

"Don't call. Don't text. Just drop the port in the lockbox at the Lexington cloakroom—corner of Thirty-Seventh and Park." He slid a thin black key card across the table toward her, but added a gentle smile. "This gets you in."

Amanda tucked the card into her coat pocket, struck by how unremarkable it looked. She lifted her eyes to his. "And once we have the clone?"

Cooper hesitated, just long enough for Amanda to feel her stomach drop, and said, "Then we start running."

The words settled between them, heavy with meaning. Promise? Warning? Perhaps something in the space between.

She remained at the table even after he stepped through the glass doors and vanished into the blur of the street. Her fingers hovered over her bag, brushing the outline of the drive—small and ordinary, yet already fracturing the foundation of her entire world.

Chapter Five

Chicago, Illinois: Two Days Later

"You made it!" Lyla said, sweeping snow from her coat with the flourish of a performer. Amanda's long-time best friend could move through a storm and make it look like a well-rehearsed dance. She was all instinct and color, equal parts hurricane and halo, the antithesis of Amanda's quiet calculation. Where Amanda tucked away anything that hurt, Lyla displayed all her experiences like art—every piece part of a larger story she never tried to hide.

"I was starting to think you'd forgotten how telephones actually work," she smiled, the voice coming through the swirl of cold before the woman herself did.

Amanda blinked, half smiling. Only Lyla would think nothing of calling from another time zone and saying, *"Meet me in Chicago,"* as though it were a perfectly reasonable Saturday plan.

As they paused inside the lobby, Lyla took a long, hard look at Amanda. "Please tell me you've eaten something solid in the last seventy-two hours," she said, one eyebrow lifting as if she were an old school marm, scolding a student.

Amanda tilted her head. "Define solid. Coffee counts if it has… substance, right? Foam is basically food."

Lyla laughed, her eyes catching the light with a brightness born of love, though a shadow of worry lingered beneath it. "Well, you *do* look like you've been living on caffeine and sheer willpower."

Amanda stepped aside, waving her hand slightly through the air. "And you look like the storm was just your runway."

"Obviously," Lyla tossed her hair back in one effortless motion, the gesture caught somewhere between red carpet and reflex.

She looped her arm through Amanda's, steering her toward the lobby's light as if they were late to something perfectly ordinary. "If I'm going to drag you halfway across the country, I might as well make an entrance."

Lyla moved with her usual theatrical sway, a grin blooming as though she'd just pulled off another small miracle. They crossed the marble floor together, heels tapping in sync, muted by the sound of people filling the entrance—luggage wheels rolling, a concierge's voice softened by distance, the faint hiss of steam from the café corner. Outside, the L train moaned across the river, its low tremor slipping through the tall glass façade like a pulse the city couldn't hide.

"So, are you going to tell me why you didn't answer a single text for four days, and I was about to lose my ever-loving mind with worry?" Lyla asked as they reached a cluster of velvet chairs near the window.

"I was off-grid."

"That's your excuse for everything now."

"It's my reality," Amanda replied, her tone quieter than she meant it to be.

Lyla paused, studying her. "Off-grid or hiding?"

Amanda smiled faintly. "Both."

"Well," Lyla said, unwinding her scarf and tossing it over the chair, "if you're going to have a breakdown, I at least got you a hotel with *incredible* amenities," she smiled, but her tone shifted. "I wasn't sure you'd actually do it—show up, I mean."

Amanda exhaled slowly, the warmth of it slipping into the small space that separated them. "Neither was I."

"Then let's make it worth the trip," Lyla said, pulling out a thin folder and holding it between them.

"Please tell me this is not a self-help workbook," Amanda grimaced.

"I'm not that worried about you," Lyla laughed. "It's worse. Corporate propaganda." She tapped her finger on the folder as she said the words, then slid the packet across the table. "The reason I had you meet me here is because I'm freelancing for a PR firm. "One of their clients is—guess who?"

Amanda gave a small shrug, the motion more fatigue than curiosity. "I haven't the slightest," she said.

Lyla's eyes widened, "Helion Technologies," she enunciated. "And you won't believe what they're calling an 'ethics campaign.' I nearly fell out of my chair when I saw the name, much less some of the cryptic language."

Amanda opened the folder. Three pages in, the words *Autonomous Deterrence Protocols* glared up at her in a crisp white font, overlaid atop a sleek navy blue header.

Her pulse hitched. "What is this?"

"It's what I think it is, right?" Lyla asked. "Like, *end-of-the-world run by robots* bad."

"Yeah," Amanda nodded.

"So, I'm not wrong. You know I can sense when things get bad, but, like, break it down for me," Lyla said. "What do they mean by all of this?"

Amanda leaned closer, scanning the line. "So, deterrence is just keeping your enemies from striking first, usually by proving you can hit back harder."

"Totally," Lyla said. "That's like the old Cold War standoff. But autonomous—" She looked up. "That means *no human oversight?*"

"Right," Amanda said softly. "A system that responds automatically if it senses an attack. No waiting for authorization. No one to say *stop.*" Her words lingered a moment, the silence around them tightening. Then she blinked, the analytical calm giving way to a sharper realization. "But—wait. How did you even get this?"

"That's why I've been trying to get a hold of you this week. I'm supposed to photograph a Helion facility here with all the executives. You'd think something this dark would be password-protected. Nope. It's their save-the-world campaign that arrived in my inbox like an ad for hand cream, Amanda. Fonts, ideal locations for inspiration, and moral decay—all beautifully aligned. And hiring me as the photographer—that can't be a subtle message. Do you think they know you've told me stuff?"

Amanda had never fully understood the Helion Group—no one outside their upper tiers truly did—but she knew enough to recognize the shape of their power. They weren't a company so much as a constellation of them, a network of industries secretly welded together beneath one name. Energy, communications, aerospace, medical tech—Helion didn't diversify; they entwined.

What unnerved her most was the way they operated: not by force or influence, but by *integration.* They slipped into places that didn't normally overlap—power grids syncing with satellite systems, analytics feeding into public health databases, transportation models whispering to supply-chain algorithms. Once Helion placed a single device inside a system, the rest followed like falling dominoes. Governments called it innovation. Helion called it efficiency. Everyone else simply learned to depend on it.

It made the world feel smaller in subtle ways, as if whole countries were running on software no one had thought to question. And Tristan—brilliant, polished, adored—had been their ideal frontman. The Ocular Grid wasn't just a masterpiece; it was the entry point into the last place Helion had yet to claim: *vision.*

Amanda traced a finger over the embossed header. "I don't know. These trillion-dollar tech overlords are not even pretending anymore." She set the paper down and pressed its corners flat, the motion practiced, and pointless—an instinct for control in a world unraveling by the minute.

"Autonomous deterrence," she said absently, her tone strained. "At Oak Ridge—the old nuclear research hub in Tennessee where the Manhattan Project was in the fifties—you know what they called it?"

Lyla hesitated, watching her with a blank stare, knowing something more was coming. The question sounded rhetorical, but Amanda's voice carried the weight of her perfect memory— she was recalling something she'd read long ago. Lyla shook her head without a word.

"Machine-guided response systems," she said, her voice monotone. "Different century, same delusion. People still think if they make the algorithm sophisticated enough, it'll develop a conscience."

Lyla shook her head. "So... you're telling me they've dusted off the apocalypse and given it a new logo?"

Amanda almost smiled. "Pretty much. Only this time, they're dressing it up as moral efficiency."

"A pragmatic end-of-days, of course," Lyla scoffed, taking a sip of coffee. "We've only ourselves to blame, I guess. So what does that look like, practically?"

Amanda hesitated, scanning the café window where traffic pulsed like a living graph. "If these slides are real, Helion's already merging defense contracts with the Grid—automating nuclear deterrence through predictive modeling. Meaning: the system that analyzes social behavior, i.e., the Grid, could soon analyze launch decisions. And whoever controls that, basically controls the world."

Lyla stared. "Please tell me that sentence is not even real."

"I wish it weren't." Amanda leaned in. "They're trying to market this thing to the whole world as an ethical safe-guard—remove emotional bias, prevent human error—but it's the same logic that built the bombs in the first place. We keep saying *never again,* and then we find smarter ways to say, well, just *maybe,* we might need these nukes someday."

Silence folded again between them, the sputtering of the espresso machine sounding suddenly intrusive.

Lyla shook her head slowly. "You know, you have a real talent for dropping world-ending information in a sentence or two."

"I'm sorry," Amanda chuckled, her eyes flickering back to life at Lyla's attempt at humor.

"Don't be. But, we may have to work on a rebrand for you, okay?" She grinned, eyes still on the folder. "So... where do you see Tristan in all of this?

Lyla knew about the breakup; she'd been the first person Amanda called. But she didn't know what those days afterward had really held. She didn't know why Amanda had gone silent, or how Cooper had resurfaced to help her peel back the layers of Tristan's life. She didn't know that Amanda had stepped in and out of Tristan's apartment again, not for reconciliation, but to learn how to dismantle the man she once thought she loved. Amanda kept all of that sealed—not out of secrecy, but because Lyla was already tangled enough in this story.

So she offered the part she could say safely.

"Where do I see him?" Amanda exhaled.

"Yeah, do you think Tristan is just creating systems? Running things?" Lyla's voice was barely above a whisper.

"Maybe both," Amanda choked. "He thinks he's preventing chaos. He believes if he can control information, he can prevent people from making the wrong choice, and he calls it 'stability.' "

"And you call it…?"

"Essentially? Tyranny—obligatory obedience. Tale as old as time," Amanda murmured. Her voice softened at the memory of their high school days. "Do you remember when we studied Hiroshima in that ethics seminar? Everyone else argued about military strategy, and you said the worst part wasn't even the blast—it was that someone somewhere along the line wrote the plan to potentially annihilate millions as an acceptable risk."

Lyla's fingers paused mid-gesture, resting on the rim of her cup. "I was being dramatic," she said.

"You were being realistic. And you weren't wrong."

For a moment, neither spoke. Outside, the light shifted against the window, gray to silver.

Amanda's gaze lingered there, on the shimmer of light against glass. *Acceptable risk.* The phrase had followed her from theory into currency. She used to write about the moral calculus of nations—how strategy could hinge on devastation, how scale made unthinkable choices feel survivable. Now she was living inside that equation, where a man's algorithm could decide whose life counted enough to spare. It wasn't abstract anymore; it was the cost measured in real bodies, real consequences.

She tore her eyes from the window, her reflection dissolving as Lyla spoke again, grounding her in the present. "So what now? Do I order another latte or an underground bunker?"

Amanda laughed, but the sound caught mid-breath, disappearing before it could become humor. Perhaps there was no graceful way to protect Lyla from what she was about to say—and no point in pretending anymore.

"I'm supposed to clone Tristan's laptop," she said. "Cooper's guiding me from the outside, but Tristan is almost never without that computer—and when he is, the security around it comes alive. I can't risk being caught; I don't even know what kind of danger I'd be in."

Lyla absorbed the words without blinking at first, her whole face pausing—not shocked, but subtly shifting, like she was rearranging the internal map she used to make sense of Amanda's life.

"So... you didn't come here because you finally wanted me to stop calling and texting?" Lyla asked slowly. "You were avoiding the task? Or delaying it?"

"Both," Amanda admitted. "And because you're the only person I trust to tell me when I'm losing perspective."

"That's easy," Lyla said, lifting her cup with a dry flourish. "You lost it three countries ago."

Amanda's smile wavered slightly but still held. "At least I'm consistent," she said, raising an eyebrow.

Lyla's gaze settled, steady and unflinching, threaded with worry but not judgment. When she spoke again, her voice dropped into a soothing cadence.

"So you're working with Cooper again?"

Amanda didn't flinch that time. "Yes," she admitted.

Lyla exhaled, the subtlest shift of breath, but it carried more understanding than surprise.

"Well," she said, leaning back, "that explains the ghosting. And the circles under your eyes. And the whole 'I'm clearly keeping twelve secrets and maybe a prototype in my purse' energy."

Despite everything, Amanda couldn't help but let out a genuine laugh.

Lyla reached across the table, her fingers brushing Amanda's wrist in a gesture so simple it steadied her.

"Just... don't cut me out again, okay? I can't help you stay alive if I don't know which disaster you're walking into."

Amanda smiled faintly. "You got it," she said.

Lyla drummed her fingers on the table. "Okay, humor me. Let's say you get what you need from Tristan's computer. What happens then? You expose him? Blow up Helion's board meeting? Upload the files to some noble corner of the internet?"

"I don't know," Amanda said. "I'm not built for endings. Just the truth."

"That's such an Amanda thing to say," Lyla muttered. Then, she leaned in and spoke more gently. "You realize you're still in love with him, right?"

Amanda blinked, startled by the definitiveness of Lyla's words. "I'm in love with the *idea* of him. The man who convinced me that ethics could be engineered, that a better world was just a matter of design. Who wined and dined me in every way imaginable."

"And now?"

"Now I see how belief becomes weaponry."

Lyla crossed one hand over the other, her voice steady. "So you're doing this to save him—or to stop him?"

Amanda's answer came after a long beat. "I don't know."

Lyla nodded slowly. "That's the problem with empathy. It makes excellent spies and terrible survivors."

"Tell me about it."

They sat for a while, watching the reflection of pedestrians ripple across the window—faces in motion, anonymous and safe.

"Do you ever think about how we got here?" Amanda asked. "We always talked about wanting to make the world better. Now the best we can do is try to keep it from collapsing."

"Stopping a collapse is still progress," Lyla said. "Sometimes saving the world looks like buying it a little more time."

Amanda laughed despite herself. "You should trademark that."

"I will. I'll print it on T-shirts if we all survive this."

Amanda's phone buzzed, muffled against her bag. She glanced at it before she turned the screen face-down, pulse skipping.

Lyla caught the shift in her expression. "That was him, wasn't it?"

"Not Tristan."

"The other him, then."

Amanda nodded once.

"You know what this reminds me of?" Lyla finally said. "That scene in *Pride and Prejudice*. When Elizabeth realizes she's been wrong about Darcy and Wickham."

Amanda arched a brow. "You're not about to compare Tristan and Cooper to Austen characters, are you?"

Lyla tilted her head, unbothered by Amanda's edge. "And why shouldn't I? Jane Austen, the Queen of Everything, doesn't get the feminist credit she deserves. And you know I'm not wrong. Because, tell me if this doesn't fit—'one has all the appearance of goodness, and the other has all the goodness itself.'"

Amanda blinked, as if the line hit too close.

"Don't act like you're too sophisticated for a little Regency wisdom," Lyla said lightly, her voice insistent with accuracy.

"You told me how the Hansens lied to both of you. How Cooper never knew about...everything. You were both victims, Amanda. And Tristan..." She hesitated, watching Amanda's face. "I'm starting to think I may have never really known him... like his pursuits and genius have only ever had the appearance of goodness."

Lyla let the words settle in the silence between them. Then she took a slow, deliberate sip of her coffee, eyes never leaving Amanda's face. The faint slurp that followed wasn't careless—it was calculated, a tiny act meant to draw Amanda out of her thoughts as she set the cup down again with care.

"Okay," she spoke discreetly, without her typical flair. "You and Cooper have a plan, at least, right? What do you need from me?"

"Nothing dangerous," Amanda said. "Maybe just a place to vanish in plain sight if things go sideways."

"That I can do." Lyla scribbled an address on a napkin, her handwriting quick and confident. "It's a co-op studio near Wabash. I've got friends who owe me favors. If you show up asking for room twenty-three, they'll assume you're a designer and practically ignore you."

"Thank you."

Lyla reached across the table, covering Amanda's hand with hers. "You've been carrying the end of the world like it's hand luggage, babe. You're allowed to set it down sometimes."

Amanda looked up, eyes bright but steady, the faintest quiver in her smile revealing the fatigue beneath it.

"I will," she said. "When it's safe."

Lyla quirked a brow, folding her arms as she leaned back. "That's what you said before Bucharest."

Amanda exhaled through her nose with half a laugh. "And yet, here I am."

"Barely." Lyla's tone was gentle, but her eyes said the rest—*you don't have to keep proving you can survive this way.*

The corner of Amanda's mouth lifted. "Barely still counts, doesn't it?"

"Only in horseshoes and hand grenades," Lyla said, grinning.

That old line of her grandpa's had followed them since high school, always surfacing at the right time. He'd toss it out with some other nonsense—like asking if they "lived around here or rode a bike"—and the two of them would dissolve into laughter. It was their shorthand for everything unspoken: *I see you. You're not alone.* Those were the kinds of lines that belonged only to them, the ones that proved their friendship had roots deeper than reason.

"I hate that I can't fix this for you," Lyla murmured. "But if anyone can walk through hell and come out breathing, it's you. Just promise me you will."

Amanda's smile was small but real. "You know I don't make promises I can't keep," she said. "But I'll try like hell."

"Come on. You need sugar before you start dismantling empires," Lyla replied, tugging her hand until Amanda rose.

They wove through tables toward a pastry counter at the front of the cafe, the air thick with espresso and conversation. A barista called out an order, steam hissed, and the women's conversation disappeared into the city's steady hum, just another secret folded into its endless noise.

Chapter Six

NYC, Tristan's Loft: Two Days Later

"Maybe they're nervous," Amanda offered, folding her legs beneath her on the couch. "You're moving fast. People get uneasy when they can't keep up."

"I don't know," Tristan huffed. He was standing as he often did, palms on the window, staring at the view. He'd often stay there for long stretches of time; he claimed it cleared his head.

New York lay pressed to the glass like a living diagram—avenues sliding past each other with a precision that was somehow both intricately designed and haphazard. At this height, noise flattened into a single unbroken line, and the city's pulse vibrated in the bones of the apartment building.

He watched, the reflection staring back at him coating his face with a sheen, like polish over steel.

He said nothing for a while, then turned, studying her. She used to think his intensity was sexy; she saw it in the way he studied everything, precise and detailed. But now, things felt clinical, like he was searching for weakness disguised as curiosity or admiration.

She squirmed in her seat.

"I'm working with people who have to keep up, Amanda. Or else this doesn't work. We have to have buy-in from all parties to really show how this can unite our world."

Amanda swallowed, half smiling. Tristan had been performing all evening. He had cooked for her again, happy to have her home after her trip to Chicago, he'd said. She knew he was tracking her every move, so there were no lies to keep track of. She had visited Lyla just as they always had—here, there, and around the world. It was nothing out of the ordinary. But when she'd come back, with nothing set in stone about whether she'd stay, they'd sat down to dinner—pan-seared sea bass, a salad he plated with accurate attention, and opened a bottle he said he'd been saving "for a night we needed to remember."

During dinner, he'd touched her effortlessly and warmly. He'd been all charm until he left the table to take a call—Helion's ethics committee wanted to pause, to "evaluate downstream implications" before approving the next round of partnerships. Afterwards, Tristan had paced the apartment, irritation flashing beneath his polished exterior as he muttered about bureaucrats who "couldn't see the trajectory of progress even when it stood in front of them." He'd said they were timid, provincial, and unable to grasp what the Ocular Grid could accomplish.

"They'll get it. They just need time," Amanda now reassured.

When he looked at her again, the smile that surfaced held just enough softness to *feel* real. But Amanda recognized the shift—the precision of a man returning to the role he chose, the perfect partner he knew how to perform.

"Stay," he said, and he meant the evening, the month, the arc of whatever he had convinced himself was permanence. He meant the next flight and the one after. He meant the couch, the bed, the chair where she liked to tuck one leg under and read, as if books could ground her.

"Stay for dessert?" she said lightly with a wry smile, trying to temper his fervor.

"Forever," he whispered, and there was kindness in it. His softness unmoored her—rationally, she knew it was possession dressed up as promise, but her heart wasn't fully convinced. And standing there—too close, too tired, too worn down by the whiplash of the last few days—she felt herself teeter on the line between wanting to trust it and knowing better.

He crossed the room to sit beside her, setting his glass of wine down on the table. His hand grazed her shoulder, lingering before sliding down her arm. "You're impossible to replace, you know that?"

Once, she might have melted at words like that. Now they only made her brace.

She tilted her head, hiding her unease behind a soft smirk. "Flattery doesn't make me stay. You know that, too."

Tristan chuckled, the sound low and rhythmic. "No. But it makes you hesitate."

She grinned as he kissed her temple, then moved his lips to her neck before a phone buzzed.

"Not another call," Amanda whispered, more out of fear that something else would upset him rather than being interrupted.

"It's probably Julius. I texted him about Helion's evaluations," Tristan said as he picked up the phone and walked into the bedroom.

Amanda waited for the air to settle, for his footsteps to carry him far enough away that she could catch her breath again. Every nerve in her body felt like it had learned Morse code: *wait, not yet, wait.*

As soon as the bedroom door shut, she felt the signal switch—a thin slice of silence opening like a fault line beneath her feet. Tristan always lowered his voice when speaking to Julius, pacing to the far side of the room so no one could overhear. It was the only predictable privacy he ever offered, and this was her window. Small and razor-thin, but real. She rose slowly, every movement calculated, listening for the familiar cadence of his voice turning low and clipped. When it came—muffled through the wall, sharp with irritation—she slipped toward his office, her pulse tightening into a steady, urgent rhythm.

The loft had no real rooms, only shifts in purpose: living area, kitchen, the open workspace he favored. The bedroom door closing signaled the only true boundary in the entire space.

Tristan's desk occupied the brightest corner against the window, its surface perfectly ordered, and Tristan's laptop was placed directly in the center. He had an almost religious obsession with it, including practices to alert him if it was ever tampered with in his absence. Every time he left the room, he angled it a certain way, checked the reflection on the screen, and memorized its position. Upon returning to work, he'd notice even the slightest shift in the lid.

And yet, Cooper's plan depended on her touching it. She put her hand on it, the closed machine warm beneath her fingers, slipping the data port—a slim, matte-black device, small enough to disappear in her hand—into the USB slot.

"Plug it in, and don't touch anything," Cooper had said. "It'll run itself. If he's got motion sensors or mic surveillance, it'll mimic background noise—same heat signatures, same electrical pulse. You'll have a few minutes before the system pings any false loop."

The device clicked on, a small green light pulsing at the edge. Her reflection wavered on the screen as she opened the laptop, and the machine hummed to life. She typed the passcode she'd memorized a few months earlier—the one she'd spotted during those early days when she was new, frightened, and paying attention to everything. Tristan had never told her. She'd simply seen it once, tucked it away, and never forgotten. Lines of code began to whir in mirrored glass, unreadable and dizzying.

Amanda glanced toward the closed door. Tristan's voice filtered faintly through—low, and impatient, full of passion and the evening's annoyances. Julius was on the other end, likely controlling the tempo as he always did.

On the screen, the progress bar crept forward with merciless precision. Folders opened and collapsed in rapid succession, each completed sector chiming with a faint, crystalline tone. The pattern of it lulled the nerves beneath her skin, pulling her into its steady count, until the door handle turned.

Her heart jolted so violently she felt the echo in her fingertips. In one motion, she pulled the drive free, tucked it into her sleeve, and nudged the laptop just enough to restore its angle.

Tristan stepped out of the bedroom and into the main living space a moment later, drained and sharp-edged, a faint charge still crackling through the room with him.

"Everything okay?" she asked, forcing calm.

"Julius thinks I should slow the full European rollout."

"Oh?" She leaned casually against the desk, praying he wouldn't notice her pulse.

"He says the optics aren't right. He wants a bit of silence before expansion."

"Do you agree?"

Tristan stared out the window, his reflection fractured by city lights. "I don't know. He's been cautious ever since Nairobi. But the Grid can't wait. We're weeks from full integration. We need all sites to activate."

Amanda moved closer. "Then maybe take a breath before you decide what to say to the partners. Sleep on it."

He stepped forward, leaning into her, brushing a strand of hair from her cheek. His fingers trailed behind her ear, resting against her neck for a moment without saying another word. When he finally turned away, moving to the kitchen for another drink, Amanda exhaled. The small device was still warm under her sleeve.

We should get away for a few days," he said, almost offhandedly, though the weight behind it was unmistakable. "My parents are already at the house in Lake Como. They'd love to see you." His smile deepened. "And frankly, I'd like to keep you close while things with Helion stabilize."

"Sounds lovely, but..." She hesitated just long enough for concern, but not suspicion, to flicker across his face. "I just don't think I can leave right now."

His expression shifted—tightening, then smoothing over in a single breath. "Why?"

She walked to the kitchen island, taking a seat on a stool. "Because you kicked me out, Tristan. A few days ago, you told me to leave. I'm still trying to understand where exactly we stand."

He stared at her, unblinking, the faintest scoff leaving his throat. "Amanda... that wasn't a breakup. You know that. It was a *moment.* You walked out before we resolved anything."

She blinked, surprised by the memory being rewritten so cleanly. "I walked out because you asked me to."

"I asked you to *give me space*," he corrected softly, as if soothing a child who had misunderstood. "And you coming back proves you know we're not done."

His hand slid to her wrist as she held his gaze. She took a breath, knowing she had to find a way to appease him.

"I didn't say we were done," she smiled. "I just need time to handle a few things before I can disappear to Italy with you."

"Things?" His voice stayed even, but the question carried a weight that had nothing to do with curiosity.

She exhaled, thinking on the fly. "The dress company called today. You know, the gown I ordered before... everything. The cancellation can't be done over the phone. They need me to come in and sign the release. If I don't handle it this week, they'll charge the next installment, and I'm not flying across the world while that's hanging over me."

"You don't have to cancel the dress," Tristan said, taking both of her hands into his. "We don't need to make decisions like that yet. Let's just... see where life takes us."

Amanda didn't waver. "I'm not canceling it because I've made a decision about us," she said quietly. "I'm not getting the dress because I need closure on what happened. If you want us to do a reset, I can't while pieces of that day are still hanging over me. And if we're going to press reset in Italy, I need to close the part that got ripped open in New York."

He studied her for a long moment, recalibrating the narrative into one he could live with. Then he nodded, his voice lowering into a practiced, reassuring cadence.

"Fine. Handle it. But don't let it pull you back into... doubts." His thumb brushed her cheek. "We're not going backward, Amanda. We're rebuilding. You coming to Como proves that."

She let her features soften into a measured and believable smile. "Then let me meet you there with a clean slate."

"Okay," he said. "Come to Como once your little errand is handled." He slapped the counter with a subtle, decisive clap. "Two days. I'll fly ahead and get things ready for us."

Amanda nodded, "I'll meet you there."

His lips curved into satisfaction, reassured and restored. "Good," he whispered, kissing her temple. "I knew you'd choose us. Now, what do you want to drink?" he asked as if they'd only been chatting about the weather.

"Surprise me," she said.

He grinned. "Always."

As he reached for a bottle from the wine rack, Amanda let her gaze drift back to the window. She'd gotten what she came for. She should've felt triumphant, but instead, there was only hollowness.

"You know, Julius was testing you with that whole Katherine giving you the prototype," Tristan said, pouring her another glass of wine. "He wanted to see whether you'd panic. You didn't." His fingers brushed her wrist, warm and reassuring. "You kept quiet when it mattered. That means something."

Amanda gave a small smile. "I'm glad you see it that way. I was really just scared and didn't know who to trust." She tipped her glass toward his as the sound of a soft clink made Tristan smile.

She saw the flicker of approval in his eyes, the kind that made him lean in and kiss her temple, murmuring something more about trust and moving forward. And for the rest of the evening, she played along beautifully. She let her shoulders soften, her laughter sound easy, and the wine slip down her throat like permission.

By the time they went to bed, Tristan's arm draped warm and heavy over her waist. The shape of her breathing was already convincing him she was safe again—anchored, loyal, his.

But Amanda lay awake in the dark, her pulse matching the faint hum of the prototype she no longer carried. Her mind traced a single path: the drive in her bag, the lockbox on Lexington, the short window Cooper said they had before Tristan synced his system again.

His sleep was light at first—he always drifted through the edges of dreams before dropping fully into them. When his breathing finally deepened, long and even, she eased out from under his arm.

When she slipped out of bed, Tristan stirred. "Where are you going?"

"Water," she whispered, trying not to give him any reason to fully wake up.

He reached for her wrist, even half-asleep, tugging her with a reflexive pull, as if some part of him refused to let her drift too far. "Stay."

Amanda froze. The pressure of his hand wasn't painful, but it was enough to remind her that freedom wasn't something he'd ever give easily.

She turned slightly, softening her voice. "I'll be right back."

Tristan hesitated, then released her. "Don't be long." He gave a low, drowsy sound, loosening his grip entirely as he slipped back into sleep.

Amanda moved to the kitchen, filling a glass just for the sound of it, her mind spinning with contingencies. She couldn't afford suspicion. Not tonight. She set the glass down and leaned against the counter, breathing slowly until her pulse leveled.

At the front door, she hesitated long enough to make sure there was no other movement in the house. Tristan hadn't moved. She reached for her coat and bag, sliding the zipper open only halfway, keeping the sound a whisper. Her fingers found the drive she'd tucked into the side pocket, and the key card beside it.

Lexington cloakroom. Thirty-seventh and Park. She repeated each detail silently, like beads on a rosary, as she slipped into the hallway.

The building was still sleepy, creating the kind of hush that carried every sound farther than it should. Her heartbeat was loud in her throat as she crossed to the elevator, then changed her mind—stairs were safer. They weren't monitored like the elevators were. Each level down felt like shedding another layer of the woman Tristan believed had come home to him. Her choice sharpened with every step: she had to break free of him, of his spell, and of the people who had placed her in his orbit to begin with.

Outside, the night air wrapped around her with a cool seriousness. New York hummed even at this hour—taxis cutting through the dark, a delivery truck unloading crates of produce, a woman on a bike weaving past with a messenger bag slung cross-body. Normal life for a city that never sleeps.

She drew her coat tighter as she stepped outside, her fingers skimming the key card in her pocket the way one checks a pulse. The streets were still drowsy with blue-gray light, traffic low enough that every passing car made her glance over her shoulder. Lexington and Thirty-Seventh lay only a few blocks ahead—near enough that she could walk it before Tristan woke, and before whatever fragile margin she still had collapsed.

She kept her pace steady, letting the city swallow her as she moved. At each intersection, she paused briefly, scanning reflections and listening for footsteps that didn't belong to her until the moment she arrived. The cloakroom's narrow vestibule offered a thin slice of shelter from the wind as she slipped inside, the door whispering shut behind her.

Amanda slid the key card through the scanner as the lockbox door eased open. She placed the drive inside, closing the metal lid with a click so soft it barely existed. She let a breath leave her mouth in a slow, controlled exhale.

Then she turned and walked back out into the city—into the glow of streetlamps, into the possibility of being caught, or into whatever came next. But when she got onto the sidewalk, two men stepped out of the mouth of a service alley, their movements too coordinated to be chance. One of them said her name. He didn't shout or question her, just stated it, like a confirmation that she was the mark he was looking for.

Amanda's instincts didn't think; they detonated. She ran, her shoes slapping the pavement, breath sharp in her chest, and the night air breaking against her face as she tore toward the corner of the block. Until, suddenly, she skidded to a halt.

Katherine stood beneath the streetlight, hands clasped, silver hair catching the glow like frost. She didn't look startled. She looked like she'd been waiting.

"Amanda," she said, her tone almost apologetic. "Follow me."

The men flanked her as gently as they could, guiding her toward a nondescript entrance between a dry cleaner and a shuttered café. There were no windows, no signage, just a black door and a key fob, one of them tapped.

Inside, the stairwell climbed in tight concrete spirals, and they ascended quickly, as if they knew she wouldn't fight—not with Katherine murmuring, "You're safe now," in a voice meant to soothe, not convince.

At the top, a metal door swung open, and the world widened as the rooftop wind seized her hair. A black helicopter crouched in the darkness like an insect, lights pulsing along its frame, blades thudding slow and heavy as it idled.

Katherine placed a steadying hand at Amanda's back. "We don't have much time," she said.

She kept moving, letting their hands guide her, realizing too late that she hadn't escaped anything. She hadn't fled. It wasn't until the city opened beneath the spinning blades that she understood—this wasn't escape. This was capture.

Chapter Seven

NYC: The Next Morning

Cooper didn't remember the walk from the cloakroom door to the street—only the sensation of New York gathering around him in a kind of restless hum, as if the whole city were holding its breath. The air was cool against his face, the kind of morning that should have offered anonymity, but instead made him feel unbearably visible. He slipped the drive deeper into his jacket, not because anyone was watching, but because he had learned long ago that danger didn't always announce itself with footsteps.

He moved with purpose, yet each stride carried a strange, suspended quiet, as though leaving Manhattan required him to peel himself away from some invisible web. Amanda's name flickered through his thoughts, not with panic, but with the steady ache of someone he told himself he had no business worrying about, and yet she was the only thing on his mind.

Crossing Lexington, he didn't allow himself to look back. A man looking over his shoulder would be conspicuous—guilty, afraid, like someone worth following. So, he kept his eyes forward, melting into the flow of the early-morning foot traffic, letting the city's rhythm absorb him—taxis angling through intersections, headlights threading the dark, a couple arguing softly under the awning of a shop. To anyone watching, Cooper was just another man going somewhere he was expected to be.

He kept walking, Grand Central rising from the pavement in front of him—its stone lions and high-arched windows emerging through the morning haze, a sanctuary carved out of time. He slipped inside, letting the grand hall swallow him whole. Buying a ticket without thinking about the destination, he chose a place where the lines would let him disappear. The important part was distance. Silence. Space enough to open the drive without feeling the gravity of Manhattan pressing between his shoulder blades.

Minutes later, he boarded a near-empty Metro-South train, settling into a window seat as the doors hissed shut. Only when the city began to slide backward did he take out the device Amanda had risked everything to give him.

And for the first time since he had done the pickup, he allowed himself to breathe.

He set the drive carefully on the fold-out table. The metal casing looked inert, almost innocently designed, a harmless sliver of technology no different from a dozen others he'd handled in his years with the military. And yet this one contained something far more volatile: Tristan Montgomery's inner world. His architecture. His intentions. His true online personality that few would ever know.

Cooper connected it to the port on his laptop and watched the first shards of data unfurl like a slow, deliberate invitation. He thought he had prepared himself for the information that made a cold shock rush down his spine.

Folders within folders. Looping structures. Self-referencing scripts. Embedded triggers that seemed to watch the watcher. The farther the train moved from New York, the deeper Cooper sank into the cacophony on-screen. The exhaustion he'd been carrying sharpened into focus.

He exhaled softly, closing his hand around the drive for a moment as though it could steady him.

This was worse than he had feared, and better than he had hoped—it had worked. He had access to it all. He started with the logs.

They opened like any other archive—time stamps, locations, strings of characters that meant nothing until you knew what lens to look through. At first, it was only volume that struck him. Endless streams of data taken from test cities, airports, transit hubs, and business districts marked as "pilot zones." The Ocular Grid watched everything its transmitters could touch: faces, movements, trajectories, the small, unremarkable maneuvering of ordinary days.

Cooper scrolled, letting the rhythm of it wash past until a pattern began to surface.

Each subject line carried more than a name or anonymized ID. There were numerical tags attached, short strings that repeated with disquieting regularity.

C.O.E.

P.C.V.

V.I.

Efficient abbreviations that kept things organized without assigning any real depth or feeling to any of the data.

He followed one thread, expanding a single subject file at random—a man in his late forties, captured dozens of times in the course of a week as he crossed the same intersection on his way to work. It was a log for the Grid, but it documented more than his presence. It logged the pace of his stride, the angle of his head, the frequency with which he checked his phone, and the length of time he lingered in front of a crosswalk before setting foot on the street.

Under the video capture, a ledger unspooled:

Cognitive Output Efficiency: 0.72

Predictive Compliance Vector: 0.91

Volatility Index: 0.08

Cooper's gaze lingered on the first line. The man had become a fraction. Not dangerous enough to worry about. Not obedient enough to praise. Simply... inefficient.

Every subject carried a similar breakdown, some with glowing internal notes about "high-range potential," others marked as "non-advancing" or "low adaptive index." Children were tagged in playgrounds, students in lecture halls, and employees entering office towers. The Grid did not distinguish between public and private life. It catalogued everything, then rendered judgment.

The Ocular Grid system was never only about surveillance. It was about sorting. *Ocular* meant eyes on everything; *Grid* meant the boxes where certain kinds of people could be placed—and kept.

What the world hadn't realized was that the Grid wasn't waiting to be born; it was waiting to be *connected*. Each "prototype" Tristan delivered—Tokyo, Bangkok, Switzerland, Nairobi—hadn't been an experiment, but a live node. Helion's purchase wasn't a stake in the future. In truth, they were only buying a leash to a system already very much alive.

The tour hadn't been a launch. Everywhere they'd had a test site or "demo," the real Grid had already been active, gathering and sorting under the guise of research.

Once Cooper realized it, the classification lattice revealed itself like a hidden watermark. An invisible hierarchy was imposed over every captured face. The Grid did not merely predict who might break a law or pose a threat—it ranked people. It assigned social value.

Cooper followed another thread, hoping to discover how that value may be assigned to a nested directory buried three layers down. The folder titles here were more cautious, abstruse enough to pass casual inspection, but direct enough to make sense to the architect who had built them.

C2B Series was one label, with subfolders containing C2B0, C2B1, and C2B2.

He clicked on the one in the middle, C2B1, seemingly at random.

Schematic diagrams took over the screen—clean, elegant, and brutally simple. An animation of a slim crescent-shaped device appeared, settling just above the ear. Microfilaments radiated outward, not piercing skin but looking like minuscule suction cups syncing to the electrical murmurs beneath it, reading the mind and transmitting messages the way satellites communicate with everyday hardware.

Earlier generations had been implanted—surgical and crude, that, once removed left scars the person would never forget. Tristan's updated model didn't need incisions. It needed only contact. A brush of metal against skin, a moment of proximity, and the device began listening.

A single conductive thread ran through the center, gathering every signal into one seamless stream. Not just thoughts in progress, but preferences, tendencies, risk metrics—tiny pieces of a person rendered into data points.

Single-lane, uni-directional when desired, bi-directional when necessary. Computer to brain. Brain back to computer.

Cooper read the annotations slowly, allowing each phrase to lodge where it hurt most.

Single-track interface sufficient for base-level modulation. Full cognitive mapping unnecessary for early-stage compliance. Reduce noise. Reduce variance. Reduce deviation.

He lifted a hand to his own temple without thinking, fingers hovering over the spot where the schematic indicated the track would rest. His skin prickled at the thought of something foreign pressed there, listening, humming, whispering. Reading his mind and controlling him with artificial intelligence.

Below the diagrams, a block of text outlined the interplay between the Ocular Grid and the C2B interface. The Grid mapped and measured. It observed behavior, inferred patterns, and projected trajectories. Over time, it built out a psychometric profile for every individual within its reach: temperament, ideological leanings, cognitive style.

From there, another layer engaged. An algorithm cross-referenced each profile with approximated cognitive output scores. The language was sanitized, couched in the rhetoric of efficiency and resource allocation, but the intent seeped through.

The people whose IQ fell below a certain threshold were flagged with red markers along a sprawling map. Too many in one neighborhood, and the system recommended "intervention."

Intervention, in this lexicon, was not a hand extended. It meant a letter in the mail or a knock at a door, the kind that arrived with smiles and clipboards and assurances that everything would be fine. The Grid did not need an implant to make its first judgments. It read the world from the outside in—public records, academic performance, purchasing patterns, biometric signatures scraped from transit hubs, even the cadence of a person's typing if they logged onto a public network could be monitored. Metadata became personality.

And once that knock came—once a household was flagged and entered into the system—its inhabitants were groomed little by little. Until eventually, someone inside that home, softened by months of curated intervention, grew trusting enough to accept a single-track interface slipped over the ear: a device that whispered back to the brain what it should think, what it should want, and what it should never imagine again.

People with "low-range cognitive output" would be selected for "augmentation trials." The language suggested benevolence—improving function, helping them "align more easily with societal goals." But once implanted, their thoughts could be nudged, their impulses softened. They could be guided away from what the system defined as disruption.

The next step sat several pages deeper, in a file that tried to hide behind a veil of clinical phrasing and mathematical modeling.

Sterilization was never named outright. It did not have to be. The word remained unspoken, tucked between lines that pretended to discuss efficiency, not eugenics.

Long-term population refinement requires a reduction in non-contributive gene-line propagation.

Gene-line propagation. Non-contributive.

Cooper read the words again, then shut his eyes for a moment. He'd heard language like this years ago—briefings that were whispered about and then buried, the kind of ideas decent people refused to put on paper. Seeing it here, in Tristan's files, made his throat tighten as if the air itself had thinned.

He sat still for a moment, letting the chill settle before he leaned in again, shoulders curled over the screen as though bracing against wind. Whatever this was—whatever Tristan had built—its center hadn't revealed itself yet. Cooper wasn't leaving this train without understanding it. He owed Amanda at least that much.

Graphs followed, projecting generations forward—curves that bent gracefully upward as the percentage of "high-value cognitive contributors" increased. Whole populations reimagined as carefully pruned orchards instead of forests. The plan was never just to watch or even to steer. It was to redesign.

Cooper scrolled through paragraph after paragraph, feeling his vision pull tight around the edges. He had sat through defense briefings where men with stars on their shoulders argued over lesser atrocities than this. Those plans had died on conference table battlegrounds because someone, somewhere, remembered the vestiges of conscience.

Here, there were no uniforms. No flags. No elected oversight. Just Tristan's voice encoded in comments and references, confident and unrepentant.

Cooper pulled out a notebook. He had started carrying one years earlier, knowing from his training that the only safe information was analog. Every two months, he burned his pocket-sized notebook and got a fresh one. This one, he'd been carrying since Tokyo. He scrawled a few words on the blank page.

The Ocular Grid makes it possible to watch everyone.
C2B1 makes it possible to tap directly into thought.
Sterilization protocols turn preference into inevitability.

He put the notebook back in his inner coat pocket and lifted one hand from the trackpad, flexing his fingers slowly, as if they belonged to someone else. His pulse had settled into a strange, cold steadiness. Shock had a way of quieting him—the worse the revelation, the more focused he became.

He continued scrolling, folders shifting from diagrams to field notes, then to projected partnership models. He saw Helion's name among a list of corporations eager to license what they believed to be the future of security and optimization.

He saw government officials—his father's name sitting too comfortably in the list—alongside private foundations, philanthropic institutions, and even space programs likely courted for their satellite networks. The breadth of it was staggering, but he forced himself onward.

He reached the last folder in the C2B chain, a modest entry simply entitled: *Candidate Archives.* It could have held anything or nothing at all—trial notes, background noise, discarded drafts. But when he opened it, the first name to greet him was hers, appearing with the measured certainty of something that had been waiting to be found.

Hopkins, Amanda — Full Profile.

The file was dense; it had not been built quickly. Years of accumulation had been layered into it, each entry stacked atop an earlier curiosity. Cooper was right about him. Tristan's interest in her had begun long before she stepped into his orbit that night in Rome.

Academic records appeared first. Acceptance letters. Scholarship offers. A glowing note from an MIT admissions committee member calling her "formidably promising." Her standardized test scores. Her early withdrawal from school, marked only by a brief line: *voluntary discontinuation.*

Tristan had cross-referenced everything. He had doubled back to high school transcripts, aptitude tests, even a math competition from a forgotten regional meet where she'd placed first without lifting her eyes from the paper.

Next came her flight records. Evaluations from instructors commenting on her reflexes, her spatial reasoning, and her ability to anticipate problems three steps ahead. Someone had once scribbled in a margin: *"She sees the whole board while everyone else is still looking for their pieces."*

An overlay followed, Amanda's entire life bent into the lines of a single theory.

High cognitive range with above-percentile emotional infer-ence.
Demonstrated capacity for pattern recognition under pressure.
Adaptive intelligence. Stubbornness threshold: high.
Primary liability: loyalty.

"Liability?" he said audibly. "Loyal is liable, wow."

The words echoed with a kind of sterile violence. He moved on, letting it fade only enough to make room for the second document branching from the same assessment.

Hopkins, Amanda — Genetic Potential.

Medical charts populated the page, rendered anonymous but familiar. Blood panels, imaging, routine visits that had been quietly harvested and recombined. Tristan had pieced to-gether a genomic portrait from whatever fragments the world had dropped about her. Health markers. Latent risk factors. Potential hereditary traits.

Tristan's own data sat beside Amanda's in a comparative column, as if this were nothing more than a compatibility test for a project that required high-grade input.

Matches were highlighted in soft gold—neurological markers, metabolic strengths, cognitive traits that aligned too perfectly to be a coincidence.

Complements were circled: the places where her intuitive brilliance balanced his more rigid logic. And then vulnerabilities—small genetic predispositions, latent medical risks, emotional traits he deemed "inefficient"—were annotated with clinical suggestions for how one deficit might "correct" the other.

Beneath Amanda's data profile, a simple conclusion was noted:

Projected offspring: high potential for exceptional cognitive output and emotional inference.
Recommendation: prioritize as primary candidate for Line One.

Tristan did not only envision a purified population in the abstract. He envisioned lineages—a family tree with a central trunk from which others might grow.

Amanda was not simply a woman he had fallen in love with. She was the cornerstone in a breeding design for superior intelligence.

Cooper's jaw tightened, the muscles flickering once along the hinge before he forced them still. It would have been easier if Tristan's interest in her had been purely clinical, a detached evaluation of ideal genes. That would have been monstrous enough. But the files revealed something more complex and insidious.

Tristan hadn't needed any implanted device to study her. Long before the Grid became something the world could name, its earliest skeleton lived inside patterns—continuous currents of behavior collected from industries that ran on precision. Aviation was one of the richest sources, a place where countless micro-decisions left small signatures in the data: the timing of a course correction, the instinct to reroute around a storm cell before the instruments insisted, the way a pilot managed fuel, altitude, or communication in moments of pressure. Most of it was absorbed into the larger flow of information he used to train his models.

Every so often, though, a pattern refused to dissolve into the rest.

Amanda's rose to the surface again and again, marked by a kind of internal coherence that the algorithms kept flagging. Her decision logic branched instead of breaking. Her instincts resolved into clarity faster than the models predicted. When other pilots followed protocol, she adapted, anticipating variables the system had not yet been taught to acknowledge. She was an anomaly, but not the kind the code dismissed, the kind it learned from. The code consistently circled back to Amanda Hopkins, trying to understand what it had missed.

Tristan studied that pattern for years without knowing the face attached to it. What began as professional curiosity became a fascination, almost an irritation, because he could never quite account for the way she thought.

By the time he finally decided to learn her name, she was no longer just an outlier in a dataset; she had become the variable the models returned to as if she were part of the engine itself, a singular intelligence moving with a logic that unsettled his own.

Earlier entries were tagged differently. Back when Tristan had first begun collecting information about her, his language was less formal, his tone almost awed.

A mind like this is rare. The combination of intuition and analytic range suggests a kind of bridge architecture. She moves between ways of thinking without strain. There is enormous value here.

Later, his notes shifted. As if somewhere along the way, data had become infatuation.

He catalogued not only her scores but her habits. What time she tended to answer flight scheduling emails, how often she adjusted her route planning to account for weather when others would have flown through it, and her propensity to hum when she worked through complex logistics—all noticed, all documented.

He had been watching long before she knew there was anything to see.

Off to the side of her profile, Cooper found a smaller file with a different name: *Elise — Dissolution Summary.*

The entry was sparse. There were no elaborate notes, no lengthy postmortems. Just a handful of lines connecting personal history to strategic aims.

Elise: socially adept, financially advantageous, aesthetically appropriate.
Liability: low-range cognitive ambition. Prioritizes societal status over structural impact.
Outcome: non-viable partner for long-term genetic optimization project.

Non-viable. The marriage had ended not because of incompatibility in the ordinary sense, but because she did not fit the genetic blueprint. Amanda did.

The thought settled in Cooper's chest like ash. He lifted his gaze briefly, not to see the world outside—whatever landscape the train was cutting through now was irrelevant—but to give his mind something to focus on that was not text or graphs or Tristan's voice running under everything like a merciless wire.

He closed the Elise file and returned to Amanda's. Farther down, the entries grew darker still. Predictions about how her temperament might respond to pressure. Estimates of how far her loyalty could stretch before it snapped. Models depicting what kind of stressors might be required to break her enough to discredit her, should she one day become a threat.

In one hypothetical scenario, she accused him publicly of wrongdoing.

The response model was chillingly efficient.

Step one: undermine perceived emotional stability.
Step two: frame objections as residual trauma from early life events.
Step three: introduce carefully curated "concern" about her mental state into public discourse.

Even her pain, if it arose, had already been quantified, mitigated, and planned for exploitation.

Cooper scrolled until the words blurred, then forced himself back into focus. It was too dangerous, now, to look away. Every line he memorized here was one more weapon he could bring to bear later.

Another piece of the C2B puzzle waited in a separate branch—a document that linked candidate selection directly to the single-track interface.

The highest-range individuals, those he deemed "worthy," would be protected, given advantages the rest of the population would never see. Their thoughts would not be policed in the same way. They would not be sterilized. Instead, they would be groomed.

The track in their brains would not restrain them; it would amplify them. Enhance focus. Sharpen cognitive processing. Increase coherence between intention and action. Where lower-range citizens were to be muted, higher-range ones were to be given a microphone.

It was engineered stratification woven into the nervous system. The cruelest part, Cooper thought, was not that Tristan saw people as raw material. That was grotesque, but not unique. Men had sought to rearrange the human race before, driven by ideology or fear or greed. The particular horror here was that the men who built this whole system assumed they were right. That what they were building was not evil but inevitable. Necessary. Beautiful, even.

In Tristan's private notes, nestled among the projections, he had written one line that made Cooper understand everything.

"Ethics must be architected, not negotiated. Left to the average mind, they degrade."

There it was: the core of Tristan Montgomery. Cooper absorbed the gravity of Amanda's situation, of the seduction she fell prey to in that moment.

Tristan did not believe he was the villain. He believed he was the only adult in a room full of children, finally taking the matches away.

Cooper sat back, the drive still glowing faintly on the table. The mission was no longer about exposing a surveillance overreach or even about dismantling a dangerous technology. It was about stopping men who had decided that entire swaths of humanity did not deserve to continue.

And threaded through that enormity was one woman he could not stop thinking about, no matter how hard he tried. A woman whose life had been dissected and fitted into a framework she had never agreed to inhabit. Amanda's real danger was no longer abstract. It was written here in line after line—her value, her vulnerability, the ways she might be broken, the ways she might be used.

He closed the last file, but the images remained. The single-track schematic. The cognitive rankings. The quiet, merciless language of "optimization."

His training urged him toward compartmentalization, toward that rigid mental shelving he had practiced out of necessity rather than instinct. It told him to take the enormity of what he'd seen and break it into manageable pieces—intelligence to be processed, threats to be ranked, next steps to be drafted with the precision of someone who lived by procedure. But those habits, learned late and never quite comfortably, felt thin now, slipping through him like water through cupped hands.

Because beneath all of that discipline lived the part of him he had never managed to train away. That part of him knew Amanda not as an abstract vulnerability in Tristan's system, but as a girl standing barefoot by the riverbank, wild-haired and laughing, the summer sky cracked open above them. He remembered loving her before he understood what love cost. He remembered losing her the way a body loses air—suddenly, catastrophically, with the kind of panic you never shake.

And now that he knew their child had lived, that Amanda had carried a daughter he'd never had the chance to meet, that their baby had been taken before either of them could touch her—the knowledge of Daisy left him gutted in a way no briefing, mission, or threat had ever managed. Every ounce of restraint he'd maintained since Amanda reentered his life felt unbearably fragile, stretched thin over old wounds that were beginning to bleed again.

He closed the laptop gently, as if the motion might soothe something inside him, then reopened it almost in the same breath. He found himself searching again—not for strategy this time, but for truth. If Tristan had scoured every corner of Amanda's history, then somewhere in this archive there should have been a trace of the pregnancy, a whisper of the girl Amanda once was, and the child she brought into the world. He moved carefully through the files, scanning medical logs, insurance data, flight gaps, anything that might hold a shadow of Daisy's existence.

But nothing surfaced. There were no clinic entries or adoption markers. No files from The Ridge.
No evidence of a teenage mother hidden away in the hills of Tennessee.

The absence itself became its own answer. Cooper sat back slowly, the realization unfolding with a cold, weighted clarity: Tristan didn't know. He couldn't have known. Every living trace of that time had been swept away long before Amanda ever crossed his path—scrubbed with the precision of a man determined to erase any threat to the trajectory he envisioned for his son. James Hansen had buried it all. Every document, every witness, every scrap of record that might have connected the Governor's heir to a girl from White Pine and the life they created too young and too alone was gone.

Cooper felt another wave of grief and fury coil through him in the same breath, neither emotion sharp enough to sever the other. He steadied his hands on the table, breathing through the ache of memories he had spent a lifetime trying not to feel.

Outside, daylight pressed gently against the window, the world moving on in indifference. He let out a long breath, the kind meant to steady, not soothe, and allowed himself one last thought before diving deeper into the archive: that somewhere between the boy he had been and the man he was trying to become lay the faint, flickering hope that it wasn't too late to save the dream of himself he had buried long ago.

CHAPTER EIGHT

Undisclosed Location, Canada: The Same Day

"Amanda," Katherine said, her voice steady even as the helicopter shuddered through the last stretch of cloud. "You're shaking." She said it casually, as if this hadn't been an abduction.

Amanda kept her gaze on the window, refusing to meet Katherine's eyes. "It's the cold," she said, though the cabin was warm enough that her breath didn't fog the glass.

The helicopter angled downward, and the landscape began to take shape—snow, a dark cut of treeline, the muted rise of a mountain pressing close behind the facility. Something about the air seemed to flatten out here, as if sound and color both quieted on approach.

"We're almost there," Katherine said, fastening her coat as the rotors eased into their landing rhythm.

The ground rose steadily beneath them, and Amanda felt the shift in her body—the subtle engagement of gravity, the way descent always pulled reality closer. Perhaps that's why she was born to fly. She didn't want to live with her feet on the ground. Up in the air, space isn't tangible.

She braced herself as the helicopter settled, skids biting into snow. Cold surged in when the door slid open, a stark contrast to the insulated cabin, and Amanda stepped out with Katherine close behind her. A current of wind spun off the helicopter's rotors and curled around them, lifting the edges of their coats and scattering hair across their faces. Amanda caught her balance with a narrow step while the escorts closed in around them.

Their footsteps met the industrial floor in a muted, syncopated cadence. Amanda hadn't expected the place to affect her again, but it did—the press of silence, the subtle hum of machinery behind the walls, the faint chemical scent of recycled air. She was struck by an awareness that this time, she wasn't being ushered toward answers but towards ultimatums. The building seemed to know it too, its silence arranged like a held breath. Amanda matched Katherine's pace without thinking, unwilling to fall behind. Whatever their demands were, she'd find a way to survive them.

As they continued walking, interior sensors recognized movement, and another set of doors parted, ushering them into a lean, silent stretch of hallway where the air seemed almost too still. Amanda crossed the threshold, feeling a concentration in the space—a soundless density that suggested whatever lay beyond this corridor was not meant for many eyes.

The doors sealed off the world behind them.

Katherine's voice slipped into the silence. "They're waiting."

Amanda didn't ask who. Something in Katherine's tone suggested that whatever answer came, she wouldn't want to hear it in the hallway.

At the final door, Katherine raised her palm to a biometric panel that lit beneath it, and the lock released with a deep, engineered sigh. Warmth spilled through the opening, and they stepped inside.

The light was soft enough to obscure faces for a beat, just long enough for her mind to process what she was seeing.

Malonga stood by a narrow table, one hand resting lightly on its edge. He carried stillness the way some people carried height or scars—something elemental to him, an inheritance rather than a choice. The last time she had seen him, he'd been a lone figure carved against a Romanian mountainside. Seeing him here flanked by shadows and strategy unsettled her in a different way. He appeared less mythic, more human, and all the more powerful for it.

She slowed just inside the doorway, one hand brushing the frame before she let it fall. She didn't dare move farther in yet.

Near the far wall, Julius remained seated with the poise of a statesman. His jacket was immaculate, tailored so precisely it gave him the air of a man arriving for a diplomatic supper rather than a covert briefing. The expression he wore matched it—a faint, inscrutable calm that invited underestimation and hid the fact that he preferred it that way. He nodded once at her entrance, his greeting all too familiar, not dismissal or approval, simply acknowledgment.

Stephen stood near the whiteboard, one hand braced lightly against the frame, the charts behind him a testimony to how long he'd lived inside this war. What struck her wasn't surprise or satisfaction—it was the way he steadied himself at the sight of her, as if he'd pictured this moment in private countless times and still wasn't ready for its weight.

And that heaviness landed somewhere Amanda hadn't braced for.

It stirred an involuntary tug, a flicker of recognition she didn't want and wasn't prepared to feel. She had spent her life believing her father was a closed chapter, a mystery sealed off. Yet here he was, and the part of her that should have remained indomitable wavered, unsettling in the quiet insistence of his presence.

She stopped just past the threshold, steadying herself on the invisible line between past and present. It was as if she'd stepped onto a fault line that had been waiting for her.

Her voice came out low. "What is this?" she whispered, though the question hung in the space, thin compared to the gravity around her.

Malonga answered, "It is time," he said softly, "to tell you the truth we have been circling."

Amanda's weight shifted from one foot to the other, a small adjustment that felt like bracing against a wave as a slow ripple went through her. Not fear exactly, but the dawning sense that the night's earlier chaos—Tristan's pressure, her sneaking out, the drop, the street, her capture—had only been an overture. Whatever stood in front of her now ran deeper, older, and threaded beneath every step she'd taken without knowing what lay beneath the ground she was on.

"You were meant to arrive under different circumstances," he said. "We expected you to come on your own. But when you left the apartment early... when you established a line of communication with Mr. Hansen, we had to assume it was compromised..."

Amanda felt her chin lift before she even chose to move it. She stepped farther into the room, planting her feet as if refusing to be spoken over. "So you had me taken."

Julius's correction cut in with practiced calm. "We *intervened*," he said—as if the distinction meant something. "Control is necessary now."

The word landed with an almost bitter humor. *Control.* Amanda felt the laugh rise in her chest, thin and disbelieving.

She looked at the four of them—Malonga, Julius, Stephen, Katherine—each of whom had, in their own way, tugged her life into new trajectories. None of them in agreement, yet all of them converging here, now, as if the tides had finally decided to sync.

Katherine lifted her hand in a simple, unadorned gesture. "Your phone," she said.

Amanda hesitated only long enough to take a breath as she reached into her coat and laid the device in Katherine's palm. The act felt strangely intimate, as if she were handing over the last piece of a life that had already been dissolving beneath her feet. Even though her phone was technically a dual version of itself—one part her authentic life, one part her monitored one—the thought of losing it felt like surrendering her identity.

Katherine didn't take a beat for any kind of emotion as she crossed to a metal tray positioned against the wall. A technician stepped forward at her approach, waiting for the signal. When she gave the slightest nod, he pulled a lever, and a hydraulic press descended with slow, implacable pressure. Amanda watched the device collapse in on itself—glass splintering, circuitry folding, the device flattening into a warped scrap of metal that held no trace of her.

She drew in a breath that barely moved her ribs. It was an inward bracing, the instinct to hold herself steady where any hint of reaction could be read as guilt or acquiescence.

Katherine returned and offered a new device, a sleek black phone that seemed almost weightless in her hand. "You'll use this now. It's clean."

Amanda's eyes moved across the room, sweeping over the faces gathered here, the tension strung like a network of tangled wires between them. She lowered herself to an empty chair, overwhelmed with the need to grip something solid.

"Why am I here?" she asked. "All of you—together—what does that mean?"

Julius didn't shift so much as settle deeper into his chair. "It means the world is closer to collapse than anyone is willing to admit, apparently."

Malonga gave a wordless, almost weary glance his way. "It means that each of us, in our own lanes, has been working to stop what your fiancé intends to release into the world. Sometimes in cooperation, sometimes in conflict, sometimes without knowing the whole picture—but always toward the same end."

"Tristan isn't—" The sentence caught, its truth fracturing under the weight of what she now knew, but Katherine stepped into the silence with a tone that held no judgment, only clarity.

"Not a monster," she said softly. "Possibly not. But his ambition outpaces his conscience. And that imbalance is often more dangerous than pure malice."

Amanda looked from one face to the next, trying to decipher the unseen architecture of this room, the history that had brought these four people—who should never have occupied the same space—to stand as if they were pieces of a single design. There was no unity in their postures, no shared loyalty, only the fragile alignment of necessity.

"You've been working together?" she said, disbelief threading through her voice despite her efforts to contain it. "All this time?"

Stephen nodded, an acknowledgment of a truth she had never been meant to uncover. "Yes," he said.

Tension gathered in her hands before she knew she was clenching them. "And me?" she asked. "Where did I fit in all of this? What did you expect from me?"

Katherine exhaled through her nose. "Competence. Discretion. A certain intuition we believed you possessed." She paused. "Some of us did not expect your... improvisation."

"You mean Cooper," Amanda said.

A pulse passed through the room; it wasn't dramatic or hostile, but unmistakably wary.

Katherine's expression sharpened. "We know you contacted him. We know he participated. And we know you completed the clone."

"I didn't know what else to do," Amanda said defensively.

"That choice put our entire operation at risk," Julius replied, voice smooth but edged. "You were meant to dissuade Tristan from some of his more unsavory ambitions and report to us directly. Instead, you run into the arms of a man whose family has spent decades shaping the narrative of power in the United States."

"And *you* didn't want that power?" Amanda spouted. "It's not like the other people in this room didn't suspect you of wanting more control than you pretend. If Tristan's in on it, aren't you?"

Julius stiffened at her words, but he held his tongue, refusing to give any dignified response to Amanda's accusation. His eyes cut toward Katherine as though seeking her intervention.

"Everyone in this room has a complicated relationship," Katherine admitted. "But, we are allies in the end. People have entrusted us to supply at least a modicum of safety in our respective countries. And so, we do our best," she said.

"And you have been sleeping with the enemy," Julius huffed.

"I have not. And he is not his family," Amanda said, without hesitation.

Malonga studied her with a look in his eyes that could have been read as respect.

"Tell us why you believe that."

Because he loves me. Because he's always loved me. Because he is the only person who understands me. Because he would die before he betrayed me. Because he is the father of my child.

The thoughts ripped through her in an instant, the last one living inside her like a bruise pressed to bone. But she could say nothing of the sort, not in a room like this. Whatever lived between her and Cooper belonged nowhere near here, even if every person understood more of their history than she wished.

So she steadied her breath and said, "Cooper wants to stop Tristan as much as you do."

Katherine's chin angled upward with a flick. "Intent and trustworthiness are not the same thing."

"Neither are loyalty and survival under threat," Amanda snapped. "Just tell me what you want from me."

A flicker of exasperation passed across Katherine's eyes before Stephen stepped in, his voice pitched low, warm in a way that was almost comforting. "We're asking for clarity," he said. "Not allegiance."

Julius exhaled once, a controlled release that felt like the prelude to a decision he'd been waiting for an excuse to make. He unfolded his hands with a ceremonial calm, but it was the kind of gesture that signaled not patience but the depletion of it. "Enough," he said—not loudly, enduring one explanation too many. "We are well past debating trust and sentiment."

He leaned forward, and the room narrowed around his focus.

"Here is what remains," Julius continued, each word measured and unhurried. "You secured access to Tristan's computer. We know it, and you know it. The destruction of your phone is to ensure that information reaches no one else. So your options are simple. First: you give us what you took. All of it."

He paused—not for effect, but to let the inevitability settle.

"Or," he said, voice still smooth, still impeccably polite, but carrying the unmistakable finality of a closing door, "you disappear. Permanently."

Amanda's stomach tightened. "Disappear?"

Malonga spoke next, presenting a gentleness that didn't soften the truth; it was simply an acknowledgement of its cost.

"During the Mossad operations of the '50s and '60s, agents who were burned were given new lives—new faces, new families, new countries. Not to erase them, but to save what remained. It is not a choice anyone makes lightly," he added, almost under his breath, "least of all the person who must live it."

Amanda stared at him, the enormity of what he had just said sinking into her skin. "You're suggesting plastic surgery and a new address in Timbuktu? That I vanish into some new life?"

"It is an option," Stephen said. "A last resort, not a threat."

"And Cooper?" The question escaped her before she could contain it, smaller, more fragile than she intended.

Katherine shook her head. "A Hansen does not simply disappear. Their lineage is... unrelenting."

"But he's in this as deeply as I am," Amanda said. "He'll be in danger too."

"Which is precisely the problem," Julius replied, his tone sharpening. "Tristan will come for him first."

"Then we stop Tristan," Amanda said, her pulse rising, "We stop him before he can get to Cooper."

Katherine's response came with a sigh. "But we cannot proceed until we know what you have." Her gaze sharpened, the weight of withheld knowledge settling into the room. "You spoke of a clone when you met him at the coffeehouse. Where is it?"

Amanda went completely still, the meaning of Katherine's words settling through her with a slow, cold clarity. *The coffeehouse.* Katherine hadn't been guessing or piecing rumors together—she was citing something heard, something captured. Amanda felt the realization unfurl inside her in one heavy sweep: they hadn't just been following, but listening, always.

Every time her phone was near, every whispered plan, every moment she thought she and her confidantes had carved out of the chaos—they had never been truly alone. She didn't have time to think about what this meant for Lyla or Melody.

A pulse of heat tightened behind her ribs, not quite fear, not quite anger, but the sharp, disorienting awareness of what a mess she'd made.

Across from her, Katherine's expression shifted with a subtler revelation of her own. It was the unmistakable flash of someone calculating a mistake in hindsight.

"We didn't intercept you," she blurted. Her face said the rest: they hadn't gotten to Amanda before the drop. They hadn't stopped her when they meant to. Whatever window they'd been working toward, they'd missed it.

For a suspended beat, both women absorbed the truth from opposite ends of the same wound—Amanda, shocked by how thoroughly she'd been monitored, and Katherine, measuring the consequences of arriving too late.

Katherine's voice slipped out quieter, though no less precise. "Where is the clone, Amanda?"

She lifted her chin a fraction. "He has it."

A collective stillness followed as Julius eased back in his chair, the movement deceptively relaxed.

"You entrusted the most volatile piece of intelligence on the planet to Cooper Hansen," he said, each word cooled to a blade's edge. "A man whose family has shaped political influence for decades."

"You don't know him," Amanda replied firmly.

"No," Katherine said, and there was no triumph in it. "But you do. And your instincts have carried you farther than any training might have."

Stephen stepped forward slightly, hands loosely folded, as if bridging the distance without crowding her. "Amanda, we are not here to punish you," he said. "We need to understand what we are working with."

Malonga nodded once, his tone even. "And to understand how quickly we must move."

Amanda met their eyes one by one—Malonga, the strategist, Julius, the tactician, Stephen, the man who shared her features, and Katherine, the woman who'd upended her life in Rome. Trust was a gift she could not offer any of them.

"I will get you access," she said. "But I'm not walking out of here blind. I need to know the plan. And I need your word—whatever the hell that's worth—that Cooper is part of it... If we vanish," Amanda finished, "we vanish together. That is my condition."

Katherine studied her for a long moment, weighing not just the request but the resolve behind it. At last, she inclined her head. "Very well. That is manageable."

The men in the room nodded. Their agreements were not spoken in unison, but layered, each one eventually muttering, "Agreed."

CHAPTER NINE

*A Remote Hillside in East Tennessee: Two Days
Later*

THE ROAD NARROWED THE higher it climbed, curling through winter-bare trees in a way that felt almost familiar, though Amanda hadn't been here in nearly twenty years. As she drove, gravel snapped under her tires, the sound oddly comforting—a steady cadence she'd once known by heart. As the car inched up the last incline, the Smokies rose around her in sweeping, silent layers, the mountains holding themselves like they always had: patient, immense, and unwilling to hurry for anyone.

Halfway up the ridge, a memory crept in—not invited, but not unwelcome either. She was fifteen again, sitting in the back seat of a borrowed truck on this very road, knees tucked tightly into her chest, the scent of wet leaves and woodsmoke drifting through the cracked window. She'd pressed her forehead to the glass, watching the trees blur together, dreaming of a future she hadn't yet given herself permission to imagine. A future full of sky, of flight, of romance, fingers laced between those of the boy she loved.

The recollection warmed her ribcage, reaching back and touching the girl she had been. It reminded her that once, before everything else, she believed in the possibility of true love. The Hansen family cabin appeared just past the crest of the hill, set far from the end of the official road, its green roof softened by the gray light. From the roadway, it looked ordinary, the kind of place that could belong to a retired couple or a family who spent summers fishing. But Amanda knew better. Places like this hid in plain sight, their magic cloaked in ordinariness.

She stepped out of the car, boots crunching through cold, brittle grass as the land fell away behind the porch in a grand sweep, revealing the full breadth of the Smokies that stretched out in blue shadows and fading ridgelines. The view wasn't just beautiful—it was disarming. The kind of panorama that makes a person involuntarily speechless, that steadies the breath whether you want it to or not.

The hill beneath her feet felt unchanged, as though no time had passed at all... as if it had simply been waiting for her to find her way back. A warm glow wavered behind the glass, pale and steady against the dimming afternoon, the anticipated but still alleviating sign of someone waiting. *Cooper was here.*

The relief hummed beneath her skin, a soft, dangerous warmth that felt far too close to that long-ago memory of wanting something impossible. Except this time, impossibility wasn't the barrier. Everything else was.

Amanda pulled her coat tighter, hands trembling. She told herself it was the cold, but it wasn't. She took the last few steps toward the porch.

The boards gave a soft, familiar creak under her weight, the sound rising up out of some distant summer and settling over this winter afternoon slipping into evening. For one suspended breath, she stood there, heart beating in a rhythm that didn't belong to missions or surveillance or controlled deception, but to something older and simpler: a girl about to see the boy she loved.

She pushed the door open.

"Hey," she said in almost a whisper as she opened the unlocked door.

Warmth moved toward her first—wood heat with a wisp of pine on its twirl, followed by the acrid edge of coffee brewed too strong and too long. The interior light was low, golden, and soft against the logs, revealing a narrow front room that opened into a wider space. Stone fireplace, an overstuffed chair, and a couch sagging just slightly in the middle; its dip a reminder of the night two teenagers learned how powerful closeness could be.

She smiled at a pair of boots that sat near the door, abandoned where Cooper had toed them off in a hurry, but it faded as her eyes moved to the center of the room, where the dining table had been transformed into a war room.

Light from the laptop pooled over the table's clutter—notes, diagrams, pages marked and re-marked until the ink blurred, the evidence of hours he hadn't slept. An abandoned mug balanced near the edge, dark stain drying along its lip; beside it, another cup cooled slowly, forgotten in the rush to uncover whatever had kept him awake.

Cooper stood behind the chair, one hand braced on the table, the other wrapped around yet another mug. Hours had carved themselves into him, softening his posture, stubble darkened his jaw in uneven shadow, and faint purple crescents had settled beneath his eyes.

The first flicker in his gaze when he saw her was not the flare of desire or relief she'd imagined he'd greet her with on the drive here, but something raw and exposed—fear, threaded so tightly with hope that it was hard to tell them apart.

"Amanda," he said.

Her name left him on a breath, and in that single syllable lived every year between them, every what-if, and her body moved before her brain caught up; the impulse to cross the room and close the remaining distance was as instinctive as breathing. For a heartbeat, it felt like this might finally be the moment when there was nothing between them but the truth of who they were to each other.

But Cooper's hand tightened on the back of the chair, halting his own movement.

"You're here," he said, as if confirming the fact for himself. "You made it."

Amanda paused midway to the table, caught in the thin, electric space where anticipation tangled with dread. She questioned whether the closeness she thought she'd be greeted with was real or just her heart filling in the blanks.

"Yeah," she managed. "I made it."

She took him in—every frayed edge and restless shift. He looked like a man who had walked too far into a storm of his own making and wasn't entirely sure how to return. Whatever warmth she had hoped might bloom between them now felt dense with static, as regret and guilt began to creep in.

"I thought..." She trailed off, unsure how much of her expectation she was willing to admit out loud.

He set the mug down carefully, conscious of how close it was to the edge. "I've been working," he said. "Since the minute I left New York."

She managed a faint, crooked smile. "So I see."

He made a vague gesture toward the table, then dragged the chair out as if only now remembering basic hospitality. "Sit. Please. You've... you've come at the right time."

"The right time for what?" she asked.

Cooper didn't answer immediately. Instead, he reached for the laptop, fingers hovering over the trackpad with a momentary hesitation that felt out of character. He was a man whose hands usually knew exactly what to do, whether on a keyboard or the small of her back. Now, they seemed to move just behind his thoughts, like he was afraid of what they might bring to the surface.

Amanda took the chair he'd pulled out, the wood cool through her jeans. The world outside looked impossibly calm, like it had never heard of surveillance algorithms, or black-budget projects, or men who thought they could audition themselves for godhood. But here, in this small cabin, their ambitions settled over her like an invisible storm.

"I need to know if you're safe," he said suddenly, looking up at her again. "Really safe. I know you got away from Tristan, but after that...?"

"Safe is a moving target," she replied. "But I'm here. They know you have the clone."

His jaw tightened. "Of course they do."

"They're not coming for you. Not yet," she added quickly, seeing the flash of alarm. "Right now, they're more interested in what you found than in dragging you into some windowless room to interrogate you. They need us. Both of us."

He gave a short, humorless exhale. "That's almost comforting."

"It's the best I've got," she shrugged.

Cooper nodded, the laptop screen brightening as he tapped the trackpad, light climbing over the angles of his face, marking the hollows that hadn't been there the last time she'd seen him.

"So," she prompted gently. "What did you find?"

He swallowed, his throat scratchy as though he'd been speaking for hours. He rubbed a hand along his jaw, searching for the least destructive way to say what came next.

"You know how Tristan talks about building a better world?" he said finally. "A cleaner one, a more refined one?"

Amanda nodded, though something in her chest had begun to sink.

"It isn't idealism," Cooper said. "And it isn't arrogance. It's calculation."

He opened a file—just one—and even from a distance, Amanda could see her own name buried in a column of coded identifiers.

"Tristan didn't fall in love with you in Rome or on an airplane," Cooper said. "He wasn't just watching you; he was running analytics to measure compatibility."

Amanda's breath caught, the cabin suddenly too warm.

Cooper continued, his voice gentling not because the truth was gentle, but because he knew it wasn't. "He knew about your testing scores when you were a kid. Your acceptance into MIT. The flight evaluations you thought no one paid attention to. He compiled all of it. Mapped it. Studied it. My guess is that night he started obsessing over you in Chicago was simply to get a real-life glimpse of the person he'd been tracking."

"That doesn't make sense," she whispered. "Why? Why me?"

"Because you fit the model," Cooper said. "Because to him, you weren't just brilliant or capable. You were genetically optimized by his standards. And he wants to replicate that. Scale it. He thinks people like you are the future...and people who don't meet that bar?" Cooper swallowed. "He believes they drag the world down."

Amanda stared at him, unable to speak.

"He's not talking about improving systems," Cooper said. "He's talking about improving humanity by force. By filtering. By...curation." The last word twisted out of him with disgust.

"He thinks he can build a 'cleaner' human race if he controls who gets to contribute to it."

Amanda's skin prickled cold, as if a draft had moved through the room. "You're saying he's been—what?—tracking my DNA? Keeping a file on me like I'm a breeding prospect?"

"He tracked your cognitive markers. Your weaknesses. Your strengths. He ran simulations on what your offspring would look like; how they'd test; what they'd contribute. Tristan didn't choose you because he loved you. He chose you because he thinks you're an evolutionary upgrade."

Amanda pressed her hand to her stomach—an instinctive, protective gesture she hated the second it escaped her. She closed her eyes, the horror settling like a stone in her lungs.

"So everything with him—everything he said, everything he made me believe—was because of this."

Cooper's answer was simply a brief nod followed by a verbal affirmation. "Yes."

The word fell between them with a density that made her stomach tighten. She gripped the edge of the table, suddenly conscious of the way her heartbeat had found a painful new rhythm, and Cooper let the moment settle before he spoke again.

"He didn't find out about the baby," he added. "If he did... we wouldn't be sitting here. We wouldn't be safe."

"You think we're safe?" she let out a nervous laugh.

"Maybe not, but I did find out, however."

"What do you mean?" she asked.

Cooper didn't answer right away. Instead, he angled the laptop so she could see more clearly and began navigating through a labyrinth of folders—some with innocuous labels, some buried three directories deep beneath decoy file structures. Lines of code, timestamps, and encrypted reference strings flickered across the screen.

"I copied some code and hacked into my dad's computers. I couldn't let the thought go that maybe he'd still have info on her," he said. "On Daisy," he added, as if Amanda wasn't keeping up. "My guess was he was the type of guy who wouldn't have lost track of someone he was trying to control. And I was right."

Cooper clicked into a folder, and Amanda felt the world constrict around the glow of the screen. The cabin, the mountains, the long drive up the hill—all of it seemed to fall backward, leaving her perched on a narrow ledge made of numbers and clinical language.

"Cooper," she said. His name came out thin, the syllables scraping against the edges of her breath. "What are you saying?"

He looked into her eyes for a long moment, and she saw it clearly—the part of him that had been stretched taut for two days, the part that had held this knowledge alone, waiting for her to arrive so he didn't have to carry it solo anymore.

"I can't... I don't know how to say this in a way that doesn't..." He broke off, shaking his head, a brief, inelegant gesture of helplessness that made him look younger, closer to the boy she remembered. "Just—look."

He turned the laptop fully toward her and shifted his hand aside.

Her gaze fell to the highlighted row on the screen. Her vision blurred for a second, the words swimming. She had once been told her baby had "gone to a better home," but this read like a clinical placement.

Sex: Female

Blood Type: A+

Projected Intelligence Band: High Potential (Composite Range: 130–145)

Health Markers: Normal physiology; elevated problem-solving markers; mild myopia; no chronic conditions; psychosocial stability within expected range.

Adoption Placement: Subject 18 – Domestic Transfer

Location: East Tennessee Developmental Assessment Home – Node 3

She read the lines once, then again, her throat tightening as a quiet shock moved through her. Breath came carefully, the way it did when the body tried to stay still long enough for the mind to catch up. She still wasn't sure what she was reading.

"Does this mean they put Daisy... in a facility?" she finally choked out.

Cooper kept his eyes on the screen as he spoke, as if saying it out loud might change something fundamental in the air between them.

"Yes. She was never adopted, Amanda. There's no family in the records. No actual transfer. Just a subject number.

They placed her in one of the state-run developmental programs—one my father pushed through funding channels years ago. It's billed as a residential support system for vulnerable children, but inside the private files, it's described very differently. Monitored living. Medical oversight. Cognitive assessments. Long-term tracking."

Amanda felt her breath catch in a place too deep for sound. The room didn't move, yet everything seemed to tilt an inch off center.

Cooper went on, keeping his voice low, as though he wished he could unsay the words even as he delivered them. "He buried the public trail, but he kept her logged in the restricted layer of their network. The file never closed. *She's still there,* Amanda. He's been monitoring her for years. I don't know what role this type of facility has in the grand scheme of things with Tristan's invention, but I can only imagine what my dad envisioned once he saw what the Ocular Grid was capable of in Tokyo."

The truth settled inside her with the cold, unmistakable weight of something she had always feared but never imagined she would have to face.

For a heartbeat, she forgot about Julius's threats and Katherine's strategies, about Malonga's measured calm and Stephen's gravity. The war around them receded, and in its place stood a single, inescapable truth: somewhere beyond these hills, a girl with their blood was living a life built on secrets and lies.

Amanda lowered her head, fingers trembling as they found the edge of the table again. "And you're sure?" she asked, though she could already see the answer in his eyes.

He nodded once, his own voice roughened. "I don't think it could be anyone else."

Amanda kept her gaze on the screen because looking at him felt dangerous in a different way now.

"I thought when you said you'd cracked something, you meant you had enough to give them. Katherine. The others. A way to stop Tristan, and then..." She swallowed. "...then maybe we'd be able to walk away."

"We might," Cooper said. "Eventually. But not like we thought."

Cooper slid his hand toward hers until only a sliver of air separated them, that narrow run of space sparking hotter than contact itself. He didn't touch her; it was worse than that. He hovered, close enough that the warmth of him traced the edges of her fingers, a phantom caress that made her pulse zoom.

When she lifted her eyes, his restraint faltered. She saw it—the hunger he'd kept caged since she'd asked him to. His breath caught, shallow and uneven, as though he were fighting the urge to close that last impossible distance. And something deep in her yielded, recognizing that they were past the point where staying apart was simple.

"I thought I came here so we could figure out how to survive this," she whispered.

"We will," Cooper said. "But now we're not just surviving it for us."

He glanced at the screen, then back at her, the words sitting between them like a vow he was terrified to make and more terrified not to.

"We're doing it for her."

Chapter Ten

*East Tennessee Developmental Assessment Home:
The Next Day*

"So Mr. Booker says if I get the shading right on the hands, he'll submit it to that regional thing," Charlee said, nearly tripping over a raised section of sidewalk and catching herself without breaking her sentence. "You know, the one with the scholarships? I mean, I won't get it, obviously, but still. It's like... a thing."

"You could get it," Daisy said.

Daisy Smith liked the walk home from school best when the air smelled like late winter—wet bark, thawing earth, and that clean metallic edge that made everything feel like it was about to change, even if it never did.

Portwell High sat two blocks off the main road, and the route back to the Cluster House cut through a neighborhood full of tired ranch-style homes and chain-link fences that had long ago given up on standing straight. The sidewalks were cracked in the same places they'd been cracked three years ago when she started ninth grade, and probably ten years before that, but the sameness comforted her. You could map your life by the chips in the concrete if you had enough time and a good enough pen.

Charlee walked on Daisy's right, talking with her hands the way she always did, fingers flaring in quick, paint-smeared arcs as she described the mural she was working on in the art room. Junie was on her left, one earbud in, the cord tucked carefully under her collar so the hall monitor wouldn't see. She nodded every so often, whether to Charlee or to whatever song was bleeding lightly into her ear, Daisy could never be sure.

Charlee snorted. "You have to submit a portfolio for that, and I have, like, three finished pieces that don't still have pizza grease on them."

"It's your signature medium," Junie murmured.

They all laughed, and for a few seconds, the cold didn't feel quite so sharp on Daisy's cheeks.

The Cluster House came into view the same way it always did: gradually. First, the top of the chimney, then the dark line of the roof, then the full spread of the wraparound porch with its mismatched rocking chairs and faded wind chime. From the street, it looked like a slightly run-down farmhouse someone's grandmother might live in, the kind of place where cookies cooled on the counter, and the TV played game shows all afternoon. Which, to be fair, wasn't entirely wrong.

Only the discreet state-plated SUV parked near the side entrance and the small, almost apologetically placed security camera in the porch light hinted that this was anything other than a normal house with too many shoes by the door.

Momma Price stood on the top step, arms wrapped around herself against the wind, gray cardigan pulled tight. Her hair was half pinned up and half escaping, the flyaway strands catching every bit of weak sunlight. She smiled as they came up the walk. It was a familiar, creased-at-the-corners smile Daisy had known for as long as she could remember.

"There are my girls," she called. "How'd the world treat you today?"

"Brutally," Charlee said. "We had a pop quiz."

"In art," Junie added.

"It was graded," Charlee clarified, as though that were a punishable crime.

Momma Price clucked her tongue sympathetically. "A graded quiz in art. That *does* feel sacrilegious."

She reached out and smoothed a stray strand of hair behind Daisy's ear, the gesture so practiced it felt like breathing. "You okay, baby?"

"Normal," Daisy said, and she meant it. "We had an assembly. They told us not to vape in the bathroom or join radical cults. Again."

"Well, those are both habits worth avoiding," Momma Price said, amused. "Dinner in an hour. And Daisy, sweetheart—Dr. Kessler wants you in the Blue Room after you put your things away."

Charlee threw her head back dramatically. "Free us from our obligations, O Lords of Science!"

Trying to conceal her smile, Daisy nodded at Momma Price. Tuesday—that tracked. Their group had Blue Room on Tuesdays and Fridays, unless there was a holiday, in which case it moved to Wednesday and Sunday. The schedule had never been written down anywhere she could see, but she could feel it all the same, in the rhythm of the week, and the way the air seemed a degree cooler at the end of certain days.

Momma Price swatted lightly at Charlee's shoulder. "Go on with you. And take your shoes off before you ruin my floors."

Inside, the house felt like a patchwork quilt that had been sewn and resewn over the years, edges fraying in places but still holding. The living room spilled into a dining area, which blended into the kitchen, and at any given hour, at least three conversations overlapped across the whole floor. Today was no exception. Two of the younger kids were draped over the couch watching cartoons, their socked feet kicking absently in the air. A teenage boy named Mateo was at the table with a battered laptop, mouthing vocabulary words in Spanish and English. Somewhere down the hallway, water thundered in the pipes because someone was taking a shower, and that activity in this old house was loud enough to be heard from space.

Daisy kicked her shoes into the row by the door, tucking them between a pair of tiny pink sneakers and a set of size-twelve boots that belonged to Elijah, who insisted he was going to play running back for the Volunteers one day.

"Back by five-forty," Momma Price called after her. "You know they like to stay on their schedule."

"I know," Daisy said.

She took the narrow back staircase two steps at a time. The stairs creaked in three reliable places—second, fifth, and eighth steps. Daisy could walk them in the dark and never trip.

Her room was tucked under the eaves, the ceiling sloped just enough to make the space feel secret. A small bed was pushed up under the window, which looked out over a field that slanted down toward a dark fringe of trees. During the summer, the field went soft and green, but now it was winter-brown and brittle, the grass lying low like it was tired of pretending to be anything else.

She dropped her backpack on the bed and sank down next to it, exhaling the day out of her shoulders. There was comfort in the smallness of the room: the dresser whose bottom drawer always stuck, the bulletin board above it with snapshots and ticket stubs pinned like proof that days had, in fact, been lived. A photograph of Charlee and Junie making faces in a photo booth. A movie stub from the time they'd taken the facility van into Knoxville and watched a superhero movie so loud they still felt it in their teeth afterward. A pressed daisy, flattened between two pieces of wax paper, taped at the corner like a private joke with herself.

Sometimes she wondered if Momma Price had chosen her name on purpose. Daisy couldn't remember anyone calling her anything else, and the file they kept in the office said "Smith," which was an answer without really being one at all.

She checked the time on the digital clock by her bed. Five thirty-two. Enough stalling.

On the way back down, the house noise folded around her: the clink of plates in the kitchen, the quick patter of Rosie's feet as she ran past with a stuffed rabbit trailing from one hand, the deeper murmur of the TV where Elijah and Mateo were now arguing good-naturedly about a game.

"Daisy, you're up," Mr. Bennington called from the end of the hall, his head already angled toward the Blue Room wing. He was in his forties, balding in a way that made him look perpetually surprised, with a kind of mild, bureaucratic patience. Daisy had never seen him raise his voice. She had also never seen him laugh.

"I know," she said, offering him a small nod as she approached.

The Blue Room wasn't actually blue—not at first glance. The hallway leading to it was just narrower and more private than the rest of the property, the walls painted a neutral shade that never quite caught the light to figure out its actual color. But once you went past the second door and the third keypad, the color changed. Not the paint, but the light.

The room's official name is the Cognitive Imaging and Developmental Metrics Suite, which is an absolute mouthful and makes all the kids roll their eyes. So, they just call it the Blue Room, because when you lie back in the chair, and the scanner comes down, the world is washed in cool, pale light, like you are underwater.

Mr. Bennington keyed in the code on the door panel, and the lock released with a soft mechanical click.

"Same as usual?" Daisy asked.

"Same as usual," he confirmed. "Scan, evaluation, ten-minute recall test. Dr. Kessler might add a new sequence, but it'll be short."

"It's always short," Daisy said. "Until it isn't."

He huffed a little chuckle that could have been classified as a laugh for someone with his stoic personality. "You know the drill," he said.

Inside, the Blue Room was cleaner than any other space in the house—too clean, Daisy sometimes thought, as if it had been scrubbed of any trace that people came here and felt things. There was the reclined chair in the center, narrow but padded, with a curved headrest and an arch of equipment that could swing down over her face like a visor. Wires snaked neatly into consoles along the wall. A glassed-in observation alcove held a desk and two monitors, where Dr. Kessler sat with a tablet stylus in hand.

"Right on time," he said, glancing up as she entered. He was in his fifties, hair graying at the temples, with the kind of thin, precise hands that made Daisy think of watchmakers or piano tuners. "How are you feeling today, Daisy?"

"Like a person with math homework," she said, climbing onto the chair. "So, you know. Mixed."

He smiled absently at that, the way he always did when he thought she was trying to be funny but didn't have time to properly respond.

"Go ahead and get comfortable," he said. "We're going to run the standard cognition series and then try a new visual-sequence task. Nothing invasive."

She'd heard the phrase "nothing invasive" enough times now that it had stopped signaling anything at all. As far as she knew, there had never been anything invasive. Just scans. Lights. Beeps. Questions.

Still, the back of her neck prickled as she settled into the chair.

Mr. Bennington moved around her with practiced efficiency, attaching small sensors along her temples and just behind her ears. They never hurt, exactly, but the adhesive was cold and sent a quick shiver crawling across her scalp.

"You know the routine," he said. "Eyes open when the lights are steady, closed when they flicker. Answer the tones when you hear them. Say 'pause' if you feel dizzy or disoriented."

"I never do," she said.

"Yes, but we still ask."

The arch of equipment lowered into place, stopping just above her face. The underside was a smooth panel dotted with small lenses and emitters, dark until the machine hummed awake. The room dimmed; the first wash of pale light slid across her vision, cool and soft.

"Begin sequence one," Dr. Kessler said, his voice now filtered slightly through the speaker near her left ear.

Daisy let her eyes stay open as the light stabilized. A soft tone sounded in one ear, then the other. She tracked them without thinking—left, right, right, left—like a private game she'd long since mastered. Numbers appeared in faint overlay in the periphery of her vision, and she repeated them back: five, seven, nine, one. Patterns flashed—triangles, circles, grids—and she pressed the thumb pad under her hand when she detected the requested sequence.

It wasn't unpleasant. If anything, it felt like a slightly more intense version of the problem-solving games they sometimes did on the school computers. The machines never shocked her, never restrained her, never did any of the things kids at

Portwell liked to whisper about when they heard where she lived.

"Do they put microchips in your brain?" a boy had asked her once in seventh grade, wide-eyed and half thrilled with his own drama.

"If they did, I wouldn't forget my locker combination," she'd replied, and watched his face fall in disappointment.

A quieter kid had chimed in after, "Then why are there so many doctors there?" It was a question asked with curiosity, not cruelty. The cruel part came when kids joked about feeling jealous of them having no parents or called them orphans on occasion.

Daisy had given the same answer she always did: "It's just how the place works. They like to make sure we're healthy." She never added how strange it sometimes felt not to wonder about it herself anymore.

The scans were just... routine. Like dental cleanings or annual checkups, necessary and acceptable. The fact that they happened every day instead of once a year was just one of those quirks of her life.

"Good," Dr. Kessler said, as the light shifted into a soft pulse. "We're going to add a new layer now. Same patterns, but faster. When you feel the vibration under your hand, name the first color you remember from the series."

The vibrations were faint, like someone tapping the underside of the chair with a single finger.

"Green," she said. "Red. Blue. Yellow."

"Excellent."

Time stretched in that strange way it always did in the Blue Room. She lost track of minutes, slipping into a narrow channel of focus where there was nothing but sound and light and her responses to both. Beyond the visor and the hum of the machine, she knew Dr. Kessler's stylus was moving, that graphs were producing themselves on his screens, that her brain was being captured in lines and spikes that would mean something to someone, somewhere.

"Last sequence," he said at last. "Close your eyes."

As she did, the light shifted from blue to a softer, warmer hue that she could feel through her closed lids. A series of tones played in an unfamiliar order, and a faint prickle swept along her skin, like static when you pulled off a sweater in the dark.

"Tell me the first word that comes to mind when you hear each sound," he said.

The sounds were abstract—chimes, low thrums, a high, almost metallic ping.

"Window," she said. "Thunder. Chalk. Flight."

The last one slipped out before she could think about it. It always did—flight, sky, air, clouds were words that didn't belong to anything she'd ever actually known, and yet lived close to the surface of her mind.

"Thank you," Dr. Kessler said, tone unreadable. "We're done."

The machine powered down with a soft descending hum, and the room brightened. Mr. Bennington's hands were careful as he peeled the sensors from her skin.

"All good," he said.

"It's always all good," Daisy replied with a thumbs up. "Do you ever get tired of saying that?"

"Do you ever get tired of asking?" he countered, with a smirk.

She smiled, "Same time next week?"

"You bet. Dinner in fifteen," he reminded her. "Don't be late. We're testing blood tomorrow, so they want everyone nourished and hydrated."

"Got it," she said.

Blood tests were less frequent—once every two months for some of them, monthly for others. The vials lined up neatly in the nurses' tray, each labeled with barcodes, numbers, and names. A little pinch, a bandage, a cookie on the way out—routine.

Everything was routine.

Back in the main house, warmth and noise wrapped around her like a blanket. Momma Price moved through the kitchen with the efficiency of someone who had fed a small army for years, wielding a wooden spoon like a conductor's baton. A big pot simmered on the stove with something tomato-based and fragrant. Garlic bread lay in uneven rows on a baking sheet, waiting to go into the oven.

"You all done?" Momma Price asked as Daisy passed the kitchen doorway.

"Yeah," Daisy said. "No new superpowers yet."

"Maybe next week," Momma Price said, smiling. "Grab some water. You look pale."

"I always look pale."

"Then grab some extra."

By the time everyone was called to the table, the light outside had faded into a blue-gray, a kind of sky that hits just before full dark, the window over the sink catching the last of it. They squeezed into their usual places—fifteen kids from ages six to seventeen and one woman at a long, scarred table that had seen more spilled milk and slammed fingers than anyone could count.

Mateo started to tell an elaborate story about a fight that almost happened but didn't in the locker room, embellishing wildly. Rosie insisted on describing the dream she'd had about a turtle that could sing. Elijah argued with Junie about which decade had the best music, even though neither of them had been alive for any decade before this one, and Daisy listened, adding a line here and there, letting the sound of everyone else wash over her. This was the part she liked best about living here: the way the noise felt like proof. Proof that she belonged somewhere. That if she disappeared, a chair would be empty and a plate would be left untouched, and someone would ask where she'd gone.

"Earth to Daisy," Charlee said, nudging her knee under the table. "You spacing on us?"

"Always," Daisy said. "It's my brand."

The girls smiled at each other and by the time the dishes were stacked in the sink and the younger kids had been herded toward showers and pajamas, Daisy climbed back up to her room. The house settled by degrees—the television growing softer, footsteps growing slower—until only the faintest murmur remained.

She closed her door, not all the way, just enough that the latch didn't fully hitch. Privacy here was a flexible concept. If someone had a nightmare or needed an extra blanket or forgot where their toothbrush was, doors stayed open.

On the small desk under her window, a notebook lay open where she'd left it. Not a journal, exactly. Journals felt like something for people who had big secrets and dramatic lives. Daisy just... noticed things. She wrote them down because it felt wrong not to, so she picked up her pen.

Tuesday – Scan – Blue Room, she wrote in the margin.

New light sequence. Asked for first word after sounds. Flight again.

She paused, tapping the pen lightly against the page.

Blood tests tomorrow. Hydrate.

Underneath, almost without meaning to, she added:

Charlee laughs louder when she's lying. Junie never finishes a story about her mom. Momma Price hums hymns when she thinks no one is listening.

Then on a fresh line, she wrote:

Sometimes it feels like this house is watching us breathe. I wish I could go somewhere.

The thought made her snort softly at herself. Too dramatic. She crossed it out with a single strike, but not so hard that she couldn't still read the words.

Daisy had never left this county, not that she could remember. She'd been told once that there had been a baby home before this house, that she'd lived there until she was old enough to walk and talk and be moved into a "more sustainable environment." The words had meant nothing to her at the time, and by the time she was old enough to care, the records were harder to find.

She had asked Momma Price once, when she was eleven, if she had any baby pictures.

Momma Price had gone very still, then smiled around the stillness. "You came to me at three," she'd said. "Already walking. Already bossy. If there are baby pictures, they're not here."

"Where are they?" Daisy had asked.

"Where they need to be," Momma Price had replied, kissing her forehead. "And you're where you need to be, too."

It wasn't a satisfying answer, but it hadn't felt like a lie either. Just... the limits of what one person was allowed to say out loud.

Now, at seventeen, the question sat heavier in her chest. Not because she wanted some dramatic reunion or tearful revelation, exactly. Just because it seemed unfair to go through life without knowing what your own face looked like before you could remember it.

She set the pen down and leaned her forehead briefly against the cool pane of glass.

In the distance, headlights traced the curve of the main road, a brief streak of light that appeared and vanished in less than a breath. She imagined the person in that car: going somewhere, coming back from somewhere, holding a life in their head that had nothing to do with this house or its routines. The thought was both dizzying and oddly comforting.

A soft knock sounded against her open door.

"Hey, baby," Momma Price said. "You okay?"

"Yeah," Daisy replied, turning back toward her. "Just...thinking."

"That's how they know you're one of the smart ones," Momma Price said, stepping inside. "You think after nine o'clock."

She crossed the room and reached for the edge of the curtain, tugging it just slightly as if to test the strength of the rod, or maybe just to have something to do with her hands.

"Blood draw's tomorrow," she reminded. "Wear something with sleeves that roll easy."

"I know," Daisy said. "They want 'clean data.'"

Momma Price's mouth curved, but her eyes flickered with something Daisy wanted to think was mischievousness. "That's what they call it," Momma said.

"You don't call it that?"

"I call it part of the job," she nodded. "Now, try to sleep. You'll eat half the kitchen if you go in there tired tomorrow."

"Is that allowed?"

"For you?" Momma Price said. "I might look the other way," she winked.

When she left, Daisy turned off the lamp and climbed into bed, pulling the blanket up to her chin. The darkness in the room was gentle and familiar. Nothing lurked in it that hadn't been there the night before.

Still, as her eyes adjusted, she could just make out the faint red glow of the tiny smoke detector on the ceiling, winking at regular intervals.

She watched it for a long time.

She'd been told once, in one of the many educational seminars they all sat through, that smoking in bed used to be one of the leading causes of house fires. People fell asleep with cigarettes in their hands. Whole families were lost.

"Technology saves lives," the speaker had said, gesturing at a slide of a sleek little detector. "Sometimes in ways you don't even notice."

And Daisy believed that. It was hard not to, living in a place where machines hummed softly in the background of everything. Brain scans, blood tests, and digital charts that she never saw but knew existed. In the morning, she would wake up, roll her sleeve, give her blood, go to school, walk home, eat dinner, and write notes in her notebook. Routine was everything.

There was comfort in the soft tick of the baseboard heater, the steady blink of the smoke detector, and the deep, even breathing of a house full of sleeping kids, folded into the care of a woman they all called Momma.

It was enough.

CHAPTER ELEVEN

A Remote Hillside in East Tennessee: The Same Day

For a while, neither of them spoke. The discovery on the screen had brought Amanda and Cooper horror with a side of direction—coordinates instead of guesses, a physical place instead of a shadowy haunting. Daisy was no longer scattered across files or coded strings; she was somewhere in the world, breathing under a specific roof.

Cooper hadn't withdrawn after their earlier brush; he'd leaned closer, as if some invisible orbit had drawn him into her without needing to ask permission.

As Amanda turned toward him, his face inches from hers, lit by the faint spill of the laptop screen, she whispered, "Cooper," not knowing what more she wanted to say.

Her voice barely made a sound; it was more of an exhale wrapped in meaning. He looked up, the instinct to protect her embedded so deeply in him that her voice made his entire body tense.

"Amanda," he said, her name leaving him like a confession.

He reached out again—not hesitantly this time, not hovering near her skin like a man afraid of shattering the moment—but intentionally. His fingers brushed the line of her hand, tracing it slowly and reverently, as though he were relearning the person he'd memorized before life had torn them apart. His touch was warm and careful, but charged with every unspoken truth tying them together.

He stood, not moving toward her so much as *giving in* to the pull he had been fighting since he was a teenager. One moment they were reaching, staring at each other across the table, breath lodged between ribs and memory, and the next he was rising, closing the distance in three slow, decisive steps.

Amanda stood too, but she wasn't meeting him halfway. She was *matching* him, matching the ache, the years, and the longing neither had allowed to fully surface until now.

His hands found her face first—warm, trembling, and reverent in a way that nearly undid her. She exhaled his name again, just once, close enough for him to feel her breath, and that was what it took for all restraint to collapse.

Cooper kissed her with the kind of need that had outlived time and all the lies meant to sever them. It wasn't soft; it was deep and certain, the desperate claiming of two people who had spent half their lives holding their breath.

Her fingers curled into his shoulder, slowly, almost reverently, as if savoring the ache before the satisfaction of finally touching what she'd been denied set in. Cooper answered with his other hand, threading through her hair, his thumb brushing the tender place just behind her ear as he drew her in unhurriedly. He was memorizing a moment he'd spent so much time reaching for in dreams.

The world beyond the cabin blurred until there was nothing but the warmth of his mouth and the low, startled sound she made against it.

When they finally pulled away from each other, Cooper rested his forehead against hers, their breaths mingling in a warm, uneven tether that felt less like proximity and more like gravity. His fingers tightened at her waist, not in possession but in something far more significant: recognition. She answered by sliding her hand along his jaw, her thumb brushing the corner of his mouth in a gesture that felt as natural as inhaling oxygen and as forbidden as touching fire.

"I'm sorry," he whispered, the words frayed around the edges. "I shouldn't—"

"Cooper." She caught his face fully, her palms framing him with a tenderness that undid him. "If you apologize for this, I will actually walk out of this cabin."

A laugh broke out of him, shaken and breathless.

"Amanda," he said, voice low, roughened but steady, "we don't have time to lose ourselves. Not yet. Not until she's safe."

The words slid through her like a second heartbeat. "Daisy," she whispered.

Amanda remained close, her fingertips still resting near his collar as if parting were a choice she wasn't ready to make. She drew one deep breath, tasting the warmth of him, the faint bitterness of too much coffee on his skin, the sharpness of the truth waiting only a few feet away on the cluttered table. And yet, beneath all of it, she felt something new.

"Tell me the plan," she whispered.

Cooper glanced at her, the ghost of a smile tugging at his mouth. Their bodies parted by inches, not choice so much as necessity, yet the warmth they'd shared lingered as Cooper's hand slid down her arm, closing around her fingers. With a steady, wordless invitation, he drew her toward the table again.

"Well, I don't exactly have one mapped out, but we can build one together," he smiled.

The word *together* sounded like a symphony to her ears, the air buzzing with an unsung melody only she could hear. And together, they turned toward his computer.

A map pulsed faintly on the screen, the way pixels do when a person's been sleeping too little and looking at blue light for too long. They shifted closer to the laptop, their bodies angled toward each other, knees touching under the table like neither could bear to break even that small connection.

Cooper pulled up a new window. "When I pulled the raw directory from my father's system, most of it was buried under generic infrastructure files. But in the metadata of Daisy's intake record, there was a facility code—KB-01. Once I traced that code through the state's residential-care registry, this is what came up."

He zoomed in.

"I decrypted what I could," he said. "There's a pattern in these maps. Knox–Blount facilities are coded KB-01 through KB-30, but only one—KB-01—is totally different."

Amanda's breath caught. "Different how?"

"Every legitimate residential program in this region has the same paper trail—state inspection logs, staffing ratios, fire compliance reports, meal audits. Even the sketchy ones still pretend to follow the rules."

He tapped the highlighted listing.

"KB-01 has none of that. No inspections. No staff certifications. No records of who signed off on the building's occupancy permit. It's registered as a *temporary therapeutic placement*... but the license number it uses belongs to a facility that shut down twenty-five years ago."

Amanda felt her stomach tighten. "So it's fake."

"Not fake," Cooper said. "Hidden. Someone went through a lot of trouble to build a shell identity around this place. And when I cross-checked the funding streams, only one wing of the property consistently received 'special projects' allocations."

He clicked once more, highlighting the back portion of the structure.

"Whatever's happening in that wing isn't residential. It's something else entirely."

Amanda went silent, comprehension catching up to the worst fear imaginable. She looked at him, questioning without having to say a word.

"My guess?" he added. "A lab."

Amanda felt a slow, cold press beneath her ribs. "A lab. For children."

A shadow crossed Cooper's expression. "That's my guess," he nodded as he continued scrolling. "Every child has markers recorded regularly. Cognitive scores, blood chemistry, reflex assessments, and behavioral data—all recorded in six-hour intervals."

"Six hours?" Amanda whispered.

Cooper's eyes darkened. "It's not a home. It's an assessment unit. A pipeline. A way to identify traits people like Tristan and my father find... *valuable.*"

A chill swept across her skin.

"You think Tristan knows about her?" Amanda asked.

Cooper hesitated with the kind of careful restraint that meant the truth was more complicated than a yes or no.

"I don't think he knows *who* she is," he said. "But I bet he knows there are kids in this program whose markers match what he's looking for. High intelligence bands. Stable emotional regulation. Genetic indicators they consider 'preferable.' And if my dad's been involved in funding this kind of shit since she was born, it's no wonder he wants to be Tristan's right-hand man."

"Preferable," she repeated, her chest constricting. "As if children are materials." She closed her eyes, unable to look at the world where truths like this existed.

"They are to him," Cooper said. "They are to my father. But not to us."

He brushed a strand of hair from her cheek, the gesture a comfort more profound than anything words could manage.

"So, do we know *exactly* where this place is?" she asked.

Cooper zoomed in, and the map constricted, narrowing through layers of data until a faint dot blinked in a wooded patch southeast of Knoxville.

"Its registry location shows it here," he said, his finger resting on the screen. "The East Tennessee Developmental Assessment Home, tucked behind a state wildlife preserve. One road in. One road out. I wouldn't be surprised if there are cameras on the tree line. But I haven't had time to see if I can hack into any of them."

The words fed a heat through her chest, rising in a quiet surge that unsettled her in ways she didn't have language for yet.

"And we're going?" The lilt in her voice rose just enough to count as a question, but the intention behind it was unmistakable.

Cooper looked at her, a kiss still warm between them, the mission unfolding like a fault line beneath their feet. He felt the corners of his mouth tug upward in pride, reaching out again, his hand finding hers, fingers lacing through in a grip that felt equal parts promise, peril, and inevitability.

"Yep," he said. "We're going."

He squeezed her hand once, firm and steady, then returned to the keys, pulling up satellite overlays, road access, and security routes.

Instead of feeling dread, she felt her insides loosen and uncoil. Crafting a plan with Cooper was not exactly a solution, but it was a solid place to stand, and it had been a long time since she'd had one of those.

"How can we get into the facility?" Amanda asked, pointing to the surrounding terrain.

"Well, there's a fire road here, but it's gated. And a maintenance path behind the north wing, but it might be monitored."

"Is there a patrol schedule?"

"Not a written one," Cooper said. "But I saw movement logs. Staff rotations move in predictable cycles—shift changes at 6:30 a.m., 2:00 p.m., and 10:30 p.m. The windows between shifts are probably the easiest to either sneak in or create a full cover entry."

"We can probably forge some papers," Amanda murmured. "Like, make ourselves some aliases."

"Yeah, that's our best chance," Cooper agreed.

Amanda closed her eyes and lowered her forehead to the heel of her hand, absorbing the truth of it. "Let's just keep our first names. I can't risk a slip-up while I'm this tired."

"Yeah, absolutely," Cooper echoed, voice low but sure. "I bet I have some documents here I can use to make us look completely official. And there's a printer upstairs. My dad always worked from here. Even on vacation."

She lifted her head, staring at the map again. "Okay, so we have a plan. How far is this from here?"

"A little under two hours," Cooper said. "If the roads are clear."

Amanda gave a humorless half-laugh. "In the Smokies? Not likely."

He smiled faintly, the expression softening the worn edges of his features, and for a flicker of a moment, she saw him as he'd been at seventeen—standing beside her truck on a humid Tennessee night, hands in his pockets, trying and failing not to look at her like she was the whole damn world. It was the same look he used to give her in hallways they weren't supposed to linger in, the one he wore when he'd slip his hand into hers beneath the table, the one that said *I shouldn't touch you... But I will.*

Years hadn't dimmed that look. If anything, time had sharpened it—carved it into something steadier, something that felt dangerously like certainty in this moment.

"Fair enough," he smiled. "We'll call it two and a half.""

Amanda felt a settling inside her, a soft click in her chest as though the world had aligned itself along a single, impossible axis. It shifted the room with a slow, gathering insistence, like the way a sunset deepens without anyone noticing until the whole room is gold.

She drew a breath. "Let's get those papers together, and then we should rest," she said as she sat on the edge of her chair, elbows on her knees, staring into the shadows. "It's strange," she murmured. "After everything... all the years, all the lies, all the distance—this is the first night in a while I've felt like the world isn't swinging out from under me."

Cooper leaned against the table, watching her. There was a gentleness in his eyes she'd always remembered, the antithesis of what she'd known other Hansen men to be. But there was something new too, something she accused Cooper of never being able to muster when they were young. It was a resolve carved deep, steady, and unmistakably into his expression.

"Maybe it's because we finally have a direction," he said. "A real one. And we're doing it together."

She nodded, exhaling slowly. "Together," she echoed, as if the word itself settled something inside her.

Silence drifted between them again, the kind that came when two people were still absorbing how much had been unearthed in only a few weeks. And how much was said after so many years of silence. Cooper worked on his computer for a while before turning toward her with a slow deliberateness that sent awareness racing up her spine. He didn't touch her, not yet. He just waited, giving her time to pull back if she needed to—but she didn't.

When he stood over her, waiting, Amanda tipped her head back to fully see his face, a breath lodging in her throat. He was looking at her as though she were the one steady thing in a life that had spun him in circles for too long.

"You keep staring," she whispered.

"I'm trying to remember the exact second I could no longer convince myself I didn't still love you," he said. His voice was low and honest in a way that wedged itself deep in her chest. "I think it was sometime around the moment I thought I lost you for good."

Amanda's throat tightened. "You didn't lose me," she whispered.

He reached down and brushed a finger along her jaw, and she closed her eyes, leaning into the touch, her hands lifting to his wrists as if afraid the moment might slip through her fingers if she didn't anchor it.

He lowered himself to her, crouching next to her chair, his lips touching her cheek, breath warm against her lips. "Tell me to stop," he whispered as desire trembled at the edges of the words.

She shook her head. "I can't," she said, a tear falling down one side of her face.

His mouth met hers, reacquainting himself with a language he once knew fluently. She rose to meet him, fingers weaving into his hair, pulling him closer as his arms wrapped around her, lifting her, guiding her backward, step by unsteady step, until the backs of her legs brushed the couch. A breath later, she sank into the cushions, his hands following, his tenderness stealing the sound from her throat as he kissed her again.

Their movements were unhurried but full of urgency all the same, as if time had bent to give them back only this opportunity—this single moment—from the years they'd lost. He pulled at her shirt, and it slipped away in quiet, breathless pauses; she tugged off his in kind, and he reached to unbutton her jeans. Need thrummed between them, the heat of his skin against hers grounding her more than any plan or promise ever could.

As he settled above her, he looked down with a question in his eyes, one she answered by sliding her hands along his back and bucking her hips, drawing him to her until there was no space left between them.

And when their bodies finally aligned, it felt less like an act and more like a return—two lives stitched back together, piece by piece, touch by touch, breath by breath.

Outside, the mountains slept. Inside, nothing did.

Chapter Twelve

Lake Como, Italy: The Same Day

Morning settled gently over Lake Como, but the gentleness only sharpened Tristan's unease. The water below the terrace carried a dull, metallic sheen, winter haze that blurred the boundary between sky and lake until the whole landscape felt suspended. He stood at the balustrade of his parents' villa—this place that had always promised a sense of inherited serenity—and felt none of it. A hollow vacancy had rooted itself in him instead, taut and unrelenting. It was a growing awareness that something in his world had tilted while he wasn't looking.

He checked his phone again, the screen washing his face in pale light. Still nothing. No messages, no missed calls. Amanda never said that she would stay, but if she had needed space again, she would have said so; if she had been interrupted, she would have sent a brief acknowledgement. Silence was not her language, not with him, he told himself. Not after the way she'd leaned into his chest on the balcony and let the city wind wrap around them like a shared breath. Even then, in her quietest moments with him—reserved and cautious—he could feel her presence. She never disappeared.

Until now—three days without a trace. And every minute of it scraped at him.

Tristan had once found pride in the restraint he'd shown with her. He had believed it mattered, in a twisted way, not spying on her when he had full capability of doing so. He had wanted to build something real, not something monitored or managed. He had stepped out of character for her, refusing to place trackers on her devices or fold her into the subtle channels of influence that are second nature to him. Even though he had tracked her for years before they started dating, he'd convinced himself that trust in a new relationship meant letting her live without shadowing her every move.

But trust was turning into a liability, and the part of him that had once romanticized the idea was shrinking by the hour.

Behind him, the villa murmured to life: staff voices drifting from the kitchen, the faint clink of china being set for breakfast, the soft echo of his mother's footsteps as she crossed the marble floors.

Evelyn paused in the doorway, her reflection ghosting in the glass before she stepped outside. Her expression, as always, revealed nothing but held so much.

"Tristan," she said, gently, "your father asked if—"

"I'm not joining them," he snapped without turning. "Not yet."

She accepted this with a small nod that he sensed rather than saw, and she withdrew without admonition or probing.

Tristan checked his phone again, not for a locator—he'd never crossed that line—but for something ordinary, something human: a read receipt, or a quick confirmation that she had landed, even a single-word reply that would anchor her back within reach. His screen remained unchanged, the message he'd sent hours before still waiting, patient and untouched. It wasn't like her. She had always been prompt with him, not allowing much time to pass before replying to his texts. Even when Tristan kicked her out of his apartment, and *he* was the first to reach out, she would heart or like the messages she didn't know how to respond to. Amanda didn't go silent without reason, and that simple truth began to thread unease through him in a way that no technical failure ever had.

He called the driver who had been sent to pick Amanda up at the airport. "Has she landed?" The man answered immediately, his professionalism almost abrasive in the face of Tristan's growing worry.

"No, signore. She did not meet me," he said.

Tristan knew what this meant: the plane had landed on schedule. Passengers had cleared customs, and Amanda had either not gotten on the flight to Italy as planned or had disappeared into the blank space between arrivals and the outside world.

Tristan thanked the driver, ended his call, and checked the bank card he'd given her. There was no recent activity. No hotel charges. No rideshares. No airport purchases. There was a trail of nothing.

He unlocked one of his encrypted systems—not to look for her, but to rule out the remote possibility that something within the Grid's data architecture had malfunctioned. He had begun to feel foolish for even checking new Grid notifications, but now a discreet system-level alert appeared from part of the network he rarely touched. It glowed into existence with a composed stillness: a Line One–associated sequence had been accessed from an unclassified node with an internal flag recommending review.

The meaning unfurled slowly, but once it crystallized, it did so with a clarity that pushed everything else aside. Tristan had not initiated a query. He had not opened Amanda's file. He had not interacted with anything connected to her biomarker signature for months, not even when he was decoding the prototype markers she carried halfway around the world. Yet the system had recognized an external access point interacting with data linked to her. It was a subtle breach, almost cautious, the kind of probing that suggested someone was following a thread with no awareness of who else might feel the movement.

He expanded the alert and saw the secondary identifier tied to the interaction. Its encryption was unfamiliar, but undeniably paired with Amanda's profile in the Line One module. Both files had been touched. And the request had originated hundreds of miles from New York City, where Amanda should have been—though the system couldn't yet pinpoint a region, only distance.

The villa behind him took on a stillness that felt almost anticipatory, as though the walls themselves recognized the shift. Tristan walked back inside, letting the warmth of the house replace the chill of the terrace. The scent of freshly polished wood, soft citrus, and brewing coffee lingered in the air—domestic notes that belonged to another version of this morning, not the one he was in.

"You look unsettled," Evelyn said gently. His mother appeared near the dining room archway, pausing when she saw him. "Is everything all right?"

Tristan took a measured breath, grounding himself before he spoke. "Amanda hasn't checked in," he said. "She didn't meet the driver. And... something on my end flagged an alert connected to her. Not something I initiated. She could be in trouble."

Evelyn regarded him with the attentive poise she reserved only for her son, though her voice carried none of the warmth she might have feigned for Amanda.

"When you say trouble," she said, "do you mean the kind that follows her, or the kind she invites?" she asked, the faintest glint of vindication slipping into her otherwise serene expression.

"It isn't trouble she stepped into," Tristan responded, not indulging her. "It's the fact that someone is probing data tied to her. Someone reached for something they shouldn't have."

Evelyn stepped aside just as Harold entered from the east hall, tightening the cuff of his wool coat, which he wore when he and his friends made the crossing to a private lodge upriver. The scent of cold air and cedar clung to him, faint but familiar, reminding Tristan of the winter tradition he'd declined.

"I thought you were joining us," Harold said, studying his son with a level gaze. "It's a clear day for the crossing. The others are already on the water."

Tristan didn't respond immediately; his father's words seemed to reach him from a distance.

"I can't go," he said. "Amanda didn't meet the driver. Her phone's dark. And there was... movement in a system that shouldn't have had any reason to light up. It's connected to her."

Harold paused, absorbing this with a seriousness that didn't require further explanation. He didn't ask what system or what kind of movement; the specifics were irrelevant to him. What mattered was the shift in Tristan's voice.

"Is it something you can handle from here?" Harold asked, though he already suspected the answer.

"No," Tristan said, his jaw tightening as he drew a slow breath through his nose. "I need to go after her. And if she reaches out to anyone, it'll be Lyla…"

He didn't add the rest aloud: that he should have anticipated this, that if he hadn't pretended trust was some noble foundation for a relationship, he would already know exactly where Amanda was. He would have controlled the variables the way he'd been accustomed to—cleanly and imperceptibly. But sentiment had made him sloppy, and now he was paying for it.

Harold stepped closer, laying a hand on his son's shoulder with the kind of restrained authority that had always guided rather than pressed. "Then there's no discussion to be had. You do what you need to do. I'll call and have the plane prepared."

Harold turned toward the vestibule, and the villa seemed to absorb the decision without a ripple. In this house, problems were not met with panic or sympathy, but with resources, precision, and an unspoken expectation: that the Montgomerys' son would rise to meet them as naturally as he had inherited the view of the lake.

Tristan felt a notification buzz on his phone before his father even exited the room—an internal memo routed through the secure Helion channel, labeled *Urgent: For Immediate Coordination.* It wasn't tagged as a crisis, not technically, but the timing unsettled him in a way that tightened the air around his shoulders.

The memo bore Julius Babb's unmistakable cadence: crisp without being cold, polished without sounding rehearsed. Julius never relied on urgency markers; he let his precision do the work of escalation.

According to the report, Helion's European liaison board was pushing back against the proposed relocation of the satellite facility. Their objections came dressed in respectable language—logistics, infrastructure, and regional optics—but Tristan knew the phrasing well enough to read the currents beneath it. Someone was working the political angles from behind the curtain, stirring hesitations that hadn't existed a week prior.

The board wanted reassurances. They wanted Tristan's presence; they wanted it quickly, and ideally, within the next two days.

Below the formality of the memo, Julius had written several lines, the kind he reserved for conversations meant to guide rather than dictate:

You know, I believe that we should acquiesce and slow things a little, but if we allow momentum to stall completely, the board will begin to imagine itself indispensable. There are cunning actors who would benefit from halting this transition, and their influence is not insignificant. Our discussions in the mountains were constructive, but the alliances forged there will remain delicate unless reinforced. Your voice, Tristan, is the one they will listen to.

There was no reprimand in it or pressure spelled out in bold; only Julius's familiar, steady persuasion—an artful reminder that timing was everything.

Tristan was halfway across the foyer when his phone vibrated again, this time with the distinct, low-frequency tone reserved for Julius. He considered ignoring it. The plane was being readied, and his bag wasn't even packed.

"Tristan," Julius said in a warm, impeccably calm voice, the kind that made every request sound like a courtesy. "Your father mentioned you were at Como. I trust the lake is treating you better than the Europeans are treating our timetable."

"Now's not the best time," Tristan said, keeping his voice level. "I'm dealing with something."

"Of course you are," Julius replied, and the softness in his tone didn't disguise the calculated way he absorbed information. "But I'm afraid the Helion board doesn't much care about our private inconveniences. They're slowing the rollout again. They want reassurances only you can give."

Tristan exhaled sharply. "They can wait forty-eight hours."

"They could," Julius allowed. "But in forty-eight hours, they may not be our problem anymore. They may be someone else's leverage."

There was a brief pause, framed just carefully enough to feel intentional. "You know as well as I do that Hansen's people are circling.

Julius wasn't sounding an alarm so much as positioning a piece on a board only he could see. His warnings always carried a quiet push beneath them, the kind that made Tristan believe he was reacting when, in truth, he was being steered.

"If Hansen's numbers keep climbing, he and his advisors will attempt to fold the Grid's European expansion into their campaign narrative. That cannot happen—not before your infrastructure is secured."

The mention of Governor Hansen sent Tristan's mind spinning. He knew Hansen was after power; that much was a given, but Julius hadn't expressed disapproval of him until now. Was Julius afraid that he would lose grip of the influence he had over Tristan if Hansen got too close? Jealousy was no stranger to the most powerful players on Earth, Tristan knew that. But it was the first time he ever questioned his alliance with Julius Babb.

"I'll address it," Tristan said. "But not now."

"I'm not asking you to abandon whatever you're handling," Julius replied. "I'm asking you not to underestimate how quickly the ground can shift when powerful men sense opportunity. We all want the same outcome, Tristan. Stability. Continuity. Protection from impulsive alliances and... sentimental entanglements that could jeopardize the broader vision."

The last phrase was light, almost affectionate—so subtle that someone less attuned might have missed the needle beneath the silk. Tristan felt heat rise in his chest, not anger, but something like recognition. He knew persuasion when he heard it. He also knew that Julius believed he was helping.

"I'll call you when I land; I'm taking a plane back tonight," Tristan said.

"I look forward to it," Julius replied, a smug satisfaction on his lips—measured, never smug. "And Tristan? Whatever demands your attention today... Do take care. Some disruptions have a way of widening if we don't address them early."

The line disconnected with a soft click, leaving Tristan standing alone again in the echoing hall. The timing felt impossible, but the expectations were unmistakable. And he had no intention of addressing any of it until he found Amanda.

Outside these walls, losing contact with someone might prompt worry or frantic calls to the police; here, it meant summoning a jet, rerouting a schedule, and rearranging the world. The hush of generational wealth insulated their lives from the contingencies that governed everyone else's. And as Tristan stepped toward the door, he felt the familiar weight of that contrast: the effortless power of his upbringing on one side, and the tremor of something far more human and uncertain—and far less willing to bend to his desires—waiting for him on the other.

Chapter Thirteen

East Tennessee Developmental Assessment Home:
The Next Day

Morning settled differently in the Cluster House
than it did over Lake Como. There, the lake swallowed sound
and light and gave them back in muted reflections. Here,
everything was more vivid, closer, hemmed in by walls that
smelled of lemon oil and laundry soap and something faintly
medicinal that never quite faded, no matter how many pies
Momma Price baked.

Daisy woke to the hum of the old furnace and the soft
creak of someone moving down the hallway. She lay still for a
moment, listening. The house always had this suspended hush
just before the day fully began, as if it were holding its own
breath along with the children inside it. Downstairs, a radio
clicked on to low music, followed by the clattering of dishes
and the bright sound of Momma Price's laughter.

"Up and at 'em, treasures," called one of the aides, her voice
pitched in an unvarying cheerfulness that felt both kind and
exhausting. "Momma's got cinnamon rolls today."

Daisy pushed back the covers and sat up, the air cool against her arms. She moved through the motions—smoothing the sheet, tucking the corners, and fluffing the pillow—as if folding herself into the day. This was how it worked here: you woke, you made your bed, you stepped into the prescribed rhythm.

In the bathroom, Daisy met her own reflection with the brief, polite acknowledgment she reserved for strangers. Some mornings she looked for a resemblance she couldn't name, as if bone structure might confess something the paperwork did not. Most days, she just smiled at herself, grateful to be alive. That was the type of girl she was—happy because happiness existed, and why would you choose sadness if you could avoid it? Not that melancholy didn't have its place, but it was a mood that moved through Daisy rather than settling into her everyday life.

By the time she reached the kitchen, the long pine table was already ringed with kids in various shades of flannel and denim, hands wrapped around mismatched mugs. Momma Price stood at the stove in her apron, sleeves rolled to the elbow, her hair pinned in the same careful twist she wore every day, as though she'd woken ready to be photographed for the brochure no one had ever actually seen.

"There's my sleepyhead," Momma Price said when she saw Daisy, a beam of pleasure lighting her face as though she were the one person they'd been waiting on. "Thought I might have to send a rescue squad."

Daisy managed a smile, the effort small but genuine. "Just taking my time."

"Well, there's grace for that." Momma Price reached for a plate, set a cinnamon roll on it with careful precision, and slid it across the table.

Daisy sat at the dining table with a glass of water beading slowly onto a folded paper towel, her notebook open but mostly ignored. The Blue Room session from the day before had left a faint warbling in the back of her mind, not unpleasant, just... present. Every time she blinked, she could almost see the afterimage of pale light behind her eyes.

Charlee and Junie had drifted upstairs as she finished her cinnamon roll to argue over which of them got the good mirror, and the younger kids were being herded toward the mudroom to find matching shoes for some kind of outdoor game. Momma Price moved through it all like she always did, a steady axis around which everyone else spun—calling out reminders, smoothing hair, plucking a T-shirt from the back of a chair, and folding it mid-stride without breaking conversation.

"Daisy, honey, you want to sit out on the porch for a bit before your session?" she asked, passing by with a tray of cups. "Fresh air helps the brain. Dr. Kessler says so."

"Dr. Kessler says everything helps the brain," Daisy laughed as she pushed her chair back and headed out the front door.

The porch boards had their own language of creaks and soft complaints, and the wind chime at the far corner muttered faintly, more metal than music. Daisy sank into one of the rocking chairs, tucking her legs up and wrapping her hands around the cool glass. From here, she could see the curve of the road where it dipped behind a line of trees before climbing back toward town.

A car's engine rolled faintly in the distance—ordinary enough that she almost dismissed it. Cars came and went from the main road all day: staff shifts, farm vehicles that serviced the next property a few miles down, occasional tourists who got lost on the mountain roads. This approaching car was different only in that it didn't slow at the usual pull-off down the hill; it stayed steady, then dropped gears as it turned onto their drive.

Daisy straightened a little, the motion automatic, as the car rolled to a stop, engine softening into silence.

For a moment, no one moved. Then the driver's door opened, and a man stepped out—tall, shoulders set in that particular way like he'd been told to stand straight since he was old enough to walk. He came around to the passenger side and opened the door, where the woman who followed carried a different kind of tension, as if she were holding herself together by sheer will.

She didn't recognize either of them, but something in their presence stirred a faint, unsettling familiarity she couldn't place. Daisy's fingers tightened around her glass.

Before anyone could speak, the screen door behind her creaked open and bumped lightly against her shoulder as Momma Price stepped out, wiping her hands on a dish towel, her smile blooming on reflex.

"Well, now," she said, voice warm enough to butter biscuits. "Not sure you're in the right place, folks."

"Good morning, ma'am," the man said, offering a forged document with practiced confidence. "I'm Cooper, and this is my colleague, Amanda. We have authorization for a placement verification. The guards waved us through."

Momma Price's gaze flicked toward the road that curved past the main house's drive, faint irritation crossing her features.

"If the guards waved you through at this hour, they were probably more interested in stayin' warm than doin' their job properly," she said. "Shift change makes them careless." She looked back at him, her tone even. "Authorization or not, I'll still need to understand who you are, and if you're in the right spot."

Cooper offered a polite half-smile, one that was all grin and performance and no warmth.

"We confirmed the address with the agency," he said. His accent held soft traces of Tennessee and, oddly, of somewhere else—another state, or maybe another life entirely. "We were told this is the East Tennessee Developmental Assessment Home. Are you Ms. Price?"

"That's me," she said easily. Momma Price's smile held, but Daisy watched the angle of it shift by a fraction, the way it always did when someone used the wrong vocabulary for what this house actually was. "We've got a number of kids under our roof," she said. "You'll have to be more specific about the placement you want to verify."

"We're looking for one of the older girls," Amanda said. Her voice was steady, but there was a rawness beneath it that no amount of composure could cover. "Her file lists her as Daisy Smith."

Daisy didn't realize she'd swallowed until the movement caught in her throat. It was a small movement—barely a shift—but Amanda caught it instantly. Their eyes met for a brief, breath-catching moment, something like recognition sparking between them. It wasn't certainty, and it wasn't proof, but in the half-light of morning, Amanda felt an ache so deep it nearly unsteadied her.

Daisy's name was not a secret here, but hearing it spoken like that—pulled out of a folder somewhere else in the world and carried all the way to this porch—made it feel newly fragile.

Momma Price didn't look at her charge. She kept her attention on the visitors for one beat longer than necessary, as if weighing their request and the power dynamic in the same breath.

"We do have a girl by that name," she said, her voice smooth and controlled. "Before anything moves forward, I'll need to confirm your documentation through the proper channels." She touched Daisy's shoulder with the kind of light pressure that conveyed both reassurance and instruction. "Go on upstairs, sweetheart. I'll call for you if you're needed."

Daisy hesitated only long enough for Amanda to feel something shift inside her again as she disappeared quietly into the house. Only when she was gone did Momma Price take the paper, holding it with a scrutinizing stare.

"Since you're already here," she said, opening the door with a composed gesture, "we'll sort this out inside. I'll contact Dr. Kessler and verify the request."

Momma Price's posture remained steady, neither welcoming nor hostile—simply a woman accustomed to managing delicate situations before they had the chance to become problematic.

"Come on in," she said. "Let's see what this is about."

The moment Cooper and Amanda crossed the threshold, the temperature of the house seemed to drop as the building became alert to their presence. The clatter from the kitchen softened, as if someone had lowered an invisible volume knob.

A cartoon still murmured faintly from the living room, but even the children's laughter felt slightly hushed, toned down because of strangers.

Momma Price led them into the small front parlor, a room used so rarely it carried a faint scent of dust and lavender sachets. Everything inside it looked arranged for a photograph that had never been taken—lace doilies perfectly centered, a crocheted throw draped over the back of a chair, a Bible open on the table to a psalm. The kind of room meant to impress donors or put state officials at ease.

"Have a seat," she said, gesturing to the sofa. "I'll be just a moment."

She closed the door behind her with a click, soft but unmistakably deliberate.

Amanda's hands trembled despite her effort to keep them still. The parlor's tidy calm only made her pulse louder in her ears. She had spent years in rooms staged like this—churches, foster homes, disciplinary meetings—but never had one felt so close to the past she'd been running from or to the future she wasn't sure she deserved.

Cooper's knee brushed hers when he sat. He didn't flinch or draw back; he let it rest against hers, hoping she'd feel the comfort in him as he did in her. The tightness in the room pressed against both of them.

"Do you think she believed us?" Amanda whispered.

"I think she believed enough not to raise an alarm," Cooper murmured back. "That's all we need for the moment."

Amanda exhaled slowly, steadying her breath. "She sent the girl upstairs."

"I noticed," Cooper replied. "Could've been routine. Or it could've been her way of keeping things contained until she verifies who we are."

Amanda nodded, but her chest tightened anyway. The girl's quick glance lingered in her mind—subtle recognition, not certainty, just a flicker she couldn't name. "She looked... startled."

"Anyone would," Cooper said gently. "Two strangers show up just past dawn with paperwork? That'll rattle any kid."

"Maybe," Amanda whispered. "But something about her..." She couldn't finish her thought.

"I know," Cooper said softly.

The silence that followed was thick, not with fear but with the weight of two people trying to steady themselves in the momentum of something irreversible.

Through a thin vent near the baseboard, muffled voices drifted—unhurried and controlled. Momma Price was speaking to someone on the phone, her tone as composed as it had been on the porch. Amanda couldn't make out the words, only the cadence: low question, brief pause, calm reply. She recognized the pattern instantly. It was the same rhythm her caretakers had used when calling the office at The Ridge, the same tone staff adopted when smoothing an unexpected wrinkle in routine without letting anyone else see the crease.

Cooper glanced toward the closed door, jaw tightening. "This plan felt smarter at two in the morning," he murmured.

Amanda huffed out a breath that wasn't quite a laugh. "We said we'd get here before dawn. Slide past sleepy guards. Ask to 'verify a placement.' Who did we think we were?"

"People with no better options," Cooper said. "And forged documents we hoped no one would look at too closely."

Amanda rubbed her thumb along the hem of her sleeve, grounding herself. "She didn't react the way I expected. Not suspicious. Just... managing us."

"That might be worse," Cooper admitted. "It means she's done this dance before." He leaned closer, voice low. "We just have to hold steady until we know whether she'll let us talk to Daisy."

A floorboard creaked faintly above them, and Amanda's chest tightened. She could picture Daisy on the other side of that sound—caught in the same machinery Amanda once was, decisions made around her as if she were an object to be repositioned. A girl shaped by the whims of influential people who were seldom questioned and almost never stopped.

When the door finally reopened, Momma Price stepped inside with her hands clasped gently in front of her, her expression composed into neutrality—but not indifference.

"Thank you for waiting," she said. "Dr. Kessler is available. We'll need to move this to his office. I'll take you down."

Amanda rose, a faint tremor passing through her legs. As Cooper stepped with her, the calm of his posture settled her more than any touch could have. He had to offer support without crossing the boundaries their cover required.

Behind them, the rest of the house went on—kids arguing over the remote, a pot lid clattering in the kitchen, someone calling for a missing shoe. Life, in all its ordinary noise, kept moving forward.

Daisy had been listening, and a sudden, vivid knowing that her world was about to tilt washed through her.

Chapter Fourteen

*East Tennessee Developmental Assessment Home:
The Same Day*

Amanda followed the soft squeak of Momma Price's sensible shoes down the hallway, every step carrying them farther from the warm chaos of the main house and deeper into the part of the building that didn't quite feel like it belonged to children.

The scuffed baseboards and thumb-smudged walls gave way to a narrower corridor painted in a neutral shade that refused to commit to a color; the air cooled by a degree, edged with the faint, sterile note of disinfectant. A door marked in bold letters with the words *staff only* stood ajar long enough for Amanda to catch a glimpse of file cabinets and a humming printer before it swung shut again. Down here, the sounds of the house—cartoons, laughter, a child complaining about socks—thinned into background noise.

She knew this architecture. Not the layout, but the intention. You could always tell when a place was built to look like a home and function like something else.

"Dr. Kessler's office is just ahead," Momma Price said over her shoulder. Her voice stayed even, that same warm, supervisory tone she used with the kids, but Amanda could hear the tighter thread beneath it now. "He's a busy man, but he does understand that we cooperate when the state needs something."

Cooper walked a half step behind Amanda, close enough that she could sense his steadying presence without needing to look at him. In the parlor, he'd slid the forged folder back into his bag with the unhurried confidence of someone who'd shown credentials his whole adult life. There had been no flourish, no theatrics—just plain inevitability. She clung to that now, to his ease, while her heart moved to a faster rhythm.

They reached a door labeled *Clinical Director — Dr. Sean Kessler, PhD, LCP.* The people who ran experiments on kids learned early how to drape themselves in qualifications.

Momma Price gave a single, businesslike knock. A measured reply came from inside, "Come in," Dr. Kessler answered.

She held the door for them, offering a courteous step-back that somehow positioned her behind them. The gesture was mild, almost gracious—yet Amanda felt the weight of it. Momma Price wanted the vantage point more than she was concerned about the welcome.

The doctor rose as they entered, a man in his mid-fifties, hair graying at the temples, thin hands that looked like they had never done manual labor a day in their life.

Dr. Kessler's office was tidy to the point of compulsion. Bookshelves lined one wall, packed with textbooks and monographs whose titles ran together in a slurry of developmental, cognitive, and behavioral jargon. Two monitors glowed on the desk, one displaying what looked like a schedule grid and the other a series of graphs in muted blues and grays. A framed print of a mountain landscape hung behind the desk, presumably to soften the room, but it was not doing its job well.

He nodded once in greeting, eyes moving quickly from Amanda to Cooper, then to the folder under Cooper's arm.

"Dr. Kessler," Momma Price said. "These are the folks who came to visit us this morning. From the state's review team."

She didn't stumble over the words; if anything, she sounded practiced, as though this scenario lived somewhere on a list of drills she ran through in her head at night. This was definitely not her first rodeo.

Her gaze flicked to Cooper in a quiet prompt as he quickly stepped forward, extending his hand.

"Cooper Gaines," he said. "Child Outcomes Auditor, contracted with the Department of Children's Services."

Kessler took his hand with a steady, understated grip.

"And this is my colleague, Amanda Lewis," Cooper continued. "Behavioral Outcomes Specialist."

Amanda offered her hand as well, feeling the subtle assessing pressure of Kessler's fingers as they closed over hers. He held her gaze a fraction of a second longer than strictly necessary, reading not just her face but the way she carried whatever authority he believed she had.

"I appreciate the quick accommodation, Dr. Kessler," she said. "We know the notice was short. The scheduling glitch was on our end, not yours."

His mouth tipped in something that might have been a smile if it had traveled as far as his eyes. "These things happen," he said. "I was not aware of a review scheduled for this quarter. But I'm told the state's priorities have been... evolving."

"That's one word for it," Cooper said lightly, drawing a slim folder from his bag. The Manila cover bore a convincing facsimile of the Tennessee Department of Children's Services letterhead, right down to the watermark. Cooper opened it to the second page, where the language turned particular.

"As you'll see here," he said, sliding it across the desk, "this isn't a facility-wide audit. It's part of a targeted review of long-term, mixed-placement environments with elevated medical and cognitive assessment frequencies. That narrows the field more than you might think. East Tennessee Developmental Assessment Home meets several of the state's criteria for closer study."

Kessler took the folder and sat, the leather of his chair creaking softly. His eyes scanned the page with quick, precise movements. Amanda watched the minute shifts in his expression—a brief tightening at the mention of "mixed-placement," a subtle easing when he reached the phrase "partner sites with historically compliant records."

"We've consistently met or exceeded state benchmarks," he said, almost reflexively.

"That's part of why you're on the list," Amanda replied gently. "The department wants to understand what's working in environments like yours. Especially in cases where children have remained in one setting for longer than average."

He glanced up at her, curiosity pricking through his professional reserve. "The state is celebrating continuity now?" he asked. "That's new."

"They're celebrating outcomes they can quantify," Cooper said. "Duration, stability, cognitive gains, absence of incidents. That sort of thing."

Kessler responded with a soft, noncommittal sound, the kind that hovered somewhere between agreement and skepticism and offered no clue about which he meant.

"And Ms. Price mentioned there was a specific case you were here to discuss?" he said, shifting the folder closed with two fingers. "We don't often get this kind of attention for individual residents."

"We're sampling from a small pool," Amanda said. She kept her voice calm and even, the way she used to in cockpit briefings when half the room didn't trust her yet. "One of the files that surfaced in our pull is a girl listed in your records as Daisy Smith."

Amanda watched the faint recalibration in him—a minute settling of the shoulders, a breath held a beat longer than before. It wasn't fear, probably not even concern, just a careful adjustment that told her he had tucked the detail away for later use.

"Yes," he said with an elongated vowel. "Daisy's been with us for some time."

"Seventeen now?" Cooper asked. "Long-term placement, minimal movement between environments, high participation in cognitive and physiological assessments. That combination is... uncommon."

Kessler folded his hands on the desk, fingers aligning with practiced care. "Daisy has a very particular profile," he said. "High potential, low behavioral risk, unusual resilience considering her early history. That makes her an ideal participant in certain state-approved programs."

"Such as?" Amanda asked, though she could already guess.

"Longitudinal cognition studies," he said. "Developmental metrics tied to executive function and adaptive coping. Nothing invasive," he added, the phrase slipping out so easily, Amanda knew he had said it hundreds of times. "Her involvement has been fully authorized at every level."

"Authorized by whom?" Cooper asked, though his tone remained mild.

Kessler hesitated for the first time. It was brief, barely a stall, but it existed.

"By the appropriate overseeing bodies," he replied. "The programs she's enrolled in are not unique to this facility. We are one node in a larger network."

It was an ordinary term in Kessler's mouth, yet it carried a different resonance for Cooper. *Network*— a reminder of the machinery behind institutions his father had built, the unseen hands that decided fates long before people realized their lives had been mapped.

Amanda's pulse picked up, too, but she kept her features neutral, trying to keep their cover as much as possible. They hadn't rehearsed what they'd say exactly, just what roles they were going to play, and they were keeping up for the time being.

"We're not here to disrupt programs that are working," she said. "We're here to verify that consent structures and oversight match the level of data being collected. Daisy's file just raised flags in our system because of the frequency and duration of certain procedures."

He looked at her more sharply then. "You think she's being harmed?"

"We think she deserves the same scrutiny you would want for *any* child under your care," Amanda said. "From what we've seen so far, this facility prides itself on transparency. This is an opportunity to demonstrate that."

The word pride always worked on men like him. It was always a safer lever than fear.

Kessler's mouth relaxed by a few degrees, and he nodded his head. "We do pride ourselves on our work, and her metrics have been exceptional," he said. "We've observed gains that align with the aims of the program. Her emotional stability is within normal limits. She has peer attachments, responds well to structure, and excels in school. From every measurable angle, Daisy is thriving."

Every measurable angle. The phrase scraped at Amanda.

"And from the angles you can't measure?" Cooper asked.

Kessler's gaze flicked to him, then back to Amanda, as if calculating which of them posed the more interesting challenge. "She has questions, like any adolescent," he said. "We address them as they arise. Stability often requires containment of certain variables."

Amanda let a small pause stretch, then filled it with the most reasonable request she could make.

"As part of our review, we'll need to see her file," she said. "Full case history, program enrollment terms, assessment logs, any incident reports. And we'd like to meet her. A brief structured interview, framed as a routine wellness check."

Kessler tapped a finger once against the folder. "You've come a long way for one interview," he said.

"It isn't only one," Cooper answered. "But hers is a priority. The state's data pull flagged her placement for long-term review. We're simply following the algorithm."

Nothing in that sentence was technically a lie. Algorithms had been deciding Daisy's life for more time than any of them realized.

Kessler considered the couple's statements, then nodded once. "You can review the file here," he said. "I don't permit sensitive records to leave this wing. As for meeting Daisy, I can schedule you into her day. She has a blood draw this morning, but we could bring her down after that for a twenty-minute interaction in the interview room."

The term carried a shadow Amanda couldn't quite shake, a reminder of rooms she'd rather forget. She swallowed it down, offering an easy, polished smile.

"That would be perfect," she said.

"I will, of course, remain present," Kessler added. "For continuity and to ensure she understands the nature of your questions."

"Of course," Cooper said smoothly. "We wouldn't want to undermine your relationship with her."

He seemed almost reassured by their compliance; men like Kessler trusted the architecture of their programs more than the children inside them. To them, a child was a sequence of metrics, and any instability was a data point rather than a feeling. It never seemed to occur to him that the behaviors he measured were often responses to being measured in the first place.

He faced the keyboard, tapping a sequence that brought up a screen of neatly ordered names. The motions were almost graceful, practiced enough to be instinctive, and Amanda felt a faint unease at how effortlessly he navigated a list that determined the course of so many lives.

"Here she is—Daisy Smith," he said, clicking his tongue. "I'll print the summary page and have the full file brought in. It may take a few minutes."

"We can wait," Amanda nodded.

Dr. Kessler rose and stepped out from behind his desk. "I'll ask Mr. Bennington to fetch the hard copy from records," he said. "In the meantime, if you'd like to see the space where her assessments are conducted, I can show you the suite. It may help contextualize the data."

He spoke with the confidence of a man who trusted the room itself to defend him. As if the walls and titles and polished surfaces would testify to the absolute necessity of this groundbreaking and much-needed information.

"That would be helpful," Cooper said.

Kessler glanced at Momma Price, who had remained near the door like a chaperone.

"Ms. Price," he said. "Would you have Mr. Bennington bring Daisy's file to my office? The state team will be with me in the imaging suite."

"I'll take care of it," she said. "I'll let the girls group know that Daisy's on a different schedule this morning."

Amanda kept her posture even, hands folded neatly in her lap, but she could feel the edges of the moment tightening. Every administrative delay, every keystroke on Kessler's screen, expanded the risk. Cooper mirrored her stillness with practiced calm, but she knew his attention was moving in widening circles—mapping the room, charting obstacles, rehearsing contingencies he hoped they wouldn't need.

Staying meant exposure. Moving too soon meant suspicion. They were balancing on a ledge disguised as a routine tour.

Kessler gestured toward the hallway that branched deeper into the clinical wing. "This way," he said.

Crossing into the corridor changed the texture of everything around them. The floor transitioned to polished linoleum, its shine catching the light like an unspoken warning. A camera in the corner monitored the stretch of hallway—not the doorway, a small but intentional choice—and the air carried a faint, sterile crispness, an institutional signature anyone would expect.

"The Cognitive Imaging and Developmental Metrics Suite is just ahead," Kessler said. "We call it the Blue Room. The children like that better than the formal title."

"A lighter name for a heavier purpose," Cooper said.

Kessler's gaze sharpened for a heartbeat, then smoothed over, as though Cooper's remark had landed somewhere he preferred not to linger.

"We've been able to contribute a significant volume of data through this facility," he said. "Our outcomes have been cited in two state-level reports and one federal grant renewal. The work we do here increases access to services that would otherwise be underfunded."

Amanda didn't interrupt, though the cadence of Kessler's explanation stirred something familiar beneath her ribs. It was the tone—the measured, orderly assurance of a man who believed in the architecture of his own logic. She had heard it before, in quieter rooms and more intimate moments, when Tristan spoke of systems, progress, and the future. He was certain he was doing right, even if rightness required bending a person until they fit the design, not that he'd put it in those terms. And neither had Amanda. It was easy to believe in his goodness, until it wasn't.

Kessler carried that same composure: the calm of a man who saw outcomes instead of people, metrics instead of memories. Listening to him felt like brushing up against a worldview polished smooth by years of reinforcement—one that valued improvement, optimization, the steady tightening of human potential until nothing unpredictable remained.

Amanda walked beside him, her expression composed, but a chill rose along her spine all the same as she listened to his detached voice. A flash of being in Tristan's apartment hit her, and she felt the weight of the truth that progress could be mistaken for love if you weren't careful, no matter who you were.

They turned the corner, and the door came into view—the same one Daisy had entered over and over, ordinary in color yet unmistakable in function. The plaque beside it read *Cognitive Imaging & Developmental Metrics,* the lettering crisp against the institutional white. Someone had placed a single blue star sticker just beneath the title, a small, almost hopeful gesture that couldn't soften the gravity of the work done inside.

Kessler entered his code, and the lock disengaged with a soft mechanical click.

"If you'd like to observe from the alcove when Daisy comes down later, we can arrange that," he said. "For now, I can at least show you the environment."

He gestured them forward with an ease that suggested this was the natural next step, the expected choreography. Amanda felt Cooper tense beside her. They had asked to meet the girl; instead, they were being ushered into the architecture of her confinement, a sanitized glimpse before the real encounter. The redirection was subtle, but unmistakable, and declining it would draw more attention than accepting it.

As Amanda stepped into the room where her daughter's mind had been mapped and measured for years without her consent, she felt the careful scaffolding of her alias pressing tight around her ribs. *Amanda Lewis, Behavioral Outcomes Specialist,* walked forward with practiced, professional interest.

Amanda Hopkins, the mother underneath, tried not to shake.

Chapter Fifteen

Roswell, Georgia: The Same Day

"Tristan?" Kyle's surprise crossed the threshold a moment before his mind caught up to what he was seeing. He stepped back out of pure social instinct, already gesturing Tristan inside his home with the courtesy of someone raised to make room first and ask questions later.

"Come in, man. Didn't expect to see you."

Tristan gave a polite, faintly apologetic smile as he entered. It was the kind of expression that could soften any intrusion into being almost charming. "I should have called. My schedule changed unexpectedly, and I found myself nearby."

Kyle snorted. "Nobody just 'finds themselves' in Roswell. What's going on, man?"

Tristan's smile remained steady. "I needed to see you. And Lyla, if she's home."

"She'll be back any minute." Kyle motioned toward the kitchen. "Coffee?"

"That would be great, thank you."

Kyle busied himself at the counter with the subdued energy of someone trying to read a situation without letting on as much. He handed a mug to Tristan. "Everything okay?"

"I'm not sure." Tristan wrapped his fingers around the ceramic, letting the warmth settle through his hands. "I just came in from my parents' place in Italy. Amanda was supposed to join us yesterday, but she didn't show. I haven't been able to get a hold of her. I thought she might have contacted Lyla."

Kyle shook his head. "No. I don't think so, but you can ask her yourself. She'll be home any second."

Tristan nodded once, absorbing the information without letting his composure crack. "I hoped she might have reached out."

The front door gave a muted thud somewhere down the hall, followed by Lyla's voice drifting ahead of her—light, conversational, carrying the rhythm of someone about to put groceries away and thinking about nothing heavier than the weather.

She stepped into the kitchen and stopped mid-stride.

Her gaze flicked once—Tristan, Kyle, the half-empty mugs—and the brightness in her voice dimmed as if someone had eased a hand over a light switch. She didn't ask what was wrong; she didn't need to.

"Tristan."

His name left her mouth like a cue rather than a greeting.

"You're a long way from home," she said, setting the grocery bag on the counter but not breaking eye contact.

"I'm looking for Amanda," he said. His tone was polite and measured—classic Tristan to wrap any and all emotions in etiquette.

Lyla's eyebrows pulled together. "Is she missing?"

"She didn't make her flight," he said. "And her phone hasn't been on. I thought she might have reached out to you."

"No," Lyla said. Her voice softened, careful not to display her own worry. "She hasn't." And that wasn't a lie.

His gaze lingered just past comfort, a smallest crack in his practiced calm.

"If she contacts us, we'll tell you," Lyla nodded.

"I'd appreciate it."

Kyle stepped forward, trying to cut through the tension with something gentler. "You sure you're not just—"

"Assuming the worst? Yes," Tristan said before Kyle could finish. "But I'm also assuming she wouldn't disappear without an explanation or a goodbye."

He set his mug on the counter—not abruptly or dramatically, but with the sort of precision that meant he needed control over something, even if it was only porcelain.

"Tristan, you dumped her, right?" Kyle laughed a short laugh. But when Tristan's eyes shot to meet Kyle's with a piercing stare, he felt an awkwardness he hadn't previously experienced with his old college buddy.

"I won't take more of your morning," Tristan said abruptly.

Lyla didn't move aside. "You're not here because you're casually concerned, Tristan," she said, her voice thin yet steady.

Tristan leaned against the kitchen counter, his eyes studying her. "I'm here because she matters," he said.

Kyle stepped in slightly, easing the air between them. "Bro, I get it. If I thought Lyla was missing a call, I'd be tearing the streets up. But I would give it some time. Even if you guys just need a little break, it'll probably blow over."

"Yeah, you're right, man," Tristan said, already making his way toward the door. "If she reaches out, please let me know," he said, almost as if he were speaking through a pane of glass neither of them could see.

"Absolutely," Kyle said, but he wasn't the one Tristan was talking to. He locked eyes with Lyla before stepping outside. "If she contacts you—even briefly—don't wait. Call me."

Lyla nodded, unable to shake the sensation that whatever hopes she had for protecting Amanda were slipping away. She moved to the window without meaning to, watching Tristan, phone already in her hand.

She flicked it awake and read the last message she'd sent Amanda—*You good? Call me if you need me.* It glowed on the screen, no soft gray, *Delivered,* beneath it, only a blank space that seemed to widen the longer she stared. It was the digital equivalent of knocking on a door that no one was behind.

Outside, Tristan wasn't rushing, yet every step carried an intent she recognized from people who never admitted to panic—men who translated fear into strategy, who let their focus harden instead of crack.

He's already charting where to look next, she thought.

Tristan shut the car door and drove off, the engine fading slowly down the street.

Lyla's fingers tightened around her phone.

"Kyle," she said, "something's *really* wrong."

"Yeah, I think you're right," he said, Kyle's even-keeled temperament reassuring her, "but if Amanda needs us, she'll call."

But Lyla couldn't look away from the road where Tristan's car disappeared. A cold certainty was settling into her chest.

"I don't think she can," Lyla whispered.

Tristan's car didn't speed; he simply eased onto the main road in one fluid motion, the engine responding with a low, restrained growl. He reached for the console without taking his eyes off the lane ahead and connected his phone to the encrypted relay embedded in the dashboard—a secure channel he trusted more than anything he'd built.

It connected with a muted chime, syncing his phone to the grid he'd built years ago and rarely used anymore. Not full surveillance feeds—that required bandwidth and clearance he didn't have from a moving car—but the system could still run patterns, scrape recent data, and flag anomalies.

He tapped a still frame of Amanda from their last photo together, one taken on the balcony, her hair pulled back, her expression softened by the wind. It felt strangely intimate to use it like this, but he pushed the thought away.

"Begin scan," he said under his breath.

The system obeyed as the console dimmed to a faint glow and the background process reached out across airport networks, public transit cameras, traffic feeds—nothing intrusive, nothing illegal, just the kind of passive facial-pattern sweep his own engineers had designed before ethics committees forced revisions. It wasn't real-time surveillance. It was a search, broad and sweeping.

Amanda should have appeared somewhere—boarding a train, passing through a terminal corridor, stepping into a café line, anything. But the console remained quiet except for the soft rhythm of the scan.

"Amanda... where did you go?" he whispered.

If she had walked through an airport, the system would have found her. If she had boarded a plane, there would have been a trace. Instead, the silence deepened. It was the kind that belonged to places hidden rather than lost.

Tristan's pulse hammered in his throat, a steady, punishing rhythm. He leaned closer to the wheel, voice dropping into the kind of low, dangerous tone that had once made seasoned analysts stop talking mid-sentence.

"Tell me where you are," he muttered, his voice slicing through the air like a blade. "Just give me something."

A soft alert blinked onto the console.

Tristan kept one hand steady on the wheel as the relay decoded the incoming alert—another faint regional tag, the same Tennessee-based node that had interacted with Amanda's data hours earlier. He felt a shift in his chest before he understood it intellectually: this wasn't some random background scrape or misrouted query. Someone at that node had reached for her signature again, however lightly, and the system had recognized the echo.

He wasn't getting full access from a moving car, but he didn't need it; even this thin thread was enough to tighten the boundaries of the map in his mind. A specific region. A pattern repeating. A path leading somewhere he could follow. His throat tightened as he drove. Whatever had diverted her, she hadn't simply vanished—she'd intersected with something human, intentional, and traceable. And that meant he still had a chance of finding her.

He merged onto the highway, the road drawing him toward Atlanta's airport with a pull he didn't bother resisting. The fear hollowing him out rearranged itself into a steady directive: if the system had touched her twice, she could be traced again.

Movement meant he could reach her. And he wasn't stopping until he did.

Sometimes Daisy felt as though her whole life had been shaped around the question of who, if anyone, had ever wanted her. It wasn't a loud, desperate wondering the way people imagined, but a quiet persistence in the places where truth tended to hide. It lived in the moments when she found herself watching someone a beat too long, hoping for the faintest echo of familiarity. That longing had a history, and it began the night she and Charlee slipped into the file room.

They hadn't gone in search of adventure. They'd gone because Daisy had reached the point where not knowing felt more dangerous than anything they might find.

Charlee had stationed herself just outside the doorway, crouched beside a half-open supply cabinet she'd been known to reorganize when the staff wasn't watching. Pads, toothbrushes, plastic-wrapped tubes of toothpaste—she'd shifted items around with casual authority, making enough soft noise to mask Daisy's movements. It was their makeshift signal system: one gentle clatter meant she was fine, two in quick succession meant someone was coming. That night, each subtle scrape made Daisy's pulse jump, but she kept moving. Determination, she'd learned, was more potent than fear.

The file room had smelled faintly of dust and old toner, like a place where stories went to be forgotten. Daisy had known exactly which drawer held the thin manila folder with her name typed on the tab, and to her surprise, it hadn't been locked. That, more than anything, had felt like a particular kind of cruelty—how something so defining could be left so casually unguarded.

Inside were the expected papers: intake forms, immunization records, progress notes written in the mismatched scrawl of overworked staff. And then, at the very bottom, the brittle corner of a document she hadn't recognized: a birth certificate.

The folded paper had crackled softly as she slid it free, the sound too loud in a room meant for secrets. She hadn't intended to open it—not truly—but curiosity had its own gravity, and her hands had moved before her thoughts could catch up. Lines and boxes then wavered for a moment, the typeface bending at the edges, the page itself resistant to being read.

Then her gaze had settled on the single line that mattered: the name in the box for *mother*—Amanda Hopkins.

It was an ordinary name, plain enough to belong to a teacher or a nurse or the woman at the grocery store who smelled like geraniums and never had enough potatoes. But on that night, under the harsh fluorescent light, it had cracked Daisy's world open. It hadn't read "Mother unknown." It hadn't been a blank space. It had been a name, *was* a name—*a real person*—someone who had signed a line or spoken a truth that had set Daisy's entire life in motion.

And once you have a name, the world rearranges itself.

She memorized the name until it felt like something delicate lodged beneath her tongue. Amanda Hopkins. A woman who had existed somewhere—laughing, crying, and making decisions Daisy would never understand. A woman who had once held Daisy's future in her hands... and let it go.

After that night, she couldn't move through town without searching women's faces. A blonde woman at the hairdresser's who wore blue eyeshadow and wedges every time Daisy saw her. The substitute English teacher, with a quick, ironic half-smile Daisy had seen reflected faintly in her own. A social worker from Washington who moved through the facility with polished distance, as if selecting it from a catalog. Daisy watched her every step, half-convinced the woman might turn and say, *There you are.*

Even women in commercials made her pause. She knew it was unreasonable, that the odds were nearly nonexistent. But longing has never answered to reason. It lived in the stubborn part of her that believed the universe dropped clues if you paid attention.

By now, Daisy was a true expert at looking for herself in strangers—cheekbones, the tilt of a brow, the cadence of a laugh. Hope was a strange thing: it made you brave enough to search and determined enough to keep searching, even when you knew the truth could undo you. Which was why, when she'd glimpsed the woman on the porch a few hours earlier—her posture rigid, her expression shaped by something startlingly familiar—Daisy's breath had caught before she could stop it.

It lasted only a moment, a flicker so quick she might have imagined it. But sometimes a single moment can transform everything.

And now, she sat curled on the bed, knees drawn to her chest, chin resting on them as the house breathed around her—the restless pipes, the sighing boards, the muted footsteps she'd learned to identify. For just a heartbeat, she wished the whole place would still itself long enough to let her think, to make sense of why strangers had shown up asking for her. Why the Amanda at their door looked at her the way she had.

Why her own name suddenly felt tethered to something larger than the file where she had first found it.

Who are you?

She wasn't sure whether she meant the visitors... or herself.

Chapter Sixteen

East Tennessee Developmental Assessment Home

Dr. Kessler appeared in the doorway with a folder tucked under his arm, his posture stiffly formal. "If you'll follow me," he said, already turning toward the corridor that branched away from administration.

Amanda exchanged a glance with Cooper. It was subtle and short, tightly held, carrying more between them than any spoken sentence could, as she stepped into the hallway behind the doctor. The fluorescent lights buzzed overhead, while the faint scent of floor polish coated the air so heavily it seemed to cling to her teeth.

"We're actually conducting our quarterly assessments today, so you're in for a real treat," Kessler said, leading them up a flight of concrete stairs, each one fitted with metal edges worn smooth by countless shoes. "You'll be able to observe almost every test we conduct here on the premises. The gallery offers an unobstructed view without interrupting the process, and the subjects won't be able to see you."

Kessler's tone carried the same administrative blandness as everything else in the building, but Amanda felt her pulse tighten with each step they climbed. She couldn't stand hearing the word *subjects* when talking about these children, and she wasn't sure she was ready to see Daisy seated under institutional lights.

He swiped a badge against another reinforced door at the top of the landing, and a muted chime sounded, followed by a mechanical click as he pushed it open.

"This is our observation deck," he offered.

A rush of cool, filtered air met them as Kessler opened the door, carrying that faint mineral scent of machines kept running long after the staff had gone home. The observation deck itself was narrow and deliberately underlit, its darkness designed to keep their reflections from interfering with the one-way glass that stretched across the far wall. Beyond it, the Blue Room opened like a hollow cavern, answering only to its own echoes.

Amanda could understand how it got its nickname. The light made everything look washed in a cool, aquatic tint. Panels recessed in the ceiling cast a pale, toneless glow that softened edges and made the air seem thick and unforgiving. Even without the scanner lowered over a child's face, the room felt submerged, as if everything inside existed a few degrees removed from the world.

Diagnostic equipment lined the perimeter: sealed cabinets, sensor arrays, and the curved track where the imaging scanner would descend during the full metrics cycle. A bank of monitors pulsed softly against one wall, their screens reflecting faint circles across the glass.

At the center of the room, Daisy sat in the reclining imaging chair, its headrest cupping her like a shell does an oyster. The scanner's circular track hovered above her crown—dormant for now, but close enough to cast the faint impression of a halo.

She rested her hands neatly in her lap, shoulders straight, chin lifted in the careful, measured way of a child taught to take up no more space than permitted. A clinician in pale scrubs arranged picture cards between them, the cool light making even the bright illustrations look muted. Daisy nodded to each prompt with a practiced composure Amanda recognized. It was the posture of a girl who understood that privacy was a myth in this place, and attention—especially in the Blue Room—was something to be survived, not invited.

"We can start with her file while the cognitive cycle continues," Kessler said, moving toward the desk tucked beneath the observation window's shadow. The lamp he clicked on gave off a weak, amber glow—warm where everything else had been washed cool and pale.

He drew out two forms and set them between Cooper and Amanda, fingers drumming once against the paper. "Confidentiality acknowledgment. It's standard."

Amanda signed with steady hands, but Cooper signed more quickly, his expression not quite as disciplined.

"Good," Kessler murmured, slipping the forms back into his folder with an efficient motion. "I'll give you space to review the logs. The clinicians will page me if they need anything. You're welcome to stay and observe any others when Daisy's finished."

He opened the door and stepped out, the soft thud of the latch leaving Amanda and Cooper alone with the Blue Room humming beneath them.

As Amanda moved closer to the glass, her breath caught—not from the scene, but from something nearly invisible. Daisy turned her head slightly toward the clinician, and in that rotation, a faint shimmer caught the light behind her left ear. A tiny pulse of reflected brightness glowed just under her skin, gone almost before it existed.

Cooper saw it too. His posture didn't change, but his voice lowered. "There. Look when she moves."

Amanda watched again. Daisy shifted, and the flicker returned. Not a stray hair catching light or a fleck of metal from an earring—she wasn't allowed to wear jewelry. It was something subcutaneous, but close enough to the surface to view in the right light—a quick, muted luminescence, like a single pixel in an LED grid flashing to life.

Amanda's stomach tightened. "That's—" she paused. "Do you think it's the same as the—"

"Data feed?" Cooper whispered, not letting her finish. "Could be... or a tracker. Something collecting information in real time." He almost couldn't let the truth be real.

But the realization was unavoidable, landing with a cold, clean finality. This corresponded too closely with what they found in Tristan's archives. They tried to keep their voices as low as possible, knowing the room itself could have ears.

Amanda could barely pull her eyes from Daisy, but she forced herself to look at the binder, grasping for any information that could help her think of a way to get Daisy out. Each page was crisp, neatly tagged, and color-coded—paperwork designed to appear transparent while revealing nothing that mattered.

Through the glass, Daisy responded to a question by lifting her hand, and the faint glow behind her ear pulsed again. Amanda couldn't help but wonder if it was ever visible outside the walls of the Blue Room.

Kessler reentered, holding another document. "One more thing. We'll need your signatures here as well," Kessler continued, sliding another form toward them. "This grants access to the quarterly reports in full. And once the metrics upload, I can arrange a short, general-questions interview for the two of you. Standard protocol for site evaluators."

"Perfect," Cooper replied. "How long does this test last?"

"Oh, not long; she'll be done shortly," Kessler said.

The tests were packaged as harmless developmental checks: first the puzzles, then the recall tasks, then the imaging lights that tracked the slightest shift in expression. Each step seemed simple, even kind, until you stepped back far enough to see the full shape of what they were actually collecting. It wasn't ordinary intelligence—not the kind teachers praised or report cards recorded—but something sharper, the kind of cognitive edge the state flagged as "high potential." Potential for *what* depended on who was doing the analysis.

A final series of lights flickered across the imaging track above Daisy's head. The clinician made a note on a tablet, then helped the girl down from the reclining chair. Daisy's feet touched the floor as lightly as if the room itself were listening.

"She did well," Kessler said, watching the clinician lead her through the secondary door. "If you'll follow me, we'll speak with her upstairs."

They walked down a quieter corridor lined with framed agency certificates and watercolor landscapes meant to appear comforting. Kessler keyed open a door to a small interview room—a space furnished like a guidance counselor's office, soft chairs and a round table placed just off-center, as if asymmetry alone could disguise the surveillance camera tucked into the corner.

"Talk to her like you would any child in care," Kessler said. "We try to keep things conversational. Nothing evaluative. Nothing that would influence her responses."

"Of course," Amanda smiled coolly.

The clinician guided Daisy in, and she moved with the tentative grace of someone accustomed to walking into rooms where adults already had a plan for her. She sat when asked, back straight, hands tucked neatly together, her eyes flicking toward each of them with a curiosity she hid almost as soon as it appeared.

"Good afternoon," Cooper said, gentle and steady. "We appreciate you meeting with us. This is just part of our routine visit."

Daisy nodded, seeming calm on the surface, though Amanda could feel the small current beneath it. She had the same alertness and self-containment as her mother. It caught Amanda by surprise, tightening deep in her chest.

"How did the testing go today?" Amanda asked, keeping her voice warm and professional.

"It was fine," Daisy said. Her tone was neutral, but her eyes darted once toward the camera before returning to them.

"Good," Amanda replied softly. "We won't keep you long. Just a few items to confirm."

They spent several minutes on safe, shallow questions—meals, schoolwork, and whether she knew who to speak to if she needed something. Her answers were careful and practiced. The kind of answers children learned in institutional settings: safe, correct, and economical.

Dr. Kessler stepped just outside the room, visible through the narrow pane of glass in the door, reviewing a chart before handing it to an aide.

Amanda felt every second thinning. *It was now or never.*

She reached into the folder Kessler had provided earlier and withdrew a clipboard with a simple form clipped to the front. The form was nothing more than a routine acknowledgement verifying that evaluators had spoken with the child—exactly the sort of thing Amanda's cover required her to "review" with Daisy before leaving.

"Before we finish," she said, offering the clipboard to Daisy, "I need your acknowledgement here. Just a quick signature or initial so we can attach it to today's report."

The note lay right on top, aligned so perfectly with the official header that it looked like part of the form: a single narrow slip bearing a phone number and the words she had rewritten three times in her head before boarding the plane.

If you ever feel unsafe, call. You are not alone. —A.

Daisy's eyes flicked to the top of the page. A breath caught—so slight it might have been imagined—but she didn't reach for the note. She only looked at Amanda, a fraction too long, as though trying to decode the space between words.

Amanda smiled lightly. "Oh—sorry." She tapped the edge of the clipboard with her knuckle. "I didn't give you a pen."

She reached into her bag, and in that movement—natural, unhurried—she slid her fingers beneath the note, pressing it gently into Daisy's palm as she placed the pen into her other hand. Daisy's grip tightened around the slip so quickly, and subtly, it might have been a reflex.

She pretended to sign the form, the pen barely touching the paper.

"Perfect," Amanda said, taking the clipboard back as though nothing unusual had happened. "Thank you."

Daisy's hand returned to her lap, curled around the secret she now carried.

Cooper stood, smoothing the front of his blazer. "We appreciate your time today," he said. "You've been very helpful."

They approached the door, and a clinician escorted Daisy out, as Cooper and Amanda watched her go until the hallway swallowed her.

Kessler returned with an easy smile. "Everything satisfactory?"

"Very," Cooper said, professional warmth coating each syllable. "You have a well-run facility here."

"We'll file our report this afternoon," Amanda added. "Thank you for accommodating us on such short notice."

Momma Price caught them on their way back through the main house.

"Y'all come back anytime," she said with her usual Tennessee lilt, which held equal parts charm and suspicion. "Always glad to have folks from the state checking in. Keeps us sharp."

Amanda laughed lightly. "We *were* impressed."

"Well, bless you for sayin' so," Momma Price beamed. "I'll take those for ya," she said, collecting their visitor badges to drop in the return bin. "Safe travels now."

"Thank you," Cooper said, holding the door as they stepped out into the afternoon light.

Only when the car doors shut and the engine turned over did Amanda finally let herself breathe—long and slow, the kind of breath that trembles at the edges because it has been held for far too long.

"Someone implanted Tristan's gadget in her," she said, voice barely audible. "And we're going to get her out of there."

The drive leading up to the Cluster House wound through bare trees and frost-dusted grass, a narrow ribbon of gravel that crackled under the car's tires like something breaking. Tristan pulled in without hesitation, parking at an angle that suggested the space belonged to him. He stepped out before the engine fully quieted, drawing a slow breath of East Tennessee's winter air; it tasted of damp earth and the faint sweetness of distant chimney smoke.

Nothing about the modest campus ahead of him—white clapboard buildings, weathered porches, and distinct orderliness—seemed like the kind of place that held children against their wills.

Tristan had always known places like this existed; in truth, he had relied on them. Facilities like the Cluster House fed data into the systems he'd built, producing the clean metrics he trusted above human testimony. He had wanted these places to be functional and predictable. But he had never stepped inside one, never smelled the sterilized air or heard the muted footsteps of children trained to be seen and not heard. His role had kept him above it all, an architect of outcomes rather than a witness to the machinery that produced them.

But when he'd zoomed into the flagged region, and the map had resolved into a blank, softened blur—no roads, no structures, just a patch of digital fog where there should have been detail—he understood exactly what he was looking at. Hidden facilities never announced themselves. They showed up as absences. And this was one he needed to see for himself.

A guard stepped out of the security booth as Tristan approached, his stance more uneasy than authoritative, as though unsure whether he ought to block or welcome him.

"Sir, can I help you?" he asked, and there was a softness in his voice that suggested he wasn't accustomed to confrontation.

"I'm here for a tour," Tristan said, and even he could hear how foreign the words sounded coming out of his mouth. "Erm, I'm a potential philanthropic partner."

He did not lie often. He didn't need to. And he didn't disguise himself ever. People came to him, opened doors for him, and rearranged schedules around him. Pretending to need permission felt like squeezing into a jacket two sizes too small.

Not that announcing who he was would help here. The Cluster House had no relationship to the network in a way that would make his name matter. And he couldn't very well explain the real reason he'd driven three and a half hours to stand on this porch—following a thread he wasn't ready for anyone to notice he'd pulled.

The guard blinked. "Nobody told us about a second visit today."

"A second?" Tristan repeated, keeping his face even as a coldness unfurled in his chest. "I wasn't aware there had been another."

"Not a tour, a state visit. Let me call up to the house, get you through. I'll need an ID," the guard said.

Tristan handed over his driver's license as the guard, apologetic and increasingly unsettled, lifted his radio. "Main house, this is Gate Two. I've got a... potential donor at the front. Says his name is Tristan Montgomery."

The name traveled like a current. A beat later, Momma Price's voice drifted through the radio with a warm certainty, tinged with the unquestioning authority of someone who ran this place more thoroughly than any clipboard ever could.

"Tristan Montgomery?" she repeated, her voice lifting with a surprised brightness she didn't bother to hide. "Well, my goodness, of course. Please, send him on up."

Momma Price never bothered with technology beyond the ancient landline hanging in her kitchen. She couldn't tell a touchscreen from a TV remote and didn't particularly care to. But tabloids—those she treated like public service announcements. She could recite divorces, engagements, and philanthropic scandals with encyclopedic precision, and she recognized Tristan Montgomery's name before the guard even finished saying it. In her world, he belonged to the constellation of people important enough to warrant attention, and she came down the stairs with the kind of excitement reserved for royalty and long-lost cousins.

The guard stepped aside at once. "You're cleared, sir. Sorry for the confusion."

Tristan nodded in acknowledgment, though his impatience vibrated beneath the surface like a taut wire. He pulled his car past the gate and into the Cluster House's gravel drive. The place looked aged but tended, with broad-planked floors glimpsed through the windows and the soft glow of lamps warming the twilight edges of the day. The porch boards creaked beneath his steps, releasing the scent of cedar and old varnish.

Momma Price met him as he entered, her wide frame solid and reassuring, and her expression one of polite surprise and immediate calculation.

"Mr. Montgomery," she said. "I wish we'd known you were comin'. We had a surprise visit from the state this morning, and it threw our whole routine off."

Tristan's gaze sharpened with precision. "A visit from the state?"

"Yes," she said, waving vaguely toward the administrative wing. "A couple of young agents. Very kind. Well-spoken. Credentials checked out. Amanda something and..." she paused, brows lifting as memory settled into place, "Cooper. That was his name. Amanda and Cooper."

Tristan kept his expression level, but the names landed with a violence that hollowed the air around him. Nothing in the room changed, but inside him everything did—sharp, sudden, and irrevocably clear.

Before he could ask anything more, Momma Price lifted the old rotary phone from the wall, dialing with decisive taps. "Let me get Dr. Kessler down here to greet you properly."

"He'll be here in a minute," Momma Price said, hanging up the phone. "Can I get you some iced tea?"

Tristan nodded politely. "Of course," he said.

Within moments, Dr. Kessler arrived with brisk footsteps and a face pulled tight with confusion. "Mr. Montgomery," he said politely, though his voice snagged faintly on an edge of unease. "We weren't informed of your visit today."

"I wasn't aware I required prior notice," Tristan replied, his tone smooth and deliberate, the kind of steady that made people straighten without thinking.

"Well, no offense," Kessler cleared his throat, "but we can't be too careful protecting our young residents." He gave a quick grin and stepped aside, murmuring to Momma Price, "I need to make a call," he said, and retreated to the far corner of the foyer, taking out his phone and lowering his voice. "Yes, this is Dr. Kessler. I need the primary oversight contact—immediately."

The call redirected, and Kessler's demeanor tightened, as though the weight of the conversation had suddenly increased.

"Governor Hansen," Kessler said, keeping his voice low but unable to keep tension from bleeding through. "Sir, we've had two unscheduled visits today. First two agents from the state, and now a Mr. Tristan Montgomery has arrived unannounced as a prospective donor. I just want to make sure we've gotten the right paperwork for this. It's highly unusual."

There was a silence so dense it felt like a pressure chamber.

"No, that wasn't authorized," Hansen's voice cut in, faintly audible even from Tristan's distance. "No personnel were sent. Who did you say they were?"

"Amanda Lewis and Cooper something," Kessler repeated, flipping through the makeshift visitor log. "They seemed legitimate. Polite. Credentialed."

"Don't assume anything. Do not let Montgomery leave. I'm on my way."

"Yes, sir," Kessler whispered, ending the call with trembling fingers.

He turned back to Tristan, trying and failing to mask his disquiet. "It appears we need to verify a few details before proceeding, Mr. Montgomery. If you don't mind waiting here in the foyer—just temporarily, until we sort this out."

Tristan's expression remained perfectly contained, though something colder and far more dangerous settled behind his eyes.

"I'll wait," he said, and the words landed with a hushed finality.

Momma Price hovered beside Kessler, their shared glance carrying the realization that something far beyond their daily routines had slipped into their untroubled home.

And upstairs, in a small room with dim lights and polished floors, a girl pressed her heel slowly into her sock, feeling the tiny folded note beneath it—a secret that warmed her like a hand closing gently around her own.

CHAPTER SEVENTEEN

Roswell, Georgia: The Same Day

LYLA HAD JUST SET her phone facedown on the counter, *again,* when the doorbell rang.

"Please be my package," she muttered, scooping a stray grocery receipt out of the way. She padded down the hall in sock feet, still thinking of Tristan's face a couple of hours earlier, that too-careful calm pressed over something brittle.

She swung the door open, and the woman on the porch stood as if she had been there for some time and had decided, very politely, not to knock more than once. Silver hair swept back from a finely lined face, wool coat buttoned to the throat despite the Georgia mildness, an umbrella folded neatly at her side although the sky was clear.

"You must be Lyla," she said.

The accent hit first—English, rounded and precise. The name dropped second, rippling like a stone in a still pond.

Lyla's fingers tightened around the edge of the door. "And you must be Katherine."

A small smile touched the woman's mouth, not quite reaching her eyes. "Guilty," she said. "I apologize for the intrusion. I was hoping we might talk. It concerns Amanda."

For a beat, Lyla just stared at her, brain running backwards through everything Amanda had told her: the dossier, the secrets, the way she had said Katherine's name with equal parts fury and reluctant gratitude.

"Of course it does," Lyla said, every ounce of Georgia hospitality wrestling with her instincts. "Apparently, this is the day people from her complicated life drop by unannounced, so you might as well come in too."

Katherine's brows lifted a fraction. "People?"

Lyla stepped aside, extending her hand like an invitation to enter. "You're about two hours behind Tristan Montgomery."

Katherine paused on the threshold, revealing the smallest fracture in her composure. It was gone almost instantly, but Lyla saw it—a brief tightening around the eyes, a recalculation.

"I see," Katherine said. "Then I'm even later than I thought."

The house smelled faintly of coffee, laundry, and the citrus cleaner Lyla pretended made her more on top of things than she was (because she definitely paid someone else to use it). Katherine stepped into the living room, her gaze flicking once around the room in a sweep that took in the framed photos, the half-finished puzzle on the coffee table, and Kyle's running shoes abandoned by the couch.

"Can I get you something?" Lyla asked, because her mother had raised her properly, even if the universe kept sending untrustworthy people to her door. "Water? Coffee? Truth serum?"

"Tea would be a miracle, but I imagine coffee is more likely," Katherine said, lips curving ever so slightly.

"Now we're speaking my love language," Lyla said, leading her toward the kitchen. "Kyle, we have another visitor!"

Kyle looked up from his laptop at the table, the same place Tristan had sat that morning. For one dizzy second, Lyla saw them superimposed—Tristan's sleek European effortlessness and this woman's contained British poise, both threaded through the same dangerous world Amanda had been dragged into.

"Kyle," Lyla said, "this is Katherine. Katherine—Kyle."

Katherine extended a hand. "Pleasure to meet you," she said. "I've heard of you both."

Kyle took her hand slowly, measuring her with a tactician's eye. "Can't say I love that sentence," he said with a wry smile. "But welcome."

Lyla busied herself with the coffee maker, partly because Katherine genuinely looked like she'd been awake for too long and partly because it gave her hands something to do. Her nerves had that too-bright, fidgety quality that only served her well when working obsessively. She loved it when she was in a flow state, but any other time, she tried to temper it.

"So," Lyla said, turning back as the machine sputtered to life. "You've clearly gone to some trouble to find us, which I imagine is fairly easy when you live in the shadows. What exactly do you want from me?"

Katherine took the question as if it were a formal invitation. "I want you to help me keep Amanda alive," she said simply. "And, ideally, to persuade her to stop running toward the most dangerous part of the board."

Lyla folded her arms. "This isn't a game of chess," she huffed.

"It is to some," Katherine replied.

"Okay, well, you're going to have to be more specific. Because so far, every time Amanda told me your name, it came with a story about being lied to, manipulated, or whisked off to another country without consent."

Katherine inclined her head, accepting the blow. "And I'm sure she left nothing out," she said. "Amanda tends to be bracingly honest with the people she loves."

"She also said you were very good at sounding reasonable while playing ten games at once," Lyla replied. "So, with all due respect, you don't get the benefit of the doubt just because you showed up with an impressive accent and impeccable cheek-bones."

Kyle choked on a laugh, and Katherine's mouth twitched.

"Sorry, you seem more like a person I'd like to photograph than play spy games with," Lyla shrugged.

"Thank you?" Katherine said it like a question, determined not to let Lyla's charm affect her. "The truth is, I am playing several games at once. But on this particular move, our interests align. Amanda's, yours, and mine."

"And Tristan's?" Kyle asked.

The briefest silence stretched tight across them, the kind that changed the color of a room.

"No," Katherine said. "Not Tristan's."

Lyla set three mugs on the table, took the chair opposite Katherine, and pulled one knee up to balance her mug on it.

"You said she's running toward the most dangerous part of the board," Lyla prompted. "Where, exactly, do you think she is?"

Katherine studied her for a long, measuring moment, as if gauging exactly where to place the first fracture.

"You know Amanda has a daughter," she said. It wasn't a question—more the soft clearing of a path.

Lyla nodded slowly. "She told you that?" Her voice was steady, but her fingers tightened around the mug until the ceramic clicked faintly against her rings.

"She told me enough," Katherine said. "And Cooper uncovered the rest once certain records were... recovered."

Lyla blinked sharply. "Recovered," she repeated, the word catching. "What records?"

Katherine exhaled. "Daisy wasn't placed with a family. She's been in state care since the day she was born."

The mug in Lyla's hands stilled as color rose and fell in her face, disbelief pulling tight across her features before giving way to something deeper. It wasn't just grief, it was outrage, and a flash of protective fury she didn't bother to hide.

"Amanda's daughter is in a facility?" she said, barely above a whisper. "All this time? And she didn't know?"

"She had no way of knowing," Katherine replied gently. "The adoption was never real. The records were sealed and buried so thoroughly she couldn't have found them on her own."

Lyla swore under her breath, "Those bastards," she said, quiet and shaken. "She's been carrying that guilt for almost eighteen years."

"Yes," Katherine said quietly. "And the tragedy is that she was meant to." Katherine paused, weighing how much to reveal. "When Hansen hired my investigative firm years ago, I was meant to track threats, not his secrets. But certain details refused to stay buried. Eventually, the pattern pointed to only one truth. Daisy was the child Hansen wanted to hide, and that was leverage used to rope Amanda in."

Lyla set the mug down as if afraid she might drop it. "And you think Amanda found her?"

"We don't think," Katherine said. "We know." She folded her hands, immaculate and still. "The new telephone I issued her is monitored. We track movement and listen in enough to confirm intent. It's the only safe way to operate at present."

Lyla's eyes narrowed. "So, they are with Daisy right now?"

"Yes. At least they were an hour ago."

Lyla leaned back, trying to take in the gravity of what she was hearing as Katherine reached into her bag and drew out a small, nondescript device. It was a cheap, gray handset that looked more like a mobile that teenagers got in the early 2000s as their first cellphone than a spy tool. She set it on the table between them.

"What's this for?" Lyla asked.

"It's for you," she said.

"Me?" Lyla scoffed.

"Yes. I want you to call her and give her some instructions. She'll listen to you at this point, not to me. I'm sure she's told you enough about me to make you realize how true that is," Katherine said.

"You're not wrong," Lyla nodded. "Amanda has told me plenty—about waking up and feeling like she'd been dropped into a Bond movie she never auditioned for," she said. "And that someone—hi, that's you—kept insisting it was all for her own good."

Katherine's gaze did not waver. "She's not wrong about the methods," she said. "There's plenty I wish I could have done differently. But the danger is more real than ever. Tristan is on the move. We believe he knows she's betrayed him. James Hansen is edging closer to the presidency with Tristan's work underpinning his vision. And we are working to prevent that union from consolidating its power."

"Who's we?" Lyla asked.

"Myself, Malonga, Julius, and a few others," Katherine said. She didn't want to mention Stephen Hopkins' name in this conversation. She'd let Amanda confide that part of the story to her friend.

Lyla dropped her feet to the floor with a thud.

"Malonga showed up in Romania. He told us not to trust you or Julius. And whatever happened to Russell Drake?" she demanded. "You guys have ruined Melody's life by killing him. You did it, right? Or was it Julius? And now you want me to get involved? I'm not an idiot," Lyla vented.

"But, you're *already* involved," Katherine insisted. "You women have not been as discreet as you think."

Lyla scoffed. "What's discretion in this day and age?" she said with a contemplative sigh.

And the weight of that simple question stuffed the room.

"So, what's your grand plan?" Kyle finally asked. "If things are so dangerous, how do you think you're going to stop these people from getting what they want now?"

"We're preparing for shutdowns. Selective grid failures. Network blackouts. We are attempting to cordon off the damage as much as possible, but there is no version of this that is… tidy," Katherine explained.

Lyla stared at her. "You're just… going to turn the lights off," she said slowly. "Like flipping breakers on the whole planet?"

"Not the whole planet," Katherine said. "Certain nodes. Certain corridors of power. Enough to prevent Tristan's version of the Grid from being fully deployed while James Hansen is in a position to weaponize it."

"And she's with Cooper right now," Lyla said. "The president-to-be's son?" She whispered the words through gritted teeth.

"Precisely," Katherine replied. "Which is why your friend is uniquely placed at the intersection of all of this, whether she likes it or not."

Lyla rubbed at her forehead. "Okay, setting aside the part where you're talking about orchestrating global chaos like it's a complicated dinner party… what does any of this have to do with my best friend rescuing her daughter from a creepy state facility? Because I'm going to be very clear with you, Katherine: I am solidly on Team Get Daisy Out."

"As am I," Katherine said.

Lyla blinked. "Come again?"

"I have no intention of leaving that girl in their system forever," Katherine said. "But Amanda's attempt to retrieve her now, with Tristan already sniffing at her trail, jeopardizes more than her own safety. It jeopardizes Daisy, and it jeopardizes the only credible chance we have to limit the damage this shutdown will cause."

Lyla gave a short, incredulous laugh. "You're going to have to draw a straighter line than that," she said. "Because from where I'm sitting, it sounds like you're asking Amanda to abandon the kid she just found so she can go back to doing your dirty work."

Katherine's gaze softened in a way Lyla did not expect. "I am asking her to survive the week," she said. "And to be in the one place where her presence can stop men like Tristan and Hansen from rewriting the future while pretending they're improving humanity. Daisy does not need a mother who dies in a hallway in Tennessee. She needs a mother alive and positioned to dismantle the system that put her there."

The words landed inside Lyla like a stone in a deep well. She hated that they made sense. She also hated that Katherine had clearly anticipated that reaction.

"Do you even hear yourself?" Lyla asked. "You sound exactly like Tristan when he talks about his work. All of you talking about 'systems' and 'humanity' as if people are pieces on a board. No wonder you talk about it like it's a game. Amanda is a person. Daisy is a person."

Katherine's jaw tightened. "I am painfully aware," she said. "That is precisely why I am here instead of on a plane back to Geneva. I am not asking you to trust me because I claim to be kind. I am asking you to weigh what you know of Amanda against what you know of Tristan, and decide which direction you want her running when the lights start to go out."

Kyle cleared his throat softly. "You said you can't go after her because Tristan would see it," he said. "But he said her phone went dark. He hasn't been tracking her..."

"He said he was 'assuming possibilities,'" Lyla added. "Which, from him, sounded worse than panic."

Katherine absorbed this, the tidy lines of her face tightening. "He told you that?"

"He was sitting where you're sitting now," Lyla said. "Drinking coffee and looking at my phone like it might give him an answer I wouldn't."

"And you didn't," Katherine said.

Lyla's chin lifted. "No. I didn't. Because Amanda clearly didn't want me to know what she was up to, so I had no information to give him anyway. Not that I would have if I could."

Lyla stared at the cheap gray phone between them. "So what exactly are you asking me to do?"

Katherine nudged the handset a few inches closer. "This number is already programmed," she said. "It routes through three layers of misdirection before it reaches the secure relay we've set up. When you text or call from this phone, it will appear as if it originated from a hardware unit that no longer exists."

"Comforting," Lyla said, coughing out a sardonic laugh.

"You cannot use your own mobile," Katherine continued, unfazed. "Tristan will be watching any number associated with Amanda's old number. He may not have been tracking before, but rest assured he has access to her cloud info now. Your calls, your texts, your location history—any pattern can be mapped. If you reach out from your phone, you might as well send him a pinned map with a trail of breadcrumbs."

"So I use this burner," Lyla said slowly, "to tell Amanda... what, exactly?"

"To tell her that Tristan has been here and is hunting," Katherine said. "To tell her the grid disruptions are coming sooner than we'd planned. And to tell her that if she wants even a chance at saving Daisy in the long run, she must get herself out of Tennessee and to the rendezvous point in Europe before the shutdown cascades. It will be much safer there."

"You have a rendezvous point?" Kyle asked.

"We have several," Katherine said dryly.

"And if she says no?" Lyla sputtered.

Katherine's eyes were steady. "Then you will have done everything you could as her friend," she said. "And I will have to rework a very fragile plan without one of our most insightful field operators."

Lyla let out a breath that felt like it had been waiting to escape since she let in their unwanted visitor. "You know she's not going to like any of this."

Katherine's smile was both derisive and fond in a way that startled Lyla. "Amanda rarely likes what I ask of her," she said. "That has never stopped her from doing what she believes is necessary."

"Yeah, well, what she believes is necessary right now is getting Daisy out," Lyla said. Her voice roughened. "She's been living with that hole in her life for seventeen years. You're asking her to walk away from the first real chance she's had to look her daughter in the eye?"

"I'm asking her to live long enough to look her in the eye more than once," Katherine replied.

"Okay," Lyla said, the word tasting like compromise. "Say, I believe you. Say I text her with this and tell her what you want me to say. What do I tell her about you?"

"Be honest. Say that I am still infuriating," Katherine said dryly. "That I am still playing more than one angle, if you think so. And that this time, I am not asking her to trust me. I am asking her to trust you—and the fact that I went through you to speak to her."

Lyla studied her. "So, you're really not one of the bad guys?" she asked.

Katherine's eyes flickered with an emotion Lyla couldn't immediately name. "I've done horrific things," she said. "I've also stopped worse ones. If you're looking for someone pure in all this, I'm afraid you'll have to look elsewhere. But I have no intention of handing Amanda Hopkins—or Daisy—to a man who thinks humanity is a design problem he was born to improve."

For a moment, Tristan's face flashed in Lyla's mind: the precision, the charm, the way he looked at Amanda like she was both a miracle and a calculation.

Lyla sighed, the sound full of resistance and reluctant agreement. "Fine," she said. "Give me the script. Then get out of my kitchen so I can decide whether I'm about to blow up my best friend's life or save it."

Katherine nodded, the faintest relief loosening her shoulders. She slid a folded card from her bag and placed it beside the phone.

"Keep to key phrases," Katherine instructed. "Avoid names, avoid geography. And when your conversation is done, please destroy the phone and leave it somewhere densely trafficked. An airport would be the cleanest option."

"You really do think of everything," Kyle said.

"Not everything," Katherine murmured. "Just the parts most likely to get us all killed."

When the door closed behind her, the house felt strangely larger, as if it had inhaled and not yet remembered how to exhale.

Kyle leaned back, rubbing a hand over his face. "Well," he said. "That was... a lot."

Lyla stared at the burner phone and the folded card, the cheap plastic suddenly heavier than any of her camera gear.

"I keep thinking about when we assumed we were close to figuring this out," she said. "About Amanda on that mountain top, having to choose between a man she thought she loved and a helicopter ride that meant she'd be forced back into this crazy life."

"She chose the helicopter," Kyle said.

"She chose survival," Lyla corrected. "And now we're here again."

Kyle rose and came around the table, resting his hands on her shoulders. "Whatever you decide to tell her," he said, "you're not doing it alone."

Lyla nodded, eyes still anchored to the phone. When she reached for it, her hand moved with a kind of reverence, as if she already sensed that whatever came next would alter the shape of everything they thought they knew.

She turned the burner on. The screen glowed to life, blank and expectant.

"All right, Amanda," she whispered. "Let's see if I can get you to pick up a phone call you don't know you're waiting for."

Chapter Eighteen

East Tennessee Developmental Assessment Home:
That Afternoon

THE SUN HAD ALREADY begun its slow, winter descent when Governor James Hansen's black SUV tore up the gravel to approach the Cluster House, the engine grinding over the rutted drive with more force than necessary. Tristan heard the sound before he saw the headlights; it wasn't an arrival but an impact. As the evening sky tilted toward a cold blue, every shape on the property sharpened as if bracing for an intrusion—the same posture everyone inside the house had already adopted.

Momma Price had pulled the curtains only halfway, and the half-open windows framed the SUV like an omen. Tristan sat where Kessler had insisted he remain—near the staircase, beneath the old grandfather clock whose pendulum kept time far too loudly for anyone's comfort. The foyer smelled faintly of bleach and the lingering sage from that morning's breakfast sausage, a cloying combination under stress.

The front door flung open before anyone could reach it, and Hansen stepped inside with authority that made the air vibrate. He didn't bother to remove his coat, the heavy wool swaying around his legs as if it, too, was irritated to be there.

"What the hell is going on?" Hansen barked, not waiting for an answer as his gaze swept the foyer and landed squarely on Momma Price.

"Governor," she said, her voice climbing into the brittle politeness she reserved for men who could shut down her entire world with one phone call. She straightened instinctively, shoulders drawn back. Her usual warmth—big, boisterous, and motherly—compressed into something smaller. Not fear of volume, but of consequence.

She dipped her head, palms pressed against the knit of her sweater, damp with nerves.

"We've been preparing the children for supper," she said—*not* mentioning Kessler at all, as though she sensed it was safer to offer only the safest version of truth. "Dr. Kessler's in his office—he'll be right out."

As if summoned, Kessler appeared at the far end of the hall, wiping his palms on his lab coat as though friction alone could absolve him of whatever crisis he'd stumbled into. He opened his mouth to greet the governor, but Hansen cut him off before a word could form.

"Kessler," Hansen barked, striding into the foyer with the force of a storm front, "you and I are going to have a very long conversation about your intake protocols. And your visitor logs. And your inability to recognize when a wolf walks through the front door dressed as some ass-backwards official from the state!" His voice reverberated against the old wood paneling, sharp enough to make Momma Price flinch as she crossed the threshold to the kitchen, happy to be out of the commotion.

Kessler stammered, "Governor—sir—we weren't expecting—"

"No," Hansen snapped, slicing the air with a gesture sharp enough to silence the room. "You weren't expecting anything today. Not a falsified inspection. Not forged credentials. Not another unannounced visitor"—his hand flicked briefly toward Tristan without granting him full acknowledgment—"and certainly not me."

He turned fully to Tristan then, the temperature of his anger shifting from broad indignation to personal offense. "You, especially, know exactly how important security is."

Tristan stayed perfectly still, every muscle coiled with precision, his gaze steady even as the room trembled with Hansen's fury.

"I was simply following a digital trail," Tristan said. "I'm as surprised about all this as you are."

Tristan wasn't the sort of man who shrank from confrontation, though the truth was that he rarely met it head-on. He'd been raised in rooms where voices never rose, and decisions were made with the stroke of a pen or the tilt of a head. Conflict, for him, had always been a negotiation, a calculation, a subtle shift in leverage.

Billionaires didn't get lectured in foyers with peeling baseboards. They didn't get summoned like wayward schoolboys or interrogated by men whose authority came from state voters instead of global markets. Yet here he was—face-to-face with a governor whose anger didn't soften simply because the Montgomery name had walked through the door—and the shock of having that fury turned on *him* settled in Tristan's chest like a cold weight.

"I'll get to you in a second," Hansen said, voice booming. "I want to see their paperwork. Now. I want every form they signed, every badge they were issued, every access point they were granted—I need to know all of it."

Kessler swallowed hard. "Governor, we—we have their signatures on the observation logs and a folder with—"

"Bring it," Hansen snapped.

He turned away just long enough for the room to release the breath it had been holding, then faced Tristan again. The expression he wore was not the public face of a governor. It was the private face of a man who was losing grip of a piece of his carefully built world.

"Don't tell me you're ready to throw your life away too," Hansen said, shoulders rigid beneath the tailored lines of his coat. His face flushed, then blanched, the color rising and falling like a tide pulled hard by panic. "That damn girl."

Tristan said nothing. Silence was his armor, his preferred tool for regaining control. But inside, a crack opened—he felt the edges of it, sharp and cold, as internal scaffolding began shifting without permission. He held still out of necessity, bracing himself against the truth he sensed coming.

Kessler reappeared sooner than anyone expected, breathless and blotchy, a thin stack of paperwork clutched in both hands as though he feared it might combust if held too loosely.

"Governor—s-sir—here," he stammered. "These are... ah—these are the forms they filled out. The signatures, the... the intake sheets—everything they, um—everything they touched."

Hansen snatched the stack without looking at him, flipping through the pages with the kind of force that suggested each sheet offended him more than the last. The more he read, the darker his expression grew.

"Unbelievable," he muttered. "Forged credentials. Improvised clearances. And this—" He jabbed a page with the back of his knuckle. "This isn't even the right version of the state evaluator form. Are you imbeciles? They faked the formatting."

Kessler swallowed hard. "Sir, they were... very convincing."

Hansen ignored the doctor as he kept flipping, the motion increasingly violent, each page turned like a blow being delivered.

"Unbelievable," he repeated. "They walked in here as if the two of them could just stroll in and out of a classified facility like they were touring a damn museum! This degree of staff incompetence here is—"

Hansen's breath hitched as he reached the final page. His thumb pressed into it, leaving a pale indentation as if to bruise the paper.

"So they saw her," he said, nodding more to himself than to anyone else in the room.

"Saw who?" Tristan asked, the words cutting cleanly through the air.

Hansen stepped closer, lowering his voice only because the words themselves didn't need volume to be devastating.

"You want the truth about that girl?" he said. "Amanda and Cooper were here. But I reckon you already knew she was. Your fiancée and my son walked in here together this morning and managed to find the one thing we've been protecting for seventeen years."

Tristan's pulse kicked, a hard, contained strike against his ribs. "Protecting," he echoed, his tone careful enough to sound almost calm. "Protecting what?"

Hansen's eyes stayed narrowly fixed on Tristan, as if the rest of the room had fallen away. "You might have noticed there was more than a little familiarity between our family and that girl?"

He kept saying *that girl* as if he were narrating something about a stranger.

Tristan managed only a nod—something that looked like understanding from a distance.

But then Hansen grinned the kind of smirk that let Tristan know his world was about to change. "Amanda and Cooper had a child," he said. "A child that neither of them was in any position to raise, and I did what needed to be done. I made sure she was placed somewhere stable, somewhere peaceful, and somewhere the press would never sniff out a scandal."

Tristan didn't look toward the stairs, eyes wide. "What?" he said blankly, the information dropping into the space between them like a stone. "You're telling me they came... they came here to see... their *daughter?*"

Momma Price entered the room without thinking it through. She'd been listening at the doorway of the kitchen as any good woman would in a house she kept, and Hansen's lip curled upward with the realization that she'd been standing there.

"The girl this woman has been raising nearly her whole life," Hansen said, jerking his chin toward Momma Price, the strain sharpening his tone. "Her name's Daisy, and she's Amanda and Cooper's. Not a paper file that floated in from nowhere. She is their child—the one I buried in bureaucracy so this would never touch my son's career or reputation. And look where we are now."

Momma Price pressed a hand to her chest, the color draining from her face. "No," she whispered. "The nice young woman from this morning... that was Daisy's Amanda?"

She drifted toward the corner cabinet—her makeshift archive of dog-eared magazines and local papers, a habit she'd never shaken.

"Lord help me," she murmured, flipping through the stack with growing urgency. "I *knew* I'd seen her before."

Nicknames and recipes slipped her mind all the time, but faces—especially the ones plastered across glossy covers—never did. She found the issue she was searching for and spread it open on the foyer desk with a trembling hand.

There, across a two-page spread, Amanda shimmered in a gold gown, Tristan Montgomery's hand resting at the small of her back.

Momma Price pointed at the photo, her breath catching. "I didn't realize... I just let her right in. I didn't know who she was."

Hansen flicked his wrist in Tristan's direction with icy finality. "That girl will ruin your life forever, son. Be glad you're rid of her."

Upstairs, the sound of James Hansen's thundering voice had traveled briskly, consonants ricocheting off old wood beams. The kids had instinctively gathered at the top of the landing in an uneven cluster.

Not all of them. The youngest kids, who didn't understand the words as much as the fear, pressed against the half-open playroom door, clutching stuffed animals, wide-eyed and silent. One older girl had joined them, whispering that it was just "grown-up talk downstairs," turning the pages of a picture book she wasn't reading.

The elementary-aged group hovered in the shared TV room, pretending to care about the cartoon still playing on the muted screen, their eyes flicking to the hallway at every spike in Hansen's tone.

The older girls—the ones old enough to sense when adults were trying a little too hard to keep them away from something—had gathered near the landing in an instinctive cluster, hovering at the top of the stairs like a human guardrail. Charlee and Junie stood side by side, both in socks, both leaning forward just enough that Daisy knew they were listening with the full force of their nerves.

Her own name rose first from the chaos below, drifting upward in a tone sharp enough to slice through the banister rail. Amanda's name followed. And then a third word—*daughter*—that seemed to unravel something inside her with terrifying speed. It wasn't a shout; it was spoken plainly, as if it were simply a fact that had been waiting in the walls all along. But Daisy felt it detonate behind her ribs.

She didn't wait to hear what came next. She turned away from the stairs and moved quickly toward the back hallway, the sound of voices dissolving behind her as she slipped toward the narrower staircase that led to the third floor. Her breath stretched thin and tight as she climbed. The fourth step, which had squeaked since she was nine years old, warned her as it always did, but she avoided it with a practiced sidestep, the kind a body remembers long before the mind makes sense of anything.

By the time she closed her bedroom door behind her, her hands were trembling. The smallness of the room—its slanted ceiling, its chipped dresser, the quilt she'd had since she was little—felt suddenly claustrophobic, as if everything she recognized had folded itself inward while she was downstairs learning she had a mother after all.

She pressed her back to the wood and whispered the name she had barely dared to let herself think all morning. "Amanda." Saying it out loud made her chest tighten, as if the syllables carried more truth than her body was prepared to hold.

The note tucked in her sock felt suddenly heavier, almost warm, as if it had been waiting for her to acknowledge it.

She crossed to her bed and pulled her backpack from where she'd hidden it under the blankets. Her hands moved on instinct—two shirts, the thick socks she wore on winter mornings, the tin of coins she and Charlee kept hidden behind the dresser, a hairbrush, toothpaste, the pressed daisy sealed between wax paper. Every item made the decision feel more real. Every breath felt louder than it should have.

A soft knock startled her. She turned quickly as the door edged open.

Charlee slipped into the room with a seriousness Daisy had only seen a handful of times in all their years together. She closed the door carefully, pressing it shut with her palm before she turned, her eyes sweeping the room until they landed on the backpack. Whatever color she had left drained from her face.

"They're in a panic downstairs," she whispered. Her eyes swept over Daisy, then the backpack, then the scattered belongings on the quilt.

"You're leaving," she said, the statement clearly devoid of any uncertainty.

Daisy's breath wavered. "I have to."

Junie slipped in minutes later, her breath fast from running. "We heard Hansen scream something about a breach," she said in a rush. "If you're going to leave, girl, it has to be now."

Daisy zipped her bag, her heartbeat too loud. "How do I get past the kitchen? Momma P. is right there."

Charlee grinned, wild and brilliant. "Leave that to us."

Downstairs, the house had erupted into a storm. The three daytime staff members hurried between rooms, radios crackling with half-formed instructions they were too nervous to complete. Doors opened and closed with restless insistence. Hansen stood planted in the center of the foyer like a man born to issue orders, his voice ricocheting off the walls as he barked directives at Kessler. Momma Price hovered near him, wringing her hands, her face a mask of worry she kept trying—and failing—to school into something professional.

The younger kids had spilled out of the playroom, wandering toward the dining room in search of supper, and the chaos of their movement only fed the confusion. All of it worked in Daisy's favor.

Charlee and Junie slipped ahead of her with the coordination of girls who had spent years learning how to move unseen inside the same walls. Junie "accidentally" upended an entire tray of cups onto the kitchen tile, the clatter rising like a flare just as Daisy crossed the threshold, hugging her backpack against her chest. Charlee intercepted one of the caregivers with a breathless story about a younger child crying in the upstairs bathroom.

The diversions layered themselves across the house—noise, motion, need—each one shifting another pair of eyes away from her. Every second they bought felt like a small miracle.

The back door was in the mudroom—a narrow space where boots dried on wire racks and brown paper grocery bags lay folded in careful stacks. Daisy reached for the handle, the cold metal closing around her fingers, and a tear slipped down her cheek before she could catch it.

Junie appeared at her side, breathless. "There might be a guard doing rounds on the west path. Go through the field. Stay low until you reach the trees."

Charlee pressed a granola bar into Daisy's free hand. "You'll need it later. And text us someday. If you can."

Emotion rose so sharply that Daisy couldn't find words. She only nodded and pulled both girls into a fierce, silent hug that smelled like winter and detergent and the only home she had ever known.

Then she slipped out. The cold hit her immediately, curling around her legs as she crossed the frost-hardened grass. The sun had already set, and the porch lights stretched long shadows behind her, but she didn't look back. The field inclined toward the dark fringe of trees that bordered the property, and she let fear propel her down into the thick of the forest.

For a moment, everything was soundless except Daisy's breath and the crunch beneath her feet. She kept moving through the trees, letting instinct choose the gaps between trunks. The ground sloped downward in a slow, familiar grade; she'd noticed it on morning runs, on fire drills, on afternoons when the staff let them collect leaves for science projects.

The adults never worried about this side of the property. It was thick with brush, and the path wound so far behind the main buildings that most of the younger kids believed it led nowhere. But Daisy had learned to listen to the outside world. On still nights, she could hear the faint rush of traffic beyond the tree line, a steady whisper of a road too distant for the staff to bother guarding.

She pushed through a final curtain of branches, her breath catching as open sky appeared ahead. The treeline broke onto a shallow ditch at the edge of a narrow two-lane road, the kind where headlights blurred in long ribbons and delivery trucks barreled past without slowing.

Her lungs burned, but she didn't stop. She climbed the embankment, mud slipping beneath her shoes as she stepped onto the shoulder. They had never imagined that the soft-spoken girl with wide eyes, the one they tested every day, had been mapping every detail of her life and absorbed each detail, storing it like a compass. No one suspected she could chart her way out of this place with such ease.

When she reached the road, she didn't let herself stop. Headlights approached from the north, distant but real, and she stepped into the shoulder, raising her hand.

A elderly woman rolled down the window, suspicion softened by concern. "You all right out here?"

"My ride forgot me," Daisy lied smoothly, her voice steady even as her heart pounded. "I just need to get to the interstate. Can you drop me off at the gas station? I don't have a phone. I just need to make a call."

The woman hesitated for a moment, but kindness won. "All right," she said. "Hop in. And you can use my phone."

Daisy climbed in, hugging her bag tight, her hand closed around the note Amanda had given her like a lifeline braided into paper.

The sky settled into that deep violet-blue that belongs only to evenings in the mountains, as Amanda steered the car toward the cabin. Cooper dozed beside her, the soft rise and fall of his breathing marking the exhaustion he'd been battling for days. The silence had lulled her into deep thought for miles, but her rationale refused to line up in any order she trusted.

Her phone buzzed against the console, the screen flashing *Unknown Number*.

She didn't answer. She hadn't answered any of Katherine's calls either, allowing her name to appear, hover, and slip into voicemail every time. Amanda had to assume this was just a veiled attempt at contact. She kept telling herself she needed a moment longer, but the truth was simpler: she wasn't ready to talk to Katherine—not when the memory of a flicker behind Daisy's ear still felt like a live wire running through her.

Then the phone vibrated again. It was long and steady enough to feel less like an interruption and more like a summons. Amanda's fingers tightened on the wheel.

Cooper stirred, his eyes opening slowly. "You should answer."

"I don't recognize the number."

"Maybe it's *her*," he murmured, and those three words rearranged the air between them.

"Already? It couldn't be," she said breathlessly. She hesitated, caught between dread and hope, then clicked the Car Play icon to accept.

"Hello?"

For a moment, all she heard was the faint rush of the car's tires against gravel. Then a breath—thin, unsteady, and unmistakably human—slipped through the line.

"Amanda?"

It was her best friend's voice, frayed at the edges and held together by sheer will.

Amanda closed her eyes briefly, steadying herself against a wave of fear that rose. "Lyla, what's happening?"

"You need to listen carefully," Lyla said. Her voice wavered, but she fought to keep it level. "Katherine came to my house. She told me everything—about Daisy, about that facility, about Hansen. And she said Tristan is already on the ground. He knows where you are."

A hollow chill opened in Amanda's chest. "How would he know that?"

"Apparently, the Grid has been in operation for some time. It's kind of like indirect data tracking, so even though you have a new phone, he can see things that link back to you." Lyla replied, breath hitching. "But, listen, Katherine was serious when she told me you have to leave the place you're in right now, and you have to do it immediately."

Amanda pulled in a slow breath, forcing her thoughts to work for her instead of against her. "Did she say if Daisy is safe?"

The silence that followed was only a second long, but it stretched like something breaking.

"She said she didn't know," Lyla whispered. "But Katherine says she wants Daisy safe, too, and right now I think we have no choice but to believe her. Please, for her sake and for yours—get out. Leave the country. I think it's the only way you'll be safe."

Amanda swallowed hard, gratitude and terror rising in equal measure. She thanked Lyla, promised to touch base when she could, and ended the call with a breath that trembled through her like a fault line finally giving way.

CHAPTER NINETEEN

Over the Atlantic Ocean: Three Days Later

"Citizens of all nations," a disembodied voice said.

The warning did not arrive as a whisper or a rumor, but with orchestral force across every screen that still held a charge and internet connection, flooding the world in synchronized interruption.

For a moment, Amanda thought the plane's Wi-Fi had glitched. The hijack hit so abruptly that even the flight attendants stopped mid-aisle, their expressions mirroring the unsettled flicker in the cabin lights. Headphones came off. Conversations thinned. A hush moved through the aircraft like a ripple crossing still water.

Only hours earlier, several major newsrooms had reported receiving anonymous packets—unlabeled documents, heavily redacted, an unfinished puzzle scattered across too many continents at the same hour. Memo fragments bearing Helion letterheads. Notes placing Governor Hansen in meetings that no journalist had ever managed to uncover. Troubling, yes—but too incomplete to prove anything. Until now.

"You are receiving this message because your governments will not tell you the truth," the voice said. "For years, your movements, purchases, communications, and biometric traces have been collected and ranked without your consent. You have been evaluated, categorized, and assigned predictive profiles by algorithms you were never permitted to see."

The screens embedded into the seat backs flashed white, then steadied into the grainy clarity of a single symbol: a smooth, featureless mask, the kind meant to erase a face rather than disguise it, haloed by a horseshoe of falling code.

Anonymity.

Not the chaotic internet folklore people joked about, but the true consortium—an unaffiliated, transnational network of technologists and whistleblowers who emerged only when corruption reached a breaking point.

Amanda felt Cooper go still beside her. She took his hand as they watched.

The broadcast shifted as images and documents came into view in rapid but comprehensible sequence, woven together with sufficient narration and eerily synchronized so that even the least technologically fluent viewer could follow.

"We have orchestrated an outage," the broadcast went on, "because of individuals whose names you may already know: Tristan Montgomery, Governor James Hansen, and the Helion Group. Their intention has been to ensure strategic superiority. In other words, they want to control everyone and everything in order to create a world they think is worthy of their time, inventions, and investments."

A photograph of Tristan Montgomery with a group of international energy delegates appeared. A scanned memo bearing the letterhead of the Helion Group. A clip from a congressional hearing in which Governor James Hansen spoke about national energy independence with an ease that now felt like a mask.

Then came the archive footage—old sovereign bond documents, faded diagrams of biometric testing, early sketches of cognitive-ranking algorithms, and notes referring to "developmental assessment centers" written in scripts that belonged to people who had never imagined their secrets would leave a secure vault.

"The public has been told these centers provide care," the voice said, "but their primary function is predictive evaluation. Children are ranked according to projected adaptability, conformity, and strategic potential. Some are fast-tracked. Some are redirected. And some disappear from the public record entirely."

Gasps broke through the stillness. The truth hit with a force no newsroom could soften.

"In a few hours, we will begin shutting down major power grids across North America, Europe, Asia, and Africa, which will go offline for seven days. This is not an accident. It is not an act of war. It is a system reset designed to decentralize power from those who believe themselves entitled to absolute control."

People began to speak over the recording, voices rising in contradictory desperation. Some demanded answers from no one in particular. Others clung to disbelief like a life raft. Cooper's hand found Amanda's in a steady grip despite everything tightening around them.

The screens flickered again, and typed script appeared, letter by letter.

Prepare. Protect one another. Stay where you are safe. Another message appeared just before the feed ended.

This is not the end. It is the beginning of the truth. Then, darkness.

For several seconds, the entire aircraft sat in a silence so complete that even the drone of the engines felt distant. Then the murmurs began—first a few scattered breaths of disbelief, then voices overlapping in a rising swell.

A man two rows ahead muttered that it had to be a hoax, while a woman across the aisle stabbed at her phone, texting and whispering, *"Come on... just connect... please."* Someone further back insisted it was a conspiracy, another begged their partner not to panic, and a soft, broken voice wondered aloud how they were supposed to get home.

A flight attendant tried to soothe a pair of elderly passengers as one of them murmured, *"Those poor children... dear God..."* The cabin filled with the unfiltered sound of people grasping for sense in a world that had just capsized beneath them.

The pilot's announcement followed, calm but strained, assuring passengers that no immediate danger existed and that they would continue to Bucharest as planned.

The final hour of the flight passed in a suspended quiet. Beneath them, across continents, the broadcast had bled into the waking world, redirecting the trajectory of nations.

When their plane descended over Bucharest, the city looked deceptively serene—winter rooftops dusted in white, tram rails glinting in afternoon light, streets moving in orderly gridlines. Nothing suggested that everything had just shifted beneath the surface.

Inside the airport, the truth was immediate. Security presence was heavy, armed officers stationed every ten meters, eyes sharp, expressions unreadable. They offered no reassurance, only vigilance.

"The broadcast hit here, too," Cooper murmured. "Anonymity must have hit every major feed. This wasn't the circle I dealt with. The operational cell... no one sees them unless they're fully inside."

Amanda nodded, feeling unsettling tension beneath her ribs—the sensation of a world rearranging itself faster than people could comprehend.

They followed a driver offering his services out into the pale afternoon, slid into the back seat, and watched the city blur past as normalcy dissipated into thin air. By the time they reached the apartment, Bucharest felt suspended, functional but fragile.

Amanda switched on a lamp and watched the bulb hesitate before settling into a reluctant glow.

"Has it started? How long before the first outage?" she asked.

"Hard to know. The broadcast could've been delayed while we were in the air," Cooper said, drawing the blinds aside.

A distant power station vented steam in an unnatural column—straight, unmoving, ominous.

"The blackout will last seven days," she murmured.

Cooper nodded. "And a worldwide outage in winter? Everything fails. Transit. Communication. Hospitals. This is going to be bad."

A tremor of memories slid through her—Tokyo's neon glare, Switzerland's serene precision, the glow of Tristan's laptop never far from his side. Everything he had built was designed to withstand collapse, not to prevent it.

"I'm sorry I ever loved him," she whispered, barely realizing she said the words aloud.

"You believed him," Cooper said, slipping his arms around her.

Cooper steadied her against the cold that seemed to seep from the walls. They watched at the window as day turned into dusk, lights dimming across the skyline in a widening ring—buildings surrendering one by one, boulevard lights extinguished, windows turning dark in slow succession, a city folding itself inward.

Amanda pressed her palm to the glass, watching the final streaks of power flicker and disappear.

Suddenly, screens around the apartment flickered to life in the dark, briefly illuminating the walls with flashes of cool light. Phones vibrated in loose tandem across the table; notifications stacked themselves faster than they could be read. It was not the cadence of government alerts or news broadcasts, but something more synchronized, as though an unseen hand had pulled every platform into alignment.

Amanda's phone lit with the same sudden clarity, her screen overtaken by a surge of reports without pause. Anonymity had reemerged with a force that felt immediate and unmistakably present.

Cell towers were still operational, images unfolding on her screen that were not archival or speculative; they were live feeds from other cities documenting being swallowed by darkness—Johannesburg, Osaka, Berlin, Toronto—each one marked by the same abrupt silence that was now pressed against her own windows. Overlaid maps updated in real time, grids collapsing in widening rings across continents, while documents, data points, and clipped segments of buried testimony assembled themselves across the footage with surgical precision, revealing a story that had long been scattered and disjointed but was now impossible to ignore.

Clips appeared from every continent. News anchors broadcasting by candlelight, their equipment powered by generators. Medical staff directed crowds of patients through emergency rooms illuminated only by backup lighting as generators whirred on. Commuter trains stalled halfway into unlit tunnels. In London, the Thames ferries drifted without power, passengers waving frantically for rescue that could not come quickly. In New York, the skyline dimmed with breathtaking finality, leaving only the silhouette of the city against a bruised winter sky. In Nairobi, people streamed through the streets with radios held high, picking up frequencies that crackled with overlapping reports from stations functioning on time-limited electricity. In Seoul, drones filmed the sequential darkening of entire districts, dominoes falling in slow motion.

Every clip carried the same pinned banner at the bottom of the frame, translated into dozens of languages:

The planned blackout has begun. Protect your neighbors. Share resources. Stay where you are safe.

Amanda watched the videos with a tightening in her throat she could not swallow down. Entire nations had been forced into a synchronized pause, and yet the immediate reaction wasn't rage or chaos. It was bewilderment, then a strange, unbidden solidarity.

People handed out blankets to strangers. Restaurants cooked what they could and gave it away on sidewalks. Parents lit candles and set them in windows so children wouldn't be afraid of the dark. Neighbors who had never spoken to each other gathered in stairwells, passing flashlights up and down the line.

Outside their own apartment, a man stood directing traffic with nothing but a reflective vest and a steady, fearless voice. Strings of battery-powered lights appeared along balconies, dotted through the night like improvised constellations.

Human instinct held, even as systems collapsed.

Amanda leaned her head against Cooper's chest, feeling the city tremble beneath the weight of its own vulnerability. "Seven days like this," she whispered.

"Seven days is optimistic," he said, pulling her hand to his lips. "A blackout this size will shake everything, but we're not alone in it. We'll figure it out—together."

They remained in the glow of the screens that hadn't lost their charge as hours passed and the world recalibrated itself in uneven breaths.

Chapter Twenty

The Blackout: Six Days In

Cooper and Amanda spent the next days in the shifting half-light of battery lamps and window glass, listening as the world recalibrated itself hour by hour—shortwave broadcasts rising and fading through static, car radios catching partially-translated emergency bulletins, the low whir of Cooper's HAM receiver giving them as many updates as they could understand. Cooper powered the handheld device from the car battery he'd rigged on the kitchen floor, adjusting the dial with the knowledge of someone who had spent too many nights in too many remote places listening to voices carried across darkened continents.

The blackout wasn't total, but to a world that doesn't operate without pulsing energy, it felt like it was—ATM machines dead, businesses completely offline, grocery stores shuttered. The circumstances were precarious, but people had begun adapting as though humanity itself had reached back into older knowledge. Water stations appeared at intersections. Courtyards filled with makeshift ovens and improvised stoves. Entire buildings agreed on shared schedules for generator use, illuminating one block for two hours before plunging it back into darkness so another could breathe.

Even in the distance, hospitals shone like anchored ships—their generators refusing to surrender.

Amanda often stood at the window, one hand resting against the glass, watching these small, ordinary acts of resilience bloom across the city. She found unexpected comfort in the way people kept tending to one another, as if they had discovered a kind of humanity that only emerged when everything else was stripped away.

That night, the sky was pale and cloudless, reflecting what little light the city still offered. Amanda drifted awake with the sense that she had surfaced from deep water—slow, groggy, and not fully sure where the boundary between dream and waking lay. Moonlight spilled across the floorboards and climbed the edges of the bed. Cooper slept beside her, one arm draped over her waist with a protective instinct that no longer surprised her.

A low vibration trembled against the nightstand. At first, she wasn't sure she had heard it correctly; the city's networks had been erratic for days, appearing only in brief flickers whenever a backup node somewhere in Bucharest decided to rouse itself. When the vibration came again—a persistent, almost urgent shiver—she pushed herself upright, brushing sleep from her eyes.

The cold of the room settled over her bare shoulders, and Cooper stirred immediately, lifting his head just enough to study her face through the dimness.

"Is something wrong?" he asked, his voice still heavy with sleep but sharpened by concern.

"I'm not sure yet," she said quietly as she reached for the phone.

The screen struggled to wake, its light pulsing once before holding steady.

"Hello?"

"Amanda?" Her father's voice crackled through the line. She assumed he had been swallowed by the blackout's chaos and his own long history of strategic absences. She wasn't prepared for the shock of hearing his voice, or the rush of complicated relief that followed.

She answered. "Stephen?"

There was no clipped hesitation on the other end, only the strained inhale of a man who had spent a lifetime avoiding vulnerability and suddenly found no way around it.

"Amanda," he said. His voice sounded frayed at the edges, stripped of its usual precision. "I'm in Romania. I need you to meet me."

Her pulse quickened with the unwelcome recognition that whatever he was about to say would alter the ground beneath her. Cooper shifted closer, resting his hand against her spine.

"What's happened?" she asked, steadying her tone despite the rising tremor beneath it.

She heard him gather himself, not for theatrics but because the words themselves were heavy and unpracticed.

"I can't undo what I did," he said, and the quiet shudder in his voice struck her with a kind of grim satisfaction. She had waited years hoping her father could feel the consequences of his own choices, and hearing it now brought an intense and complex ache. "But I can give you something I never managed to give myself."

Amanda closed her eyes, feeling Cooper's fingers curl around hers beneath the blankets, as if reminding her she was not meeting this revelation alone.

"Stephen," she said, "what are you trying to tell me?"

This time, his breath broke audibly.

"I found her," he said. "Daisy's with me."

Amanda didn't remember crossing the room so much as feeling the apartment narrow around her, as though every object had stepped aside to let the moment pass unimpeded. Cooper was already out of bed, tugging on jeans and a sweater, watching her with the kind of quiet steadiness that made the whole world feel less breakable.

She didn't remember walking through the stillness toward the location Stephen had sent. Amanda barely felt the cold. Her thoughts were a single, fragile thread stretching toward a girl she had loved for eighteen years without ever being allowed to know her.

For most of his adult life, Stephen Hopkins had been the kind of man the world preferred not to see—one of those rare operatives whose influence stretched farther than the structures that claimed to employ him. Nations built entire agencies around chains of command and oversight committees, but men like Stephen existed between those lines, shaping global strategy in the quiet spaces where bureaucracy had no reach.

To the public, he never existed. To governments, he was the only operative who made sense to hire. He had been the silent architect behind half a dozen political reconciliations that never made the news, the strategist whose fingerprints could be found on operations attributed to agencies that had never once spoken his name. Intelligence circles treated him not as a colleague but as a force—one that could be consulted, rarely challenged, and never ignored.

His ethics were rarely simple but always deliberate: he believed that power, left unattended, behaved like a living thing—ravenous, self-replicating, and eager to devour what it was meant to shepherd. Stephen saw it as his responsibility, perhaps even his penance, to keep the worst impulses of nations from consuming the rest of the world.

Companies hired him when their internal protections failed. Governments hired him when their governments failed. Alliances formed, fractured, or quietly disappeared at the edge of his advice.

He was the kind of man who returned phone calls from presidents only when it served a purpose, who could push MI6 and the CIA into reluctant cooperation purely because he understood their vulnerabilities better than they did. The agencies never called him their superior—not formally—but they deferred to him with the uneasy respect of organizations that understood the balance of power was not entirely in their hands.

Katherine had worked with him for years. People often mistook her for the one in charge, and she never corrected them. Stephen wanted it that way.

Because the truth was simpler and far more dangerous: he was the person she answered to when the world threatened to veer toward catastrophe. He was the rare operative who treated her not as a subordinate but as an equal—except when the stakes surpassed even her experience. And when they did, she listened. Everyone did.

He had been the gravitational pull behind so many veiled moments, the figure slipping through doorways, issuing precise instructions, gathering intelligence with the detachment of a surgeon evaluating a wound he intended to close. It was not love that drove him. It was not ambition. It was something rarer—an unwavering conviction that the world, left to its own devices, would eat itself alive unless someone stood in the quiet places and declared that today would not be that day.

So when Stephen said Daisy was safe—when he said *we brought her in*—it meant he had mobilized an entire invisible infrastructure to retrieve her.

Not because he hoped Amanda would forgive him, or because he wanted redemption. But because, for the first time in his uncommon life, the mission and the person were the same.

And Stephen Hopkins never failed a mission.

The rendezvous point appeared at the end of a narrow, unlit street—a disused service yard behind an old municipal building, the kind of place chosen precisely because no one had reason to pass through it. A dark car idled there with its headlights off, the silhouette familiar even at a distance.

Stephen stood beside it, coat unbuttoned, posture straighter than his expression. He looked like a man who had run out of deflections and was standing in whatever truth remained.

The passenger door opened, and Daisy stepped out slowly, as if measuring each step against a world that had fractured beneath her feet. Her posture was taut but unbroken; her eyes moved over Amanda's face with a recognition that hit like a physical force.

For a single breath, she didn't move.

And then she did, crossing the distance with a certainty that left no air between them, and Amanda felt the girl's arms close around her as though the years that had separated them had never stood a chance.

CHAPTER TWENTY-ONE

*The Reemergence: Two Days After the Total
Blackout*

A SAFE HOUSE NEAR an airfield had been chosen for its forgettability. It was the sort of place people drove past without registering—a low structure tucked against the side of a larger hangar, its existence implied more than declared. Inside, a generator kept the lights and heat at a functional level, but the room's true warmth came from the familiarity of the faces that gathered there.

Katherine sat at the end of the table, hands curled around a mug she had not sipped. Julius stood near a wall of outdated paper maps. Malonga rested in a chair opposite Katherine, composed and attentive. Stephen hovered near the door, the shape of him more familiar to Amanda now than she would have predicted days ago.

"It held," Julius said. "Longer than expected."

Malonga inclined his head. "The safeguards triggered as planned. Reactors stabilized. Containment held."

"The world will never know how close it came," Katherine said in a tone that suggested she wasn't sure whether they should be grateful or quietly ashamed.

Stephen shifted. "And Helion?"

"Cut off," Julius answered. "Their influence came from the illusion of invincibility—the outage shattered that. And thanks to the corruption files, any attempt to rebuild will expose their dependencies."

Katherine added, "They mistook reach for immunity. A miscalculation, I daresay, they won't recover from."

Stephen's gaze sharpened. "And Tristan? Hansen?"

Katherine's reply was crisp. "They are exposed. Financial trails, Hansen's private state contracts—all inconveniently discoverable. I doubt they'll be prosecuted; men of this calibre rarely are. They'll simply vanish into the shadows, a whispered cautionary tale no one bothers to finish."

Julius exhaled. "I did have high hopes for Montgomery when I met him. I wish this felt more like victory."

"It rarely does," Katherine murmured. "Back to our stations?" she asked as the corner of her mouth twitched upward.

"I've got a plane to catch," Malonga nodded.

They all lifted their mismatched mugs in a quiet salute. There was no pride in it, no ceremony, just acknowledgment of a catastrophe prevented and a job well done.

What vanished during the power outage were the systems that had become too interconnected and dependent on a single digital architecture. Anything tied to this infrastructure went dark instantly—communication satellites, high-density data centers, financial exchanges, civilian internet providers, even aviation networks.

But not everything belonged to that world.

The blackout had broken the global network, but it left behind enough scattered threads for people to stitch a new version of connection together.

Across cities and borderlands, pockets of connection survived for reasons that seemed almost accidental. Some networks endured because they were too old to fail in the same way—copper landlines, radio towers broadcasting with stubborn analog insistence, small regional providers running on hardware that had never been designed to speak to anything larger than a few towns.

Others survived by virtue of caution. Intelligence agencies and diplomatic missions maintained private intranets sealed off from public routing, air-gapped systems built precisely for moments when the rest of the world might falter. These remained functional, though isolated, illuminating small islands of communication in an otherwise unlit sea.

And then there were the improvised efforts, the ones that emerged from the little warning people had and were piecemealed together only after the worst had passed. Engineers wired routers to generators. Neighborhoods formed mesh networks from phones and laptops, each device connecting to the next in a fragile chain of proximity. Amateur radio operators transmitted bursts of encoded data across bands that hadn't been busy in decades. Cafés and embassies, once power returned to their block or their backup systems, reopened their Wi-Fi to anyone who could reach it.

Many hospitals reported casualties when their generators failed before staff could move patients to non-digital systems. Major cities experienced a surge of panic—grocery shelves emptied faster than they could be replenished, and markets plunged. The world bent under the strain, but it did not break.

Most people had heard the news about the attempt the once-favored billionaire had at global domination. But they didn't know about the corruption files inconspicuously deployed across continents, a coordinated interference seeded into every active prototype of Tristan's system—files that unravelled the architecture from the inside, corrupting innumerable data the years had collected.

They did not know that Katherine had remained in North America to oversee the breach, that Julius had flown to Asia, that Stephen had been in an underground hub in Europe, and Malonga had returned to take charge of the African sector. They only knew the lights had gone out, and eventually, in pieces, they had come back on.

What mattered was that the Ocular Grid had been stopped before it matured into something irreversible. In the weeks that followed, governments offered their evasive explanation—an infrastructural cascade, a catastrophic failure of over-connected systems. It was the version polished enough for press conferences and steady enough to keep markets from buckling further. Anonymity's warning was dismissed as opportunistic chaos, their accusations folded into political rhetoric.

The truth was quieter than any of the theories: the blackout had been intentional, but not malicious. It had been the only way to keep the world from slipping into the kind of control no government would ever acknowledge it had nearly embraced.

Someday, history books would settle on a simplified narrative that was tidier and easier to teach. But only a few people knew better. And they would not be writing a press release.

Lyla was mid-rant when the connection sputtered, her face freezing in a comically indignant expression before smoothing back into motion.

"...and I swear, if one more person tells me to 'lean into uncertainty,' I'm going to mail them my laundry and see if that helps their spiritual growth."

Amanda huffed a quiet laugh despite herself. The video call wasn't perfect—pixels blurring at the edges, sound lagging half a beat—but Lyla's presence pushed through the glitches like sunlight through thin clouds. Behind her, the familiar sprawl of her kitchen came in and out of focus: a mug by the sink, a camera bag on a chair, Kyle moving in the background with the easy competence of someone who had learned long ago how to orbit his wife's chaos without being pulled under by it.

"I missed your rants," Amanda said. "Really missed them."

Lyla's face softened for a fraction of a second before she covered it with mock offense.

"Excuse me, ma'am, I am an international artist and occasional photographic genius. I do not rant. I editorialize."

"You editorialize about socks?"

"They deserve advocacy," she said.

Kyle's voice slid in from offscreen, laughing as he spoke. "Baby, are you yelling about socks again?"

Lyla pointed vaguely in his direction. "Don't undermine my platform, Mr. Grant. Every damn office is up for grabs at this point. I could win *any* election, and you know it."

He smiled. "I'd vote for you any day," he said, leaning in, kissing her, then waving to the screen. "Hey, Amanda."

"Hi, Kyle," she returned.

"Now go," Lyla shooed her husband away. "I need quiet while I'm talking to my best friend in the whole world, who almost got herself vaporized by global espionage, thank you very much."

Amanda let the words settle. *Best friend. Whole world.* The ache that had built like a knot in her chest over the last months loosened, just enough for her shoulders to drop a fraction.

Amanda smiled, small but genuine.

"I talked to Melody. I mean, she called me," Lyla said, changing the subject before Amanda's smile could break. "She and the boys are still in Croatia near the coast. She said she'd call again sometime when she can. Just wanted to give a sign of life. She goes by Maria now."

Amanda blew out a breath. "Of course she does. Good for her. I can see it now—Melody in baggy linen, the boys all wrestling around her on the floor of a century-old house..."

her pretending she doesn't miss dressing in a trench coat and figuring out the craziness her husband left behind."

"She sounded…lighter," Lyla smiled. "Like she's finally standing on ground that doesn't move."

"I'm glad," Amanda said.

"Anyway, just so you know, there's no writing me out of the script because you're changing locations. I will be your one and only Spyce Girl, on retainer, world tour, no expiration date."

Amanda's eyes stung as she laughed, blinking against the hot tears.

"Can you at least pretend to be worried about your *own* safety?" she asked.

"Oh, I'm very worried," Lyla said. "Have you met me? I attract trouble like it's a brand partnership. But since we don't know when those are coming back, I have to also worry about my bestie."

Amanda smiled. "I'll text you my permanent address when we find a place," she said.

"You'd better," Lyla said. "Because when this new world calms down, fully expect me to show up in Romania with cameras and matching Spyce Girl trench coats—with another for Daisy, obviously—and a plan to make us look like the moody heroes we were always destined to be."

Amanda laughed out loud. "Please, I am *not* interested in memorializing what we've been through. Let's just plan on climbing the peaks together and getting you the most amazing views to capture, okay?"

"Deal," Lyla said. "I am, however, deeply interested in capturing the part where you get to live a life that's actually yours. I would like front-row seats to that premiere."

"Consider yourself on the list," Amanda smiled.

"Good," Lyla answered. Her expression then turned more serious, the humor resting gently on top of something older and steadier.

"I know everything's about to shift again. And I don't understand half of what you've been carrying. But you need to hear me say this: I'm not going anywhere. Not really. Even if we go months without talking, even if networks fail again, you change numbers and names and hair color. You and I? We'll always be us."

"I know," Amanda said softly, another tear escaping her eyes.

What felt like only a moment later, the call ended, and the room felt immediately quieter, but not empty. Lyla's voice lingered in the air like the tail end of a song.

On the shore of Lake Como, Tristan Montgomery's villa glowed with the faintest thread of generator-fed light; the estate's backup systems held a thin, steady pulse, rationed carefully. Inside, the staff moved as though afraid to disturb the fragile order of a world still stitching itself back together.

Tristan had not left his office. The dark screens of his computers reflected only his outline—once the king of circuitry, now a man staring at the ruins of his own design. He had tried every hidden channel, every buried access point, every private route into the Grid's architecture. Each attempt led to the same stillness. It wasn't an error or a denial. There was simply absence, as though the system had withdrawn its recognition.

He turned toward the window. Lake Como, a mirror of the sky, offered no solace. The water was a muted sheet of grey-blue, the mountains distant and impassive.

The realization of his isolation carried a strange, familiar ache—one that drifted backward, pulling at the seams of memory until a much earlier scene took shape.

He had been eight, maybe nine—the year his father deposited him at a boarding school, with the instruction to *prove himself useful.* There had been an observatory on the roof, a glass dome he'd discovered by following a draft of cold air up an iron staircase long after curfew. He remembered pressing his hands to the chilled metal of the telescope mount, the way the stars settled him more clearly than any adult ever had. They stayed where they were meant to stay. They behaved. They aligned.

Later that year, he built a model ecosystem—paper mountains, a fragile irrigation channel, lights timed to simulate seasons. He never forgot the moment the system collapsed. A single burned-out bulb, only one variable out of his control, and the entire structure dimmed. He'd stood there in the dark, the failed project before him, and realized how quickly beauty collapsed without precision. Order had seemed the only antidote to the randomness that had shaped his childhood: a father who measured affection through achievement, a mother whose departures were as rhythmic as tides but never announced.

The ache of that old truth returned now, subtle as a bruise pressed from the inside.

Tristan dragged the curtains closed. Without the glow of screens, the office looked almost ordinary: a glass of water, a perfectly aligned stack of notes whose relevance had evaporated with the outage.

He grew up believing that loneliness was simply the tax one paid for being exceptional. It became easier, over time, to trust equations more than people. Patterns were more measurable than affection. Humans disappointed, but systems didn't. Those failed only when a disappointing human introduced error, and error, he decided, was a kind of moral weakness.

So ideology did not arrive for him like a revelation. It drifted in, almost tenderly—through academic papers that framed optimization as benevolence, through think tanks that spoke of human *improvement* as inevitability, through private conversations with men who admired efficiency more than empathy. The wayward thinking threaded itself into him the way roots find cracks in stone.

By the time he reached adulthood, he didn't see it as extremism. He saw it as clarity.

And when he found Amanda—brilliant, composed under pressure, intuitively attuned to complexity—he believed the universe had at last confirmed him. The ideal companion for a perfected world. A partner who would never threaten the symmetry he cherished.

Not only had he proved himself useful, but *they* would prove themselves useful—for posterity. But Amanda had gone and proven herself a disappointing human like the rest of them.

Tristan lowered himself into the chair, fingers poised above the dead keyboard. There had been a time when the smallest movement of his hands sent entire infrastructures humming. Tonight, the machines did not answer—but his mind did, sparking with the familiar precision of a man who had never stopped believing in his own abilities.

He knew he would try to rebuild. He always had. Obsession was not a flaw but the marrow of his genius, the force that had carried him through every closed door of his childhood and every open one he later gained access to. The candle near the window thinned to a trembling wick, casting the room in a muted, uneven glow as he stared at the dead screens, seeing not absence but possibility—the blank page before the next architecture.

Because Tristan Montgomery knew one thing for sure: doors were constructs.

And constructs could always be rebuilt.

Epilogue

Romania: Five Months Later

THE DRIVE FROM BRAŞOV to Constanţa stretched east beneath a sky already leaning toward summer. The mountains fell away behind them until only low, rolling fields remained, washed in gold-green light that hinted at the season to come. The warm wind through the cracked window carried the scent of tilled earth and new grass, and the rhythmic whir of passing tractors blended with the steady pulse of the road.

Cooper drove with one hand on the wheel and the other resting lightly against Amanda's knee, grounding them both. Daisy sat in the backseat, her forehead against the glass, watching the villages pass by in a blur of ochre rooftops and slender church spires. She had been quiet since dawn—not withdrawn, but deep inside herself, preparing for what the day required. Amanda caught her reflection in the mirror, careful not to look for too long, not wanting to make the moment heavier than it already was.

Romania held them gently. Even after the blackout, the country moved with a resilience that felt instinctive. Power flickered on and off in the mountain towns, but people still sat outside cafés, still traded recipes and laughter in the markets, still trusted the old ways more than the systems that had failed them. Amanda felt it settling into her bones, the ease of a world that valued what could survive no matter the threats that came and went.

Their farmhouse on a hill outside the city had become a sanctuary—the closest thing to home Amanda had allowed herself to imagine in nearly two decades. Cooper repaired the shed and cooked dinner most nights, singing off-key in a way that dared the universe to argue. Daisy painted quietly, guarding her watercolors like fragile pieces of herself she was only beginning to uncover. Some mornings, Amanda woke not to fear or urgency but to the simple sound of her family breathing in the same house.

But today, peace felt thinner, and threaded with uncertainty.

The implant had become a presence no one named directly, but all three of them felt the weight of it constantly. Daisy agreed to the removal, but the calmness with which she agreed unsettled Amanda more than a refusal ever could have. It was the stillness of someone who had learned that pain too often arrived disguised as help.

Andrei had understood immediately. Russell's old Romanian contact—now friend, translator, and steadying force—listened without interrupting, then simply nodded as though confirming the last piece of a puzzle he had been studying quietly. Within two days he had located a trusted surgeon; within three he had a plan. He placed a folded slip of paper in Amanda's hand, name and address written in firm strokes, and assured her, with the weight of a man who never wasted his promises, that she could trust this doctor.

So they were on their way. Long before the sea appeared, the air changed—threaded with the faint brine of an unseen horizon. Gulls called overhead, their cries thin and distinctive, and then the water revealed itself in a widening band of steel blue beneath a lowering pewter sky. By the time they reached the small harbor, the cool breeze greeting them as they began to get out of the car.

Daisy stepped out, closing her eyes for a moment, as if tasting the salt on her tongue. The breeze stirred her dark hair and brushed color into her cheeks, but Amanda saw the tension still coiled along her shoulders. She placed a hand gently at the center of her daughter's back, and Daisy leaned into the touch just enough for Amanda to feel it.

"Are you ready?" Cooper asked.

Daisy nodded, swallowing hard.

The clinic sat tucked behind aging warehouses, its grey door peeling, a pot of rosemary trembling beside the entrance. Inside, the space was compact and clean, the air cool and faintly antiseptic. There was no receptionist, only a narrow counter with a bell.

A door at the end of the hall opened, and the surgeon appeared—broad-shouldered, silver at the temples.

"Hello, I am Dr. Istrate," he said. "Amanda, yes? And Daisy."

His accent softened the edges of his English, and the gentleness in his eyes reached Daisy before any words did.

"And this is Cooper," Amanda added. "Daisy's father."

The doctor accepted the information without surprise or commentary, as if parentage were simply another clinical fact to catalog—important, but not dramatic. He couldn't know the weight it carried here.

"We have a small team today," he said. "Enough for safety. Not enough for attention." His meaning was unmistakable.

He faced Daisy fully. "It is a straightforward procedure. You will be awake at the beginning so we can speak. After that, we sedate you. You will sleep through the removal and the first part of recovery. Nothing happens without your approval. You understand, da?"

Daisy nodded.

He offered a small, encouraging smile. "Good. I will prepare the room. Take a moment together."

When he stepped away, Amanda turned to Daisy and held her arms gently.

"You are safe," she whispered. "Nothing in that room is stronger than you."

Daisy's breath trembled. "What if it hurts?"

"It might," Amanda said honestly. "But only for a moment. And then it will be gone."

Daisy nodded, her voice barely audible. "Okay. I don't want it in me anymore."

"Then it ends today," Amanda reassured.

Daisy squeezed her mother's hand once before letting go and followed the surgeon down the hall.

Amanda pressed her palm against the cool wall, grounding herself, and Cooper guided her to a bench near the window where the sea churned under a shifting sky.

"She's stronger than what was done to her," he said quietly. "Stronger than all of it."

Amanda nodded, though her eyes never left the door.

The hour stretched painfully long, until at last Dr. Istrate stepped out and motioned for them.

"She's awake. She's come through beautifully," he said.

Daisy sat propped on the narrow bed, a blanket around her shoulders. A small square of gauze covered the skin behind her ear. She blinked up at them, still a little groggy but lucid.

"How do you feel?" Amanda asked.

"Light," Daisy whispered, a small laugh catching in her throat. "Like everything's quieter."

Behind the doctor, on a small metal dish, lay the implant—narrow, metallic, shockingly ordinary.

"Let's get you dressed," Amanda murmured.

The clinic released them without fanfare, the door closing softly behind them as if aware of what had just been laid down inside its walls.

Outside, the Black Sea greeted them with warm, salt-bright air. Daisy lifted her face into the breeze, her expression shifting and softening like sand under their feet. They took off their shoes, and Amanda and Cooper followed her toward the water.

A narrow stretch of beach curved along the coastline, streaks of sand patterned with the retreat of earlier waves. Daisy stepped onto it slowly, as if testing her own steadiness and Amanda stayed close but didn't touch her, letting her choose the pace.

Daisy walked a few steps, shoes dangling from her fingers. She paused where the waves reached thin ribbons of foam along the shore. The wind lifted Amanda's summer dress, and a laughed burst out of them both

Daisy turned to looked out at the water as though seeing it from newly cleared eyes, then she turned back to see them—both of her parents.

"Can we go home now?" she asked softly.

The word struck Amanda with a force she hadn't expected. She exchanged a glance with Cooper—a shared, quiet astonishment, as fragile and immense as anything they had faced together.

"Yes," Amanda said, her voice breaking into a smile. "We can go home."

Back in the car, Daisy curled her knees to her chest, watching the sea recede through the window.

"We'll come back on vacations, right?" she murmured.

"Of course," Cooper replied, as though it were the most natural promise in the world.

Amanda reached for his hand, their fingers intertwining on the gearshift. Daisy wasn't talking about travel; she was staking a claim, shy and certain all at once. She wasn't preparing to leave them when she turned eighteen. She was choosing to stay.

The road lifted into broad fields and orchards, the sky slowly brightening as if the horizon itself welcomed the three of them back. Daisy rested her head against the window, her breath evening out as the miles passed beneath them.

She wasn't healed. None of them were. But they were healing, moving in the direction of something better, something earned, and that was enough. When the first sign for Brașov County appeared, Amanda felt her shoulders loosen, as though the land itself were welcoming them back. And for the first time since the world went dark—possibly for the first time in her life—she allowed herself to believe that what they were building wasn't something to move away from, but run toward.

She had finally found her place to land.

Author's Note

December, 2025

In the winter of 1989, I watched the evening news, sitting in the living room of our small home in St. Louis, Missouri. A newscaster was telling us about the Cold War, about its victories and democratic triumphs, while a small image of a dictator, sentenced to death, flickered in the corner of the screen. It was called a "mock trial," the reporter said—Nicolae Ceaușescu and his wife, Elena, had been sentenced to death for atrocities I don't remember them listing, but I'm sure they did. I was in my first year of high school that year, and the country of Romania was a place on a map I'd memorized the capital city of in seventh grade geography class. In case you don't remember: it's Bucharest, not to be confused with the bordering country, Hungary's Budapest.

I had no way of knowing then that Romania would become my second home—the place where I would live nearly half of my married life up to this point. Because in 1989, on the other side of the world, a boy did more than watch a news report. He gathered around radios tuned to forbidden frequencies and listened as a man from Radio Free Europe told them their country had been liberated from the clutches of a tyrant.

If only it had been so simple.

What neither of us could have predicted was how our wildly different, yet eerily parallel, upbringings would help us understand each other years later. After all, I may have grown up in one of the freest nations on earth, but my family followed a charismatic spiritual leader who drafted his own commandments and turned us all into pint-size informants—reporting on each other's slip-ups, policing one another's behavior, and shaming us into compliance. To the point where we overlooked unreported crimes until the preponderance of them became impossible to ignore. I sometimes call it a cult—not to be dramatic or sensational, because it needs no embellishment—but because naming it helps me place a frame around what happened to those inside its walls.

As fate would have it, that boy came to the US for school and met that girl, and the two of them fell in love. Fewer than ten years after the wall came down—and the Cold War was touted as over—they chose to build a life in a country still finding its sea legs after decades of authoritarian rule. The questioning and unraveling of how I'd been raised was inevitable there, in a place reconstructing its own identity as I was also doing. The road was both beautiful and painful, as all growth tends to be.

The many lessons I've learned, the experiences I've had (all the locations mentioned in this series are ones I've been fortunate to either live in or visit), and many of the conversations that shaped me are woven through its pages. Some of the lighter truths: When Amanda tells the story in Book One about having singer friends, I wanted a little nod to my own friends who sang backup for Michael Bublé when he came through my hometown of St. Louis. Another: During a trip to the Canary Islands, I climbed to the top of Mt. Teide with my husband on the island of Tenerife—not all the way, just from the cable car station—because, obviously.

And then there are darker truths: being in a facility where I wasn't allowed to leave campus without signing out with an escort—a place where strange rituals and lessons were lauded as God's work, and etched phrases like, "I might not fit, but I'm not going to quit," in my memory forever. Knowing girls whose babies were taken from them because they had "messed up," as if their sexual activity determines their entire worth—as if babies were commodities rather than beloved human lives like they claimed. As if a man's role in the equation meant nothing, and a girl's choice to protect herself and secure her own future would be an unpardonable sin.

Through the years, I learned the truth about the propaganda behind the Satanic Panic I was forced to watch videos about, the unfounded reports of weapons of mass destruction in Iraq, and the exaggerated Soviet threats that shaped generations (and perhaps made us all live in a self-fulfilling prophecy). This knowledge allowed me to view my own oppression through a new lens—one that compels me to write.

The year I left America to live abroad, the high school mass shooting at Columbine that seemed to popularize this heinous pattern took place. I heard about it, of course, but the gravity of its truth barely brushed my children as I raised three little ones far from guns and violence. Until I didn't. When I returned in 2013, I felt as though I'd stepped into an America I didn't fully recognize. Not completely foreign—but changed. And I too had changed.

Writing this series has been my way of making sense of that dynamic. Of understanding that no person, no place, no system is entirely good or entirely bad, and that balance only comes from weaving together questions that haunt me with truths that ground me.

Like Amanda, I have sometimes felt like a "flight risk," and this concept became the perfect way to depict both the danger and beauty of chasing your own path. I hope I've captured that nuance among these pages. I've long been fascinated by the lingering shadows of the Cold War and the realities of espionage, and these threads naturally draw me toward darker, high-stakes stories.

The globe still turns beneath nearly twelve thousand nuclear warheads—some ninety-six hundred poised in active stockpiles, most held by Russia and the United States—a reminder that the Cold War's ghost continues to trail behind us, whispering its unfinished history.

Yet my life is anchored in love—peaceful moments with a devoted spouse, a meaningful family life, and the belief that tenderness can and does exist alongside chaos.

I wanted Amanda's journey to mirror that coexistence: the verity that danger is real, but so is love. And at the end of the day, I hold to the conviction I try to live by—life is messy, but love endures and, sometimes, even conquers. So perhaps it's true—what millions of us have been lucky enough to sing in splendid melody for decades—all we need is love, love, love.

May you find it, may you live it, may you be it. Love from me to you, my fellow global citizen. Love to you.

Research Resources

My gratitude goes to the many podcast creators whose work feeds my audio obsession, the filmmakers who dedicate their careers to investigation and education, and the many authors who pen their experiences and findings in a profoundly human way—each has enriched my research behind this series. I will forever be thankful for the lives of the women who have gone before me, walk alongside me, and inspire me to use my voice for those who come after. I am equally grateful to those who allowed me to ask difficult questions, and validated memories some might prefer I leave behind—thank you for your courage and your kindness. The following list is not exhaustive by any means, but it highlights some of the sources that helped me ground Amanda's world in truth.

Podcasts:

The Spy Who by Wondery

The Making of Musk by CBC News

Liberty Lost by Wondery

Preacher Boys Podcast by Eric Skwarczynski

A Little Bit Culty by Sarah Edmondson and Nippy Ames

Television:

Turning Point: The Bomb And The Cold War by Netflix

American Manhunt Osama Bin Laden by Netflix

Shiny, Happy People by Amazon Studios

Let Us Prey: A Ministry of Scandals by Investigation Discovery

Flavours of Romania by Charlie Ottley

Books:

Outrageous Acts and Everyday Rebellion by Gloria Steinem

The Spy Who Saved the World: How a Soviet Colonel Changed the Course of the Cold War by Jerrold L. Schecter and Peter S. Deriabin

I Must Betray You by Ruta Septys

Finding Me by Viola Davis

Wayward by Alice Greczyn

A Thousand Tiny Paper Cuts by Katherine Spearing

On Being Human by Jennifer Pastiloff

A Well-Trained Wife by Tia Levings

And so many more. Another heartfelt thank you to those who report, write, and create stories that help us make sense of this life. I am in awe of the human experience at every turn, and those who choose beauty are who drive me to continue my own pursuit.

About The Author

Shelly Snow Pordea is a storyteller at heart, known for her exciting novels that connect, heal, and spark meaningful conversations. She first captured readers' imaginations with *Tracing Time*, a time-travel romance series that remains a fan favorite in its category. In 2021, Shelly and her brother placed in a top screenwriting contest for a co-written family drama based on their experience growing up in a cult—an exciting step into the world of film storytelling.

Her 2024 novel, *The Cheating Wife*, was inspired by a real incident of public shaming—a woman's property vandalized with the words "cheating wife" scrawled in graffiti. "After witnessing graffiti on a woman's property, blatantly accusing her of being a 'cheating wife,' I knew I was going to write a story about how far we've come—or haven't—from the days of public shaming and scarlet-letter-wearing," Shelly says. "The patriarchy is alive and well, and this book is my attempt to remind us all to take a look at our part in it."

Shelly is also the author of the *Flight Risk Spy Series*, which follows a high-flying heroine who stumbles into the world of espionage. She has based the travels of her protagonist, Amanda, on locations she's been lucky enough to visit. She and her family maintain a residence both in Brașov, Romania and St. Louis, Missouri.

Beyond her professional pursuits, Shelly is a dedicated mother to three incredible adults, loving wife to her favorite guy, George, for nearly three decades, and Buni (boo-nee) to two enchanting, magical grandchildren. She invites you to join her journey on social media, where she shares her insights and creative endeavors. Follow her @shellysnowpordea for a glimpse into the world of a multifaceted storyteller and advocate.

Also by

Shelly Snow Pordea

★ ★ ★ ★ ★

"A fun, engaging travel adventure with a female James Bond vibe that keeps you turning the page."

Books in *The Flight Risk Spy* Series:

The Night We Met – One encounter changes Amanda's life forever. March 2025

The Last Flight from Tokyo – Amanda's hunt turns deadly as she races against a ticking clock in Japan. June 2025

The Flowers of May – Back on American soil, Amanda discovers betrayal blooms closer to home than she thought. September 2025

Unfollowed – When everything goes offline, Amanda's past is sure to catch up with her. December 2025

From chance encounters to near-deadly escapes, this high-stakes series takes Amanda across continents, through smoky backrooms, and in a race against time. Each book peels back a layer of deception as Amanda learns that flying under the radar might just be the hardest thing of all.

Fasten your seatbelt! This spy series is a trip you won't want to miss.

"So original, imaginative, and captivating."

The *Tracing Time Trilogy*, **Book 1:** When Anna Wright's husband disappears abroad, her search for the truth draws her into a time-bending experiment that will test her love, her courage, and the very fabric of history.

Book 2: Fourteen years later, Anna and David's daughter Maggie uncovers her family's hidden ties to a secret time travel program, and finds herself pulled into a past that refuses to stay buried.

Book 3: A new generation steps into the fight as Maisy discovers her destiny as part of a family of time travelers—and leads the charge to free them from The Company's grip once and for all.

★ ★ ★ ★ ★

"A story that stays with you long after you've finished."

Morgan Conner had it all—until the words *cheating wife* appeared spray-painted across her property, turning her world upside down. Suddenly, her picture-perfect life is in pieces, and the whispers of her community grow louder by the second.

Caught in a storm of judgment and betrayal, Morgan must dig deep to fight for her truth and her survival. In a society where appearances often mean more than facts, can she rise above the scandal and find her own voice?

Dive into this powerful story of resilience, redemption, and breaking free from the expectations of others.